Critical Accl

MW00714905

"The posthumous publication of this novel, which was
rejected by one major publisher in 1960 and never resubmitted,
is an event to be welcomed for the additional insight it provides
into the life and work of one of Canada's most distinctive
writers." — *Canadian Literature*

"A significant piece of work by a man who was one of the
country's most powerful writers. Those who are collectors
will certainly want this one." — *The Daily Gleaner*

"*The Wanton Troopers* is a remarkable book, which will remain
in the reader's memory long after it is read. The characters of
the mother and father are brilliantly drawn and cause a deep
sympathy, as lasting as any." — David Adams Richards

"A powerful novel." — *Dimensions*

"Nowlan touches some deep truths about what it means to be
an abused, bewildered, terrified child." — *Books in Canada*

"The assurance of the prose reminds us of the adolescent
world portrayed by the great masters — Proust, Joyce and
Lawrence — and nowhere is this more evident than in Nowlan's
capturing of the boy's first awareness of sexuality, his first
adolescent love." — *The Halifax Mail Star*

"Impressive and memorable." — *The Kingston Whig-Standard*

"Well worth reading." — *The Vancouver Sun*

"A mature work heralding the poetic voice that is Nowlan's
claim to an enduring place in the annals of Canadian
literature." — *CM Magazine*

Poetry by Alden Nowlan

The Rose and the Puritan, 1958
A Darkness in the Earth, 1959
Wind in a Rocky Country, 1960
Under the Ice, 1961
The Things Which Are, 1962
Bread, Wine and Salt, 1967
The Mysterious Naked Man, 1969
Playing the Jesus Game: Selected Poems, 1970
Between Tears and Laughter, 1971
I'm a Stranger Here Myself, 1974
Shaped by This Land (with Tom Forrestall), 1974
Smoked Glass, 1977
I Might Not Tell Everybody This, 1982
Early Poems, 1983
An Exchange of Gifts: Poems New and Selected, 1985
What Happened When He Went to the Store for Bread, 1993
The Best of Alden Nowlan, 1993
Alden Nowlan: Selected Poems, 1996
Alden Nowlan and Illness, [2005]

Fiction by Alden Nowlan

Miracle at Indian River, 1968
Various Persons Named Kevin O'Brien, 1973
Will Ye Let the Mummers In, 1984
The Wanton Troopers, 1988

ALDEN NOWLAN

The Wanton Troopers
With an afterword by David Adams Richards

Edited by Laurel Boone.
Cover image detailed from a photograph by Charles Scriver.
Cover and interior page design by Julie Scriver.
Printed in Canada on paper containing 100% post-consumer fibre.
10 9 8 7 6 5 4 3 2 1

Library and Archives Canada Cataloguing in Publication

Nowlan, Alden, 1933-1983
       The wanton troopers / Alden Nowlan; with an afterword by David Adams
Richards. — Reader's guide ed.

ISBN 978-0-86492-546-6

      I. Title.

PS8527.O798W3 2009   C813'.54   C2009-903135-3

Goose Lane Editions acknowledges the financial support of the Canada Council
for the Arts, the Government of Canada through the Book Publishing Industry
Development Program (BPIDP), and the New Brunswick Department of Wellness,
Culture, and Sport for its publishing activities.

Goose Lane Editions
Suite 330, 500 Beaverbrook Court
Fredericton, New Brunswick
CANADA E3B 5X4
www.gooselane.com

To my mother and my father
in forgiveness

Notes to the First Edition

Alden Nowlan wrote his first novel in 1960, when a Canada Council grant allowed him to take a leave of absence as a reporter for the *Hartland Observer*. A year later, he published *Under the Ice,* while two other collections of poetry, *The Rose and the Puritan* (1958) and *A Darkness in the Earth* (1959), had already appeared. So *The Wanton Troopers* came from an especially creative period which would extend to the poems of *Wind in a Rocky Country* (1960) and *The Things Which Are* (1962).

Nowlan hoped that a success with this novel would free him from the drudgery of work on a small-town newspaper. Yet it seems he submitted the manuscript to only a single publisher. His motives for holding back were not simple — for while he used elements of *The Wanton Troopers* in later prose writings and even the name of its hero for *Various Persons Named Kevin O'Brien* (1973), the novel is emphatically not a piece of juvenilia or the sort of failure writers prefer to forget.

D. Peter Thomas
Publisher, Goose Lane Editions
1988

Notes to the Second Edition

As Peter Thomas foresaw, *The Wanton Troopers* was well received, and its continuing popularity has made a new edition imperative. Various minor changes and one major change have been made to the text. A few small grammar and transcription errors have been corrected, and spelling and punctuation have been made as internally consistent as possible without intrusiveness. Dialect has remained as Nowlan imagined it, except that accepted spellings have been used when feasible (*wanna*, for instance), and elisions have been moved from verbs to auxiliaries (*could a-done* has become *coulda done*).

The one major change occurs at the end of the book. The copy text for this edition is the typed manuscript in the Alden Nowlan Papers at the University of Calgary Library; it is a carbon copy, corrected in pencil in Nowlan's hand. It is one page longer than the copy text used for the 1988 edition, which had lost its last page. The final words of the 1988 edition, "Please God," occur at the end of the last line at the bottom of the second-last page of the Calgary manuscript, and it is easy to see why no one perceived that a page was missing. However, as readers of this edition will see, there can be no mistake: at last *The Wanton Troopers* has its true ending.

Susanne Alexander
Publisher, Goose Lane Editions
2009

The wanton troopers, riding by,
Have shot my faun and it will die.

— Andrew Marvell

One

It was raining so hard that Kevin thought God must have torn a hole in the sky and let all of the rivers of heaven spill upon earth. The cold spring rain hit the roof with the force of gravel, rattled down the walls, and splashed black and silver against the tawny window panes. It felt good to be in the house, safe in the sleepy warmth and lamp-glow of the kitchen, breathing the soporific aromas of smouldering millwood and burning kerosene.

A clock ticked on the shelf above the pantry door, scarcely audible above the strident clatter of the storm. The kerosene lamps, one on the table by the window and the other on a shelf above the cot, threw out inverted cones of orange-yellow light that shimmered until they were dissolved by the shadows in the corners of the room. On the ceiling above each lamp, there whirled a golden halo.

His mother had set the wash tub in front of the stove. She took buckets of cold water from under the sink and emptied them into the tub, then added hot water from a pan boiling on the stove. Steam rose in sibilant clouds, glistening ghostly as it was absorbed by the dry air.

"Come, Scampi," his mother said.

This was her private name for him. He stood on a towel while she undressed him. His body relaxed into will-lessness, went limp as she removed the shirt his grandmother had made for him from bleached-out flour bags. He liked the way in which the room became a violent ferment of darkness and light while the shirt was being pulled over his eyes. And he liked her hands, their deft union of firmness and gentleness.

His father dozed on the cot. His grandmother had long since gone to bed. This was a private moment, shared only by him and his mother. He never loved her so much as when she bathed him and readied him for bed.

Outside, over the oozing, dun-coloured fields, down the overflowing creek, through the gurgling swamps, and across the cedared hills, the wind howled like a drowning beast. Inside, there was warmth and light and the music of his mother's hands on his body.

She undid buckles and buttons and let his denim shorts slide down his legs. From May to November, he never wore underwear. He stepped out of the ring of cloth around his ankles and into the tub, recoiling as the cold rim touched his back. He leaned forward, away from the ring of cold.

Now, there was the clean, acid smell of soap in his nostrils, the foam and film of soap in his hair and across his shoulders and down his back. He closed his eyes and sank into little-boy inertia, every muscle dormant, every cell in his brain passive and inert.

Around his thighs, hips, and belly, the water's warmth coaxed the energy out of his every pore. His knees and chest were prickled by the sharper heat of the stove, little slivers of heat shooting into his flesh.

She rubbed a washcloth over his face. He drew back a little as the soap bit his eyes and nostrils. She put her hand against the back of his head and made him keep still — and he liked the peremptoriness of her gestures. Like the stinging needles from the stove, this mild discomfort accentuated their intimacy, made it more sweet.

He might have been a part of her body. She washed him as she washed her own hands. He was, all of him, hers: not the smallest part of him belonged any longer to himself. And in this surrender, there was a pervasive peace, an ecstasy of negation.

She kneaded suds into the soft fat of his belly, and he sank into the weightless dimension between wakefulness and sleep. When she made him stand up, it was as though he were coming awake.

Wind still pounded the house; rain was a rumbling landslide on the roof. With each gust, the lamp by the window flickered and the door shook on its rusty hinges. But he was only dimly aware of these things. She scrubbed his legs, rubbing his knees until they stung, the pressure of her hands softening as they ran up and down his thighs, tickling him so that he writhed and giggled. On the cot, his father — that man of ironwood and axe blades — continued to sleep. Upstairs, his grandmother was dreaming of crowns and trumpets and of the golden streets of Jerusalem. When his mother dried him with a towel made from a flour bag, she stroked him so briskly his body glowed as though it had become phosphorescent with sensuous fire.

Finishing, she draped the towel around his hips, like a loin cloth.

"Me Jane. You Tarzan," she laughed.

Their communion of warmth had ended. Now, as he always did at such times, he felt a feverish desire for sound and action. He threw his arms around her and squeezed, exerting all his strength.

"Ohhhhh! You're hurting me!" she cried in mock pain.

"I'm the king of the great bull apes!" he boasted. "You wanta hear me give the cry of the great bull apes, Mummy?"

The previous fall, they had gone to the motion picture house in Larchmont, and, ever since, Tarzan and Jane had been a game between them.

"Oh! You forgot! I'm not Mummy, I'm Jane!"

"Sure! You Jane! Me Tarzan!"

He threw back his head and howled until he was out of breath. She laughed again and slapped his posterior playfully.

His father snorted, shook himself, and sat up on the side of the cot. Rubbing his eyes, he glared at them angrily.

"For Chrissakes, Kevin, do yuh have tuh make so damn much noise!" he roared.

Kevin blushed and stared at the floor. Water that had dripped from his body as he stepped out of the tub lay in the little valleys in the warped linoleum.

"Yer gittin' too big tuh act like a baby," his father growled. He fumbled in the pockets of his jeans, found tobacco and papers, and began rolling a cigarette.

"Yessir," Kevin mumbled.

Shrinking with shame and self-contempt, he thought of how pitiful was his own skinny, almost hairless body in comparison with that of his father. Judd O'Brien's arms were bludgeons, and his horny, yellow fingernails reminded Kevin of hooves.

"Come to bed, Scampi," his mother said.

She laid her hand on his shoulder. With a scowl of irritation, he drew away. He hated her when she caressed him before his father, for he knew that Judd despised all caresses as symptoms of weakness. Even now, so it seemed to Kevin, Judd eyed him with undisguised contempt.

She took his shoulder again. This time her fingers dug into his flesh. He knew that she had sensed the reason for his withdrawal and that she resented it.

"Come to bed, Scampi," she commanded him.

She took the lamp from the shelf and, carrying it in front of her and above her head, led Kevin to his room at the other end of the house.

Setting the lamp on a chair by his bed, she helped him into the worn-out shirt of his father's that he wore as a nightdress. The air in this room smelled vaguely stale. It was strange how the odour of a room indicated the amount it was used. The air here contained just a hint of the staleness to be found in the unfurnished rooms upstairs.

He wiggled under the patchwork quilts, under the grey wool blankets that his uncle Kaye had stolen from the bunk house of the last saw mill in which he had worked. His mother put the lamp on the floor and sat in the chair by his pillow. At this end of the house, the storm was muted; water running from the eaves splashed almost gently against the window.

She leaned over him, and again he inhaled the aura of her presence: the scent of her perfume that always reminded him of wintergreen and lilacs; the pungent, comfortable odour of her body, the smell of grease and cooking oils and sweat.

"Do you love me, Mummy?"

This was the beginning of a nightly ritual.

"Yes, sweetheart, I love you."

"How much do you love me, Mummy?"

"Oh, I love you a thousand million bushels, sweetikins, a thousand million bushels."

"I love you too, Mummy."

The words, spoken in a drowsy monotone, were, in reality, not words at all, but sound-units in a charm. They were *abracadabra,* a charm against the dark powers of the night.

"Let's say our prayers now, Scampi."

"Yeah."

He chanted, running syllables together so that the prayer was broken, not by words, but by the rhythm of his breath.

Now I lay me down to sleep,
I pray the Lord my soul to keep.
If I should die before I wake,
I pray the Lord my soul to take.
God bless Mummy and Daddy,
and Uncle Kaye, and Grammie O'Brien,
and God bless everybody.

Two

The morning was bright and boundless, the air electric with that sense of freedom, of infinite distances and open spaces, that comes on a sunlit morning following a rain. Kevin had breakfasted on milk, toast, and porridge flavoured with molasses. Now he was walking down the gravelled road, toward the school house.

He kept to the soft shoulder of the road, where there was no gravel to sting his bare feet. The odour of the mud made him think of the strangely pleasant stink of horse manure and fresh-ploughed earth. A purple mist hung low over the fields and drifted lazily through the jungle of alders, willows, and mullein lining the overflowing ditches. Little beads of moisture adhered to the almost invisible hair on his legs, chilling him.

From the thickets came the shrill, toy-like song of the wood pewee and the raucous cry of the red-winged blackbird. Over the hill, on the intervals beyond the railroad track, great flocks of crows were cawing. Kevin noted that each crow cawed three times. Caw! Caw! Caw! He could not remember ever having noticed this before. Caw! Caw! Caw! Three caws each time. Never more, never less.

Reflected sunlight glistened on daisies, dandelions, and buttercups. The rain had raked petals from the wild rose bushes and many of them had been blown on the coarse gravel, where they lay, soggy but still delicate and velvety.

He came to a place where the road was bounded on both sides by barriers of spruce, stunted pine, and fir. It was colder here, because the trees shut out the heat of the sun, and the trees were dark; even at noon, all evergreens seemed to be dreaming of the haunted darkness of midnight.

Coming out of the woods, he passed the saw mill. This place both attracted and frightened him. The steam engine pulsed with ferocious, relentless power, pounding until the long, low, shed-like building shook on its log foundations. At intervals, the big saw emitted its scream of agony and triumph: the agony of the cleanly sliced log, the triumph of the luminous disc and its invisible, irresistible teeth.

There were five saws in the mill, Kevin knew. He had gone there many times, carrying tobacco or a lunch to his father. The biggest saw was called the splitter and Judd was known as the splitterman. When a slab dropped from the log carriage, Judd seized it and hurled it down the rollers to the slab sawyer. When a board fell free, he grasped it and, half-turning, threw it on a rack, from which it was taken by the edgerman. Judd had worked in the mill every summer since his fourteenth birthday.

The slab saw hung between two hinged beams. Cutting a slab into stovewood lengths, the slab sawyer gripped a metal bar attached to the beam and jerked the saw toward him, steadying the slab with his other hand. Twice in the years that Kevin could remember, slab sawyers had lost fingers, and once the swinging blade had ripped off a man's hand...

The edgerman trimmed the strips of bark from the edges of the boards. He stood about twelve feet from his small, twin saws and worked them with a long wooden lever. The saws could be moved in accordance with the width of the board. As each board was thrown, screeching, from the jaws of the edger, it was grasped by the trimmerman, whose saw tore off its ragged ends.

When these saws were working at full speed, they ceased to be substantial, metal things and became rings of nebulous, convulsive light. Kevin could remember moments in which he could hardly resist an urge to thrust his hand into one of these luminous rings. There had been times when his desire had become so strong that he had felt his stomach contract in fear as he turned away. He wondered if the men who worked in the mill ever felt tempted to throw themselves into these hypnotic whirlpools. In the twenty-five years that his father had worked at the mill, three men had been killed.

Steam billowed from the great, guy-wired stack and spurted from the exhaust pipe over the well. The saliva-light odour of steam mingled with the acrid tang of green sawdust. The mill-yard was full of men, all of them working furiously with logs and lumber. Even Stingle, who sometimes got drunk with Kevin's father, walked ahead of his team of yellow oxen, twirling his black whip over his head. The oxen had gentle eyes in their huge, stupid heads. Zombie-like, they plodded behind their driver, their heads bent low under the red yoke with its leather straps studded with brass and copper rivets, red knobs attached to the tips of their inward-curving, yellow horns.

The oxen hauled a drag, called a log-boat. All of the oxen in the world were named Broad, Bright, Star, Lion, Buck, or Brown. Horses, Kevin liked and sometimes feared; for these beasts, he felt only pity. No matter how often it was beaten, a horse retained a little glimmering spark of wildness. When let out to pasture on Sunday, even the old, sway-backed nag that pulled the sawdust cart would sometimes toss her head and neigh like a high-spirited colt. Kevin feared the teeth and hooves of horses, but something in him responded to the secret light he saw in their eyes, the freedom and grace that could never be wholly destroyed by work or punishment but ended only with death, because its life was inseparable from the life of their bodies.

The oxen were strong, but their strength was as lifeless as that of the steam engine. They did not husband their strength, as horses often did. When yoked to a load, they pulled as hard as they could from the first, and they continued to exert all their strength until they were halted by their teamster. Under the lash, a horse would cringe or strike out with its hooves; an ox accepted pain as stolidly as it accepted changes in the weather.

"Hello, Mister Man," Eben Stingle said.

"Hi."

"If yuh don't hurry, yer gonna be late for school. Then, most likely, yuh'll git stood in the corner."

Eben laughed, revealing tobacco-stained false teeth. Kevin grinned. He thought the joke inane, like most of the things men said to boys. But he always grinned when anyone smiled at him. The response came instinctively, and he was hardly aware of it.

Beyond the mill, the road re-entered the woods. Poplar, maple, birch, and cedar grew here, crowded so close together that they sucked the life from one another's roots. The trunks of these trees were so small that Kevin could have spanned them with his hands, but they grew to great heights, stretching upwards toward the sun.

The school house was about a mile from Kevin's house. He turned into the yard now. The tin-roofed, whitewashed building sat in the centre of a half-acre field, surrounded by flat and almost lifeless grass. A ragged and faded Union Jack hung limp from a pole opposite the door. Little crayon sketches of animals were pasted to the foggy glass of the windows. Approaching the open door to the porch, Kevin felt his stomach tie itself into a familiar giddy knot, his throat throb with the raw dryness of fear.

He entered the semi-darkness of the porch. Half a dozen boys lounged against walls studded with coat-hooks. Among them were two husky fifteen-year-olds in Grade VI: Riff Wingate, whose grin revealed a mouthful of broken, yellow teeth and whose breath stank of decay, and Harold Winthrop, whose face was pocked with feverish, red pimples and who liked to boast of the things that he had done to girls. To Riff and Harold, school was a ribald joke. Next summer, they would be peeling pulp or sawing slabs at the mill.

"Well, if it ain't Key-von!" Riff laughed.

Kevin reached for the knob of the inner door. Lifting his leg lazily, Harold barred his way.

"What's yer hurry, Key-von? Don't yuh like the company?" Harold smirked.

Ashen-faced, his hands by his sides, Kevin said nothing. Av Farmer stepped forward, a pudgy, fox-eyed boy of about Kevin's age. Kevin's terror of this boy was so abject that he could not muster sufficient pride to hate him.

Harold, Riff, and the others pressed close, grinning, their eyes bright with anticipation.

"The man spoke tuh yuh, Key-von," Av leered. "The cat got yer tongue or somethin'?"

"Mebbe he ain't learnt tuh talk yet," Alton Stacey guffawed.

Women said of Alton that he was pretty enough to be a girl. But his cunning had saved him from Riff and Harold. He had come to Lockhartville from Ontario, and he had cultivated the reputation of a sophisticate, a reputation he had enhanced by teaching Riff and Harold to shoot craps in the woodshed behind the school house. In these games, Alton invariably lost, and neither Riff nor Harold ever taunted him because of his resemblance to a girl.

"Show Daddy if the cat's got yer tongue!" Av demanded. He

grabbed Kevin's collar and shoved him against the door. "Come on now, show Daddy!" The others giggled.

Kevin went limp. His paralysis was too negative a thing to be described as fear. His blood was water, his heart and brain ash. All feeling was dead. The room was a vibrating blur.

"Show Daddy, Key-von!"

Idiotically, he stuck out his tongue. The boys howled and danced with excitement. Kevin wished that he could sink through the floor, sink to the dark centre of the earth and cower there forever.

"Key-von's got a tongue! Cat didn't git it, after all!" Av shrieked.

"Did yuh see that! Did yuh see what Av done!" Riff was almost hysterical with joy.

Av reached out, grabbed Kevin's nose with one hand and his chin with the other, yanked his mouth open.

"Yessir, he's got a tongue!"

"Key-von's got a tongue!"

Mercifully, the bell rang. Av threw Kevin aside like a worn-out toy. The boys brushed past, elbowing him. Blindly, he stumbled after them into the class room.

Kevin believed that every one of these boys was stronger, tougher, and braver than he. Secretly, he envied their courage and strength and wanted to be like them. But he consoled himself by the conviction that when they grew up they would be only pulp peelers and mill hands. They would live all their lives in Lockhartville, fenced in forests and rivers, and at last they would die here and be buried in the cemetery behind the Anglican church. But he — ah, he would be a lawyer, a doctor, a member of parliament, and one day he would come back here, wearing a black suit and a shining white shirt, and then he would spit in their eyes! And, in thinking this, his eyes and mouth took on that insolent, faintly contemptuous look that made them hate him.

Thirty children, ranging in age from six to fifteen, were seated at three rows of desks. The desks and seats in each row, made of scarred wood and rusting metal, were linked together so that they reminded Kevin of the cars in a train. Frayed canvas maps, rolled up like scrolls, hung over each of the three blackboards. The air was heavy with the smell of chalk, soap, sweat, and the stale crumbs of yesterday's sandwiches.

Miss Roache, the teacher, sat facing the children from behind her desk at the front of the room. Kevin slid into the seat that he shared with Alton Stacey.

"Good morning, class," Miss Roache enunciated.

"Good morning, Miss Roache," they chanted.

Kevin never joined in such chants. He thought the meaningless singsong sounded idiotic. The children used a peculiar tone when they spoke in school, an undulating croon with the emphasis falling in unexpected places. It was as if they were reading words in a language they could not understand.

"Class, stand," said Miss Roache.

With a clatter, the children got to their feet. They all of them derived a bit of sly excitement from this business of getting up and sitting down. The boys rattled the metal parts of their desks, the cotton dresses of the girls rustled like a windswept grain field.

O Canada
Our home and native land,
True patriot love,
In all thy sons command!
With glowing hearts, we see thee rise,
The true north, strong and free,
And stand on guard, O Canada!
We stand on guard for thee!

The older girls did most of the singing. Their voices, a little spiteful with self-conscious assurance, rang out above the drone of the younger children. The older boys grinned and were silent.

"We will bow our heads in prayer."

Again the mindless, undulating croon:

> *Our Father, which art in heaven,*
> *hallowed be Thy name,*
> *Thy kingdom come, Thy will be done,*
> *on earth, as it is in heaven.*
> *Give us this day our daily bread*
> *and forgive us our trespasses*
> *as we forgive those who trespass against us,*
> *and lead us not into temptation,*
> *but deliver us from evil,*
> *for Thine is the kingdom and the power and the glory,*
> *forever and ever. Amen.*

"Class, be seated."

There was another clatter and rustle, another little thrill of excitement and derision, as they resumed their seats.

"Now we shall take our Testaments and have our morning Bible reading."

Kevin took the small black book from the niche in his desk. His paralysis was lifting now. He was settling into the inertia of the school day.

Sunlight poured through the eastern windows, changing the crayon animals on the glass into grotesque abstractions. Miss Roache read aloud while the children stared with unfocussed eyes at the books that lay open before them.

Follow after charity and desire spiritual gifts, but rather that ye may prophesy. For he that speaketh in an unknown tongue speaketh not unto man, but unto God, for no man understandth him; howbeit in the spirit, he speaketh mysteries . . .

The voice droned on. Kevin's body became a vegetable. The children might have been so many carrots and turnips, propped up in their seats.

Therefore, if I know not the meaning of the voice, I shall be unto him that speaketh a barbarian, and he that speaketh shall be a barbarian unto me. Therefore, let him that speaketh in an unknown tongue pray that he may interpret . . .

He stared at Miss Roache, observing that she nodded as she read, her head bobbing up and down. She reminded him of a dog eating: the little, furtive sideways glances she cast when she raised her head. He remembered how she had wept the previous winter when some of the big boys, led by Harold and Riff, threw snowballs through the open door and onto the stove. The steam had swirled up like fog, and Miss Roache had wept and sent the children home. That day, Kevin had wanted to weep with her. He had wanted to go to her and say that it didn't matter, that Riff and Harold were fools, that she should not let them hurt her. But, of course, he had done nothing of the kind. And the next day, she had beaten little Normie Fenton, the smallest and shyest boy in the school, until his hands were red with blood . . .

Brethren, be not children in understanding; howbeit in malice ye be children, but in understanding be men . . . But if there be no interpreter let him keep silence in the church; and let him speak to himself and to God . . .

She shut the book with a gesture of relief and finality. A little ripple of movement swept from child to child, like a ripple on the surface of water.

"Current events," Miss Roache said, as she dropped the book in the drawer of her desk.

Every morning, Miss Roache talked for fifteen minutes on world affairs. To most of the children, these events were less real than the incidents in radio serials and comic books. Often, when asked to provide some news item for this period, the younger children related something that had transpired in *Buck Rogers*, *Superman*, or *Mandrake the Magician*. But, in listening to Miss Roache tell of the horrors taking place in the great world beyond the creek and the cedared hills, the world beyond Larchmont, beyond even Halifax, Kevin decided that this world, for all of its superficial foreignness, was in most ways only an extension of the world of his father and the mill.

Today, Miss Roache talked about Hitler, about his imminent capture and about the punishment that should be meted out to him. Kevin shuddered when she said it had been proposed that Hitler should be killed slowly with knives, a bit of his flesh being cut away each day. During the Bible reading, Miss Roache's voice had been a dull monotone; now it became shrill and emphatic. She said that she considered the death with knives too merciful. Hitler should be locked up in a cage and carried all over the world, so that persons everywhere could come and spit on him. He should be fed pig feed, but only enough to keep him alive, because if he were allowed to die, he would be no longer capable of suffering. In the cage, he might survive for years, and, in time, he could be brought to the little hamlets on the back roads, to places like Lockhartville... And every night he could be burnt with hot irons and beaten with whips, and the greatest doctors in the world would be on hand to see that he did not die.

Having heard Miss Roache deliver such monologues every morning for more than a year, Kevin had long ago decided that he sympathized with Hitler. In his pictures and especially in the caricatures that Miss Roache tore out of the Halifax newspapers and showed to the children, the tousle-haired, toothbrush-moustached man looked funny and pitiful. He made Kevin think of Wallie, the half-witted hired man at the Mosher farm. When Kevin saw Wallie he did not know whether to laugh or to cry. He felt the same indecision when he saw Miss Roache's cartoons of Hitler.

If they ever bring him to Lockhartville, I'll help him get away from them, Kevin vowed silently. For a little while each morning, Kevin was a dedicated Nazi. He wished he dare leap into the aisle, throw up his arm in a salute, and shout, Heil Hitler!

Three

Kevin decided that when he grew up he would be king of Nicaragua. For months, he had been fascinated by the idea of becoming a king. From the little glassed-in bookcase that composed the school library, he had taken a book entitled *A Boy's Life of Napoleon.* The book fired his imagination. He decided that when he became a man, he too would make himself a master of men and empires. Searching through an atlas for a likely country, he regretfully abandoned France, Spain, Germany, and Italy as too large and powerful. He doubted his ability to enlist sufficient volunteers to overthrow their governments. Finally, he chose Nicaragua, a tiny, purple blotch on the map. Yes, he would make himself ruler of Nicaragua. In his exercise books, he drew up time schedules and plans of campaign, fording rivers with a movement of his pencil, eliminating frontiers with a swipe of an eraser. In 1953, when he was twenty, he would raise an army of free-booters — perhaps one hundred men. They would seize a ship and sail to the Caribbean. In 1954, he would be crowned king. His Majesty Kevin I, by the Grace of God and the Constitution of the Kingdom, Commander-in-Chief and King of Nicaragua. Then, perhaps in 1955, he would invade Honduras and annex it to his domain. In 1957, he would plant his flag in El Salvador. In 1958, he would lead his troops into the capital city of Guatemala. By 1960, he would be Emperor of Central America.

With wax crayons, he made designs for flags, settling finally on a golden cross with a golden circle on a field of white. And he invented names for ships and regiments, pages of them. He would christen his first battleship *El Gringo*, and his personal bodyguards, whose uniform, which he spent an entire evening designing, bore a strong resemblance to the garb of a guardsman as depicted in *A Boy's Life of Napoleon*, would be known as King Kevin's Royal Hussars.

He supposed he would have to marry. Kings needed sons to continue their dynasties. And Princess Margaret Rose was only a little older than he... Then he remembered that Napoleon had divorced Josephine because she could not provide him with an heir. This puzzled him. He asked his mother: "Why couldn't Josephine have any children, Mummy?"

"Josephine who, sweetikins?"

"You know, Josephine, the one that married Napoleon."

Laughing, Mary threw her arms around him. She slid her hand inside the back of his shirt and ran her fingers up and down the little bumps in his spine. This was one of her favourite ways of caressing him.

"Oh, Scampi darling, you ask the craziest questions!"

He drew away sulkily. "I don't see nothin' crazy about that."

"No, it isn't really crazy. Just funny, sort of. But I don't know, lamb. I really don't know why Josephine couldn't have children. I suppose someday you'll find out all about it. When Mummy's little sugar baby gets to be a man, he's going to know all sorts of wonderful things."

Grandmother O'Brien spoke from her rocker, beneath the clock shelf. "Yer spoilin' the boy, Mary. Yer spoilin' the boy with yer foolishness."

Mary stroked Kevin under the chin and winked at him.

"We're poor people," Grandmother O'Brien said. "It ain't fittin' fer people like us tuh put on airs."

Mary winked at Kevin again.

Grandmother O'Brien said this often, to rebuke what she called the false pride of Kevin and his mother. "People like us should be willin' tuh take what's handed out tuh us. We're poor as dirt and allus will be. Puttin' on high and mighty airs ain't gonna change things none."

To ease the perpetual pain in her stomach, Martha O'Brien held a brick, heated on top of the stove and wrapped in an old wool sock, against her waist. She lived on crackers soaked in milk until they'd become an oozing pulp, but her soul was nourished on the flesh offered in sacrifice to the God of Abraham and of Isaac and of Jacob.

"The O'Briens has allus been poor, boy. But they allus knew their place. And they was allus willin' tuh work. The same with my people, the Havelocks; when a man hired a Havelock he knowed he was a-gonna git a day's work outta him. Yuh never caught a Havelock givin' hisself no stud-horse airs. They knew what they was and they never pretended tuh be nothin' else. I don't like that false pride I see in yuh, boy."

"Oh, my goodness, Grammie! Scampi just asked a simple little question!" Mary's voice rose in irritation.

Martha adjusted the pin in her black, bowl-shaped hairdo. "Mark my words, Mary, yer a-spoilin' that boy. Children should be seen and not heard, I allus say, children should be seen and not heard." Rocking complacently, she looked at Kevin with undisguised disapproval. "If that was my boy I'd Josephine him! I'd Josephine him out in the garden with a hoe. There's work tuh be done here. Ain't no earthly use of Judd workin' his heart out every night after he comes home from the mill. Put that boy out in the garden. Put him tuh work around the barn. He's big enough tuh work if he's ever gonna be!"

"Oh, Grammie, Scampi is only a baby. Things were different when you were young. You don't realize that, Grammie."

"I realize a long-legged cockalorum like that one should be doin' his share of work around the place instead of askin' questions about women havin' children."

Mary drew Kevin's face against her breast. "When Scampi grows up, he's going to work with his brain. His hands are going to be soft as a girl's — like the hands of the men who work in offices and stores in Larchmont. When he's a man, my baby is going to have nice, soft, pink hands just like he has now. You wait and see."

"Eh!" This sound, half snort and half grunt, was Martha's way of dismissing them as hopeless. She rocked vigorously, hugging her brick.

There was nothing that Kevin found more frustrating than his grandmother's sermons on the certainty of poverty and the duty of humility before one's betters. He writhed in vexation when she told him, as she often did, that within four years he would be working in the mill. He hated her for the grim satisfaction he detected in her voice. And his hate was made more vicious by the thought that she was probably right in her prediction.

Martha did not undress at night. She lay fully clothed on her bed, and when the pain became unbearable she came downstairs and heated bricks. Then, in the darkness, with the brick clutched to her belly, she rocked and sang hymns. Often, Kevin awoke and heard her voice rise like the cry of a ghost in the darkness at the other end of the house.

This was the hymn that she most often sang:

There is a fountain filled with blood,
Drawn from Emmanuel's veins,
And sinners plunged beneath that flood
Lose all their guilty stains.

E'er since by faith I saw that stream
Thy flowing did supply,
Redeeming love has been my theme
And shall be till I die.

Four

The mail had brought a letter from a lawyer, demanding a further payment on the house. Kevin and Mary knew that Judd would be angry when he read this letter and so, to postpone the crisis as long as possible, she hid the cellophane-faced, sinister-looking envelope under a stack of mail-order catalogues and love-story magazines on the shelf above the cot. She did not show it to Judd until late Sunday afternoon.

On Sundays, Judd liked to do little odd jobs around the house and outbuildings. He half-soled his work boots, sewed patches on his overalls, which were stiff and black with pitch, plugged holes in pots and glued handles on broken cups. Sometimes, he even repaired a clock. Kevin had seen him devote all of an afternoon to making a clock hand from a bobby pin.

Kevin loved to watch Judd manipulate an awl or a needle. He sat in drowsy entrancement while Judd tapped nails into leather or broke a thread between his teeth. Judd preferred to work seated on the swing in the wagonshed doorway. Here he could enjoy the sun yet avoid being observed by persons who passed on their way to church. In the planting season and again during the harvest, Judd spent his Sundays in the garden, and many times Kevin had seen him leave the field hurriedly and conceal himself behind the woodshed to elude the eyes of passing churchgoers. Judd himself never went to church.

Late in that afternoon, Judd decided to patch one of his gum rubbers. He sat on the swing and removed the punctured boot. Squatting in the couch grass by the weather-beaten wall, Kevin watched him rub the damaged spot briskly with a file. Now the sun was on the other side of the wagonshed and great, triangular shadows crept across the heath toward the smoke stack and the trees. Robins and starlings slowed their movements and quickened the rhythm of their singing, as they always did at dusk. Kevin chewed a blade of grass, letting its juice, which smelled and tasted of fermentation, fill his mouth. Mosquitoes moved in from the swamps and began their dusk song, so ponderous compared to the shrill, stabbing sound they emitted during the day. Insects lit on his bare arms and legs, falling silent as their needles pierced his skin and sucked his blood. He brushed himself continually and scratched at the hard, reddening lumps on his forearms and thighs.

Judd squeezed glue from a tube and lit a match. He made the flame stroke the rubber like a tiny, scarlet brush. Then he adjusted the patch carefully and pressed it down hard with his palm. The job finished, he grunted in satisfaction and laid the boot aside to let the glue harden and set.

Leaning back in the swing, he extracted a yellow-brown quid of chewing tobacco from his pocket, blew away the bits of sawdust that had stuck to it, and tore off a chew with his teeth.

"Soon be dark," Kevin said.

He had known better than to speak before his father finished his task. The man smiled. Judd laughed rarely, except when he was drunk, and he seldom smiled.

Judd gestured toward the sky.

"Pretty, ain't it?"

"Yeah," Kevin agreed.

As always, their voices, in speaking to one another, were formal, muted with shyness.

"Skeeters botherin' yuh?"

"A little bit, mebbe."

"Ever hear the story about the Irishmen and the skeeters?"

"Gee, no."

Kevin shook himself and changed his position in the grass. The ground beneath his body was turning cool.

"Well, it seems as though there was two Irishmen that hadn't never seen a skeeter in their life... I dunno, but I guess there ain't no skeeters in Ireland. Mebbe, this is the only country that's got skeeters. I dunno... Anyway, that don't matter none. The story is, Pat and Mike was campin' out fer the night — in a tent. And they was bein' skinned alive by skeeters. Why, they was skeeters big as sparrows! And they stung jist like bumble bees! And after a while, Pat and Mike decided to blow out the lantern so the skeeters couldn't see them! Well, that was all right for a spell, but then the lightnin' bugs started comin' in. And Mike wakes up and sees them lightnin' bugs and he grabs the quilts off Pat and he says, 'Wake up, Pat. Bejabers,' he says, 'They're comin' back with lanterns!'"

Judd chuckled and repeated the words: "Bejabers, Pat! They're comin' back with lanterns!"

Kevin doubled over with laughter. He always responded almost hysterically to his father's rare jokes, not as much because they were funny as because he was overjoyed to find his father in a mood for such stories. Now he laughed until tears streamed down his cheeks and he gasped for breath, and Judd, chuckling complacently and chewing his tobacco, repeated the line again and again.

"Bejabers, Pat, they're comin' back with lanterns!"

*

When they went into the house, Mary, observing Judd's apparent good humour, gave him the letter.

"I don't know what made me forget this," she said. "It came in the mail yesterday, but I forgot to tell you..."

Judd crushed the envelope in his fist. He went to the cot and sat down with his head in his hands. After a long moment he said, "The damn' lawyers will hound a man tuh death. They'll badger a man right intuh his grave."

Mary and Kevin sat in silent watchfulness, afraid of what might come next.

"I never should of bought this damn shack," Judd growled. "I shoulda knowed better than to of bought it."

"Maybe Hod Rankine will lend us the money," Mary said.

Hod Rankine was the owner of the saw mill.

"Yuh think I'd ask that bastard fer anythin'? He wouldn't give a man the parin's off his toenails!"

Kevin choked back a giggle. Judd glared at him hatefully. "What's so damn funny?" he roared.

"Nothin'," Kevin gulped. "Nothin'."

"Eh! Yuh won't think bills is so damn funny when yuh start payin' them yourself. I wasn't much oldern you when my old man put me out tuh dig fer my livin'."

"Judd, he didn't do anything," Mary interjected.

"It's little enough that he does, that's for certain," Judd snapped.

He rose, went to the stove, and threw the wadded, unopened envelope into the fire. Blue-tinted flame shot up as he slammed down the lid. He kicked the stove viciously and reached for a stick of wood.

"Kevin!"

Kevin sat up straight, tingling with fear.

"Why the hell didn't yuh fill this woodbox?"

"He forgot, Judd."

"I didn't ask you. I asked him. Let him speak for himself."

"I forgot, Daddy," Kevin quavered.

"Eh! Yuh forgot! I forgot, Daddy." He mimicked Kevin's shrill piping. "I forgot, Daddy! That's all I ever heard outta you! It's about time I gave yuh somethin' tuh make yuh remember! It's about time yuh get another dose of strap oil, Mister Forgetter."

"Judd!"

"Don't yuh 'Judd' me! I got a good mind to take him out right now and blister his arse for him! Lazy little bastard!"

Kevin mustered his courage. "You're jist mad because you got that old bill! That's what's the matter."

"Talk back tuh me, will yuh!" Judd roared. "Talk back tuh me!"

"He wasn't saucing you, Judd."

"I'll decide for myself whether he's sassin' me or not! Come on, Mister Big Breeches."

Kevin looked at his mother. She turned away.

"Come on!" Judd bellowed.

Kevin rose from his chair and followed him through the door.

The strap was a strip of peeling orange leather, fourteen inches long and three inches wide. It hung from a peg in the section of the barn in which Judd stored hen food and the blocks of pressed straw which, when broken open, made bedding for the cows. If Kevin's relationship with his mother reached its apotheosis when she bathed him and readied him for bed, his relationship with his father attained its epitome through the strap.

Judd took the strap from its peg and sat on a block of straw. Kevin's stomach felt as though it had turned to rock. His mouth was clogged with invisible dust, the moisture of his tongue and throat transferred to his clammy palms.

"All right, Mister Big Breeches, take down yer pants."

Judd tested the strap on his own palm and grunted. Trembling from head to toe, Kevin unbuttoned his short pants and let them slide from his numbed fingers and down his quivering legs. No act in life filled him with greater shame than this. This was the ultimate violation, the final degradation. He hated his father and himself; all of his will was channelled into the wish that they both of them would die.

"Might as well come over and take yer medicine. Ain't gonna taste no better no matter how long yuh wait."

His chest heaving with his agonized efforts to breathe, Kevin went to his father. The man seized his shoulders and bent him across his knees.

He felt his father's body tense as he raised the strap, heard the sharp intake of his breath.

"Yer gonna remember this fer a long time, Mister Big Breeches. This is one thing I can promise yuh, yuh won't fergit!"

Kevin shut his eyes and clenched his teeth. I won't cry this time, he vowed fiercely. No matter how hard he beats me, I won't cry. I won't cry even if he kills me.

WHACK!

Kevin's body jerked. He bit his lower lip savagely. Judd's free hand clamped down on his back like a vise.

WHACK!

"Yer gonna learn not tuh talk back tuh me, Mister Big Breeches!"

WHACK!

To his horror, Kevin felt his eyes fill with tears. No, he thought desperately, I won't cry. I won't let him make me cry. I won't. I won't. I won't.

WHACK!

The pain was the striking of a clock. Each stroke fell like a gong, then shivered away into the silence. And before the long, quivering pain had wholly died, the clock struck again.

WHACK!

This time, Kevin cried out. "I hate you! I hate you! I hate you!"

WHACK!

"I hope you fall on the saw! I hope you kill yourself!"

His father increased the force of the strokes. Nothing in the world was real except pain and the rhythm of the strap.

WHACK!

"I hope the saw cuts you in two! That's what I hope!"

WHACK!

"When I grow up, I'm gonna kill you! You wait and see if I don't! I'm gonna kill you!"

WHACK!

"I'll teach you, Mister Big Breeches! I'll teach you!"

WHACK!

Kevin was weeping now. His vow forgotten, he sobbed, howled, and writhed. The pain was lava in his hips and thighs.

WHACK! WHACK! WHACK!

Judd whipped him slowly and methodically, drawing a deep breath each time he lifted the strap.

WHACK!

"I'll kill you! I swear to God, I'll kill you!"

WHACK!

"Shut yer mouth, boy, or yuh won't be able tuh sit down fer a week."

WHACK!

He was blubbering now, mindless, undone.

WHACK!

"You're hurtin' me! Please don't hurt me!"

"This is supposed tuh hurt. If it didn't hurt, yuh might git to like it."

WHACK!

"Please don't, Daddy! Please don't spank me so hard!"

WHACK!

"I'll fill the woodbox, Daddy. I won't forget again! I'll never talk back again, Daddy."

He blatted like a baby.

WHACK!

"I didn't mean the things I said to you, Daddy. Please, Daddy! I didn't mean it!"

WHACK!

"I won't do it again, Daddy! I promise I won't ever do it again!"

WHACK!

Then, as always, came the defeat, the final surrender.

"I love you, Daddy," he whimpered, meaning it. "I do love you. Please, Daddy — don't hurt me. I love you."

This was defeat. He had been conquered. His soul, finding it impossible to escape the pain, ran back and embraced it. He had been beaten until he was no longer capable of hate, no longer capable of rebellion. It was finished.

His father lifted him to his feet. He stood blubbering, his buttocks burning and pulsating, his pride a handful of chaff.

"Take that strap and hang it back on its peg."

Kevin obeyed, wiping his eyes with his fingers.

"Put yer pants on and go wash yer face," his father commanded. "Yer blubberin' like a girl." The man's voice was no longer cruel, contained even a hint of apology and pity. Kevin wished he would beat him again. He was convinced that he deserved to be beaten until he died.

In his room, his mother bathed his yellow and blue welts with witch hazel.

"I hate him, Scampi. I hate him when he does this to you," she said. He knew that she had been weeping. And suddenly, he hated her for her weakness. He was angry that she had spoken of his father in such a manner. He felt that he had deserved his whipping. It had been a purgative, cleansing him of secret sins. He was a vile, worthless thing and he loved his father for having thrashed him.

Five

The first time that Kevin saw a picture of Abraham Lincoln, he was startled by the man's resemblance to his uncle Kaye. The most striking similarity lay in the eyes; the eyes of Lincoln, like those of Kaye Dunbar, were withdrawn and yet not aloof; they seemed to look at the world with a mixture of compassion and ironic amusement. When Kaye walked into the yard, Kevin ran out to meet him. Of all the grown men whom Kevin knew, Kaye was the only one of whom he was never, even for a moment, afraid.

The gangling man with the sad-happy eyes grinned at him. "Hiyuh, Namesake," he said.

Kevin's middle name was Kaye, and in his earliest years he had believed that this identity of names established some sort of occult bond between them.

Kevin blinked. "Hiyuh, Namesake," he responded.

It was a beautiful, shining day. In Kaye's presence, all of Kevin's senses opened like the ripe buds of flowers. The former owners of the O'Brien house had planted rose bushes and a lilac hedge. These had been allowed to run wild, and now tiny rose bushes dotted the unmown grass of the front yard like the banners of Lilliputian lances. In the field on the other side of the road, daisies, buttercups, and devil's paintbrush swayed gently in the breeze. Brown, purple-blue, and orange butterflies fluttered in the translucent air. Robins flitted low over the flowers. Occasionally, a goldfinch flew up from its secret place in the grass.

"I was wonderin' if mebbe you'd like to go swimmin'," Kaye drawled. He broke off a rose from the bush nearest his feet and stuck its stem between his teeth.

"Gosh, sure!" Kevin shouted.

"Better go ask your mother if it's okay."

"Yeah, jist a second. I'll be right back."

Kevin whirled and ran like a spooked deer to the house.

A few minutes later, they climbed the sagging pole fence separating Judd's garden ground from the heath. Kaye and Kevin walked up the hill, past raspberry and blackberry bushes, through alder thickets and around the rotting stumps that spoke of the time, many years before, when this had been lumber woods. Kevin inhaled the swampy odour of alder bark, the medicine-sharp scent of wintergreen, the sweet vapour of wild strawberries. Rabbits hopped out of the bushes, stood long enough to take one astonished glance at the man and the boy, then bounded back into hiding. As they came to the top of the hill, close to the woods, a fox shot across Kevin's line of vision and was gone so quickly he was not certain whether it had been a real fox or only a dream.

After walking about a mile down an abandoned logging road, they came to a tangle of raspberry bushes, birch saplings, and alders. Kaye had come here so often that he had beaten a path, like a tunnel, through the bushes. The opening was hidden by leaves and branches. Kaye pushed these aside and he and Kevin entered, as though going through a door.

At the other end of the tunnel, they emerged into brilliant sunlight and stood on a table of green-gold grass, overlooking a stream of glittering water. The birches growing on either side of the stream met high in the air, forming an inverted funnel. Sunlight stood in the funnel like a shaft of incandescent gold.

"Mighty nice here, eh?" Kaye said.

"Yeah."

Kaye squatted on the ground. Kevin threw himself down beside him. The sun was so bright that the blond fuzz on his arms and legs shone like moonlight against his chestnut-coloured skin. He lay down and felt the faint, not-unpleasant roughness of pebbles and twigs under his hips and back.

"You hear the grass growin', Namesake?" Kaye asked.

Their conversations almost always began with something like that.

"No. I guess not," Kevin answered dubiously.

He laid his ear to the ground and listened.

"No, I guess I don't hear nothin'," he said.

Kaye said nothing. Kevin continued to listen.

He held his breath. It was true! He heard it! The sound was so soft it seemed like a whispered message from the dark centre of the earth.

He sat up.

"I hear it!" he yelled. "I hear it!"

"Thought you would." Kaye grinned complacently.

"Don't make much noise, does it?" Kevin asked wonderingly.

Kaye pulled a handful of the sparse, lacklustre spears and ground them to dust between his palms.

"Pretty poor grass," he explained. "Can't expect grass as poor as this to make much noise growin'. Good timothy and alfalfa now, you'n hear them all right. Especially at night. Everythin' grows faster at night."

"Gee, why?"

"Oh, I dunno. I guess in the daytime everythin's kinda leanin'

49

back and soakin' in the sun. Not sleepin', mind you. Just kinda leanin' back and thinkin', like. Then at night all that sunshine begins to burn and sizzle inside of everythin' under the darkness, and after a while everythin' just starts to grow, kinda."

Kaye thought deeply for a moment.

"You know, don't you, that the sun don't really go out at night?"

"Gosh, yes. We learnt that at school."

"Well, I dunno if you learnt this at school. But I guess mebbe in the daytime the flowers and grass and everythin' get their sunshine from above, then mebbe at night when everythin's all dark on top of the earth, mebbe the sun's down underneath shinin' up at their roots. Mebbe that's how it is. I ain't sure. Mebbe I was wrong the first time. I dunno."

"You dunno?"

"Nope. Nobody knows hardly anythin' when it comes right down to it. I just kinda keep thinkin', that's all."

"Gosh," Kevin said. "Gosh."

They stripped themselves naked and jumped down to the narrow gravelled shelf at the water's edge. Kevin went barefoot through almost the entire summer, so the soles of his feet were like cowhide. Even so, the sharp stones cut into the soft skin of his toes. He followed Kaye into the water, its stroking warmth caressing first his ankles, then his calves, then his thighs, and finally his hips. He began to swim, entering a dimension as unearthly as the science fiction worlds of Mars and Venus.

Swimming was almost the only physical act in which Kevin functioned without self-consciousness and with ease and grace. His uncle, who had taught him, told him that he swam like a fish, like a trout or a silver salmon. He and Kaye swam far down the stream, shouting to one another. And when they became weary, they swam back, climbed up the bank, and lay in the grass, with their wet arms shielding their eyes from the sun. In the pink-tinged darkness behind his eyes, Kevin thought mysterious, incommunicable boy-thoughts. He thought of Kaye, whose life-spirit overflowed like a creek in freshet. He thought of the foxes barking in the distance, dog-like but with jungle wildness, and of the squirrels scampering and chattering, the humming midges and quick-whirring grasshoppers. As he fell asleep he heard, from every direction, the singing of unseen birds and the almost inaudible whisper of the leaves and grass.

Kaye lived in a cabin on the creek road, about two miles from the O'Brien house, and Kevin had often visited him there. Kaye had built the cabin from warped boards, which he had carried on his back from the mill. Its roof and walls were covered with tarpaper, secured by spruce slabs still clothed in their aromatic bark. The door hung on leather hinges and was locked with a wooden button. The windows could not be raised or lowered. In summer, Kaye simply drew the nails and lifted out the glass. Flattened cardboard beer cases had been nailed to the inner walls to keep the wind from getting through the cracks between the boards. On these sheets, in red ink, were the names of breweries and advertisements for stout, lager beer, and pale ale. Kaye had further decorated the walls with pictures torn from magazines: pictures of lions, tigers, elephants, and near-naked women. Kevin liked the animals, but he thought the women looked fat and foolish, and he could not understand why his uncle liked them.

The sink pipe went out through a hole in the wall, so that water poured into the sink drained out on the ground just outside the door. On coming to the door, Kevin's nostrils were always rasped by the lye-harsh stink of soap suds and dirty water. The cabin's single room was furnished with a table and two benches, all made from wooden packing cases, a stove made from an oil barrel, and a bunk on which a mound of loose straw, covered with wool blankets, took the place of a mattress.

To Kevin, this did not seem an unusual type of dwelling. Many of his cousins lived in similar cabins in Bennington, Frenchman's Cross, and Ginsonville. The difference was that this cabin was filled with the life-spirit of Kaye Dunbar. Even when he was absent, the echo of his laughter and the reflection of his grin seemed to touch everything — the rifle that rested on a rack of antlers above the door, the old violin hanging over his bunk, the beer bottles and Wild West magazines cluttering the grime-grey floor.

Kevin had spent many evenings here with Kaye. He would lie on the bunk, breathing the clean smell of straw and the stale smell of the blankets, and read stories about Billy the Kid or Wild Bill Hickok, while his uncle fried bacon and eggs, opening the door of the stove and resting the frying pan on the bluish-red coals.

After they had eaten, Kaye would play the violin and sing in imitation of Wilf Carter and Jimmie Rogers, his favourite cowboy singers. He would sing of hoboes and of freight trains and of herding cattle at night under vast, prairie skies, and Kevin would hug his knees against his chest and rest his chin on his knees and sway in time to the music, feeling a dark sweet sadness such as he felt when he woke and heard a locomotive whistle wail in the night.

Next to his violin, Kaye's most prized possession was a pearl-handled revolver. On Sundays when Kaye, Kevin, and Mary visited Kevin's grandmother Dunbar at Ginsonville, Kaye would sit on the backstep and shoot clothes pins from the line that hung between the corner of the cabin and a fir tree beyond the privy. The pins would snap and fly into the air and Grandmother

Dunbar would rush out shouting and brandishing a broom. "Kaye Dunbar! Have yuh gone clean crazy?" Grandmother Dunbar would yell as she laid the broomstick across his shoulders. Kaye would laugh and empty his pistol in the air and Grandmother Dunbar would go back in the house, shaking her head and saying she did not know what she had done to deserve such a son. But Kevin would detect a little ghost of a smile in her eyes and at the corner of her toothless mouth.

Judd disliked Kaye. He said that he was "no good," pronouncing the two words as one, with the inflection he used in speaking of one who was too lazy or too weak to work. Both Judd and Martha O'Brien could forgive anything of a man or a woman who was willing and able to work. Martha would sometimes halt in the midst of a denunciation of a drunkard or an adulteress to say that well, after all, he or she was not afraid of work. "They'n say what they like about him — he weren't never scart of work," Martha would assert, holding her hot brick against her belly. And Judd would agree. "Hard work never kilt nobody yet" was one of his favourite sayings.

Often, Judd, and many of the other men of Lockhartville, spoke of Kaye, and others like him, with hatred and rage. "I been makin' my own livin' ever since I was a young gummer of fourteen," Judd would complain. "I've peeled pulp until my back was ready tuh break. I've chopped logs when it was fifty below in the woods. I've man-handled boards in the mill when it was ninety above in the shade. I've hoed potatoes and I've milked cows and I've slaughtered pigs and I've pitched hay. And what have I got tuh show fer it? Not a damn thing. Not a goddamn thing. Now, there's Kaye Dunbar — he ain't never done an honest day's work in his life and he's livin' a damn-sight better'n you and me! It don't seem right. A man like that should be made tuh work, goddammit! Somebody should take a Dutch whip tuh him and whip him every mornin' and every night fer a month! Then he'd be ready tuh work, by God! Hard work never kilt nobody yet. A man was put on this earth tuh work. It jist makes me sick tuh see a big, husky shyster like Kaye Dunbar sittin' on his arse while the rest of us work our guts out! It jist makes me sick to my stomach, by God!"

At potato planting time or during the haying season, Kaye sometimes hired out to a farmer for a few weeks. But, for the most part, he lived by his wits. He was familiar with every acre of forest land in Connaught County, and during the trout fishing and deer hunting season, he guided sportsmen who came down from Halifax. Kevin walked in fear and awe of these men. They were doctors and lawyers and bank managers and Kevin considered them the rulers of the world, with their soft, womanish hands and clipped, insolent speech. They wore beautiful new garments of scarlet and khaki and such boots as he might have chosen for his Royal Nicaraguan Grenadiers. And they carried fascinating things: canvas gun cases, sleeping bags, Thermos bottles, and silvery rum flasks.

Kaye himself hunted for ten months of the year, ignoring the laws restricting seasons and bag limits. He killed — and ate — deer, moose, rabbit, porcupine, beaver, and bear. And he stole — a hen from a nearby farm, a gallon of molasses from the barrel in the shed behind Biff Mason's store.

Kevin was shocked by Kaye's thefts.

"It ain't right," he said. "You know it ain't right, Kaye."

Kaye looked at him in such innocent astonishment that Kevin laughed.

"How come yuh figger it ain't right, Namesake?"

"Because it ain't, that's why!"

"That ain't no kind of an answer. Why ain't it right, that's what I wanta know?"

"Because God says it ain't right. That's who!"

"What duh you mean — did God come up to you one day and put his hand on yer shoulder and say, 'Look, here, Mister Kevin Kaye O'Brien, I don't like stealin'.' Is that what happened?"

"Oh, gosh, you know better'n that! It's in the Bible, 'Thou shalt not steal.' God wrote it down and put it in the Bible. Grammie O'Brien says God wrote every word in the Bible. He took His finger and wrote it all on stone, and…"

"Huh! What you think it means, though — 'Thou shalt not steal'?"

"It means what it says! Anybody could see that! It means you shouldn't ought to have taken that barrel of kerosene from the saw mill. It means…"

"How do you know that's what it means?"

"Because it says so!"

"Listen, here, Namesake, it don't say anythin' of the kind. It jist says 'Thou shalt not steal.' It don't say what stealin' means. You gotta figger that out for yourself. Now you think it was stealin' fer me to take that barrel of kerosene, huh?"

"Sure, it was. You stole it. You told me yerself that you…"

"Hold on a minute! I never told you I stole it! I never stole a thing in my life. I never said no such a-thing."

"What duh yuh call it then, if it ain't stealin'?"

"What do I call it? I call it equalizin', that's what I call it. Now if I'd taken the last bite of food outta somebody's mouth, I'd figger that was stealin'. I ain't never took a thing that I didn't need more'n the man I took it from needed it. I needed that kerosene so I took it. Hod Rankine's got enough money to buy a thousand barrels of kerosene. Me takin' that one little, biddy old barrel was jist equalizin'. If I got anythin' he needs more'n I do, he's got all the right in the world tuh come and git it. I won't say a word if he takes somethin'…"

"But you ain't got nothin' that he needs!"

"That's right, Namesake! And that's what I mean by equalizin'!" Kaye sat back with a smirk of triumph.

"Oh, gee whiz, nobody can explain anythin' tuh you, Kaye!"

Kaye grunted and yawned while Kevin pouted. Then Kaye began making faces: cat-faces, toad-faces, snake-faces. In spite of himself, Kevin snickered.

"Equalizin' is what I call it," Kaye said again.

Six

Kevin often reflected on the difference between his mother and the other Lockhartville women. Where she skipped like a little girl, they trudged like spavined mares. The things that made her open her mouth in laughter made them close theirs in pale-lipped anger. Where she was pliant, they were unyielding. When she became soft and warm, they turned hard and cold. She was a solitary white birch sapling, surrounded on all sides by towering black spruces.

Angered, she did not, like other mothers, invoke the authority of parenthood and scold him from a pedestal of superiority while he stood hang-dog and chastened. She quarrelled with him; they bickered like children. And if, at last, she threatened to report him to his father, he felt that she had betrayed him; he despised her as he would have despised a child of his own age who had threatened to tattle to an adult.

If she told him to shut up, he would tell her that she could shut up herself. They would stand facing one another in the kitchen, yelling at the tops of their voices, while Grandmother O'Brien watched, her lips curled in contempt, from her rocking chair. If she slapped him, he would kick her shins. If she pinched him, he would pull her reddish-brown, shoulder-length hair until she yelped.

But they did not quarrel about anything that really mattered.

Small disagreements provoked storms of rage and recrimination. The big disagreements, when they came, brought only silence and hurt.

Kevin had seen his mother spring from her chair in the midst of supper, snatch up food and dishes, and run with them to the pantry. This meant that she had spied an approaching visitor. Mary was bitterly ashamed of their bread and potatoes, humiliated by their cracked plates and tarnished cutlery. When the visitor entered — usually a mill hand or a mill hand's wife who fared no better at home — the table was clear and the chairs stood in their usual places around the kitchen. But Kevin always suspected that the intruder had peered through the window or, somehow, seen through the walls. Every grin, every glance at the pantry door meant that he was slyly ridiculing Mary's impassioned efforts to conceal their shame.

"Only a damn fool would come tuh a man's house at supper time," Judd would say, after the visitor had gone. "Frenchmen and Dutchmen is the only people I've ever seen that didn't have better sense than tuh come tuh a man's house at mealtime." And Kevin would promise himself that when he became a man he would obtain for his mother the most costly foods and the most beautiful china in the world.

He already knew that even in Lockhartville there were two classes: the rich and the poor. Here, the rich were the half-dozen farmers and their families. These people possessed automobiles, electric lights, and telephones. When their children finished eighth grade, they were sent to high school in Larchmont. Some few even went on to college. One or two, over the years, had become doctors or lawyers. The farmers took trips to Ontario and to the United States. The wives of the more successful bought their clothes in Halifax. When they dined, their tables were covered with white linen and they used special knives to butter their bread.

The poor were men like Judd O'Brien and their families. Those men were mill hands, farm hands, pulp peelers, and loggers. Six evenings a week, they lay smoking or dozing until it was time to go to bed. On Saturday night, almost all of them got drunk. Often they stayed drunk until they went back to work on Monday morning. Each year there were months in which they could find no work at all.

At fifteen or sixteen, their children left school. The girls got married and the boys went to work. Most of the boys became rural labourers, like their fathers. A few of the more imaginative and ambitious ones, like Kevin's uncle Leonard, found steady jobs as railway section hands, grease monkeys, and attendants at filling stations. Men like Judd O'Brien regarded men like Leonard Dunbar with a mixture of envy and distrust. Len and the others who worked twelve months of the year at Larchmont and Bennington liked to boast of their high wages and of the praises showered on them by bosses who wore white collars and ties to work. "Big-feelin' bastards," Judd spat contemptuously.

Mary had been born in Lockhartville. But she spoke of the village in the manner of one who had come here from Halifax, or even from New York. "I don't understand these Lockhartville people," she would say. "I've never seen such people in all my life!"

Her father had been a farmer, one of those who were driven off their farms during the depression. Judd told Kevin that his Grandfather Dunbar had been a rogue and a braggart. The old man had devoted years to searching for Captain Kidd's treasure, which, according to legend, had been buried on the Nova Scotia coast. And in his last years, he had left his wife and family and gone to New Brunswick, where, so rumour claimed, he had become a preacher for some obscure sect. When Mary spoke of the herd of Ayrshires which her father had once possessed, Judd guffawed and said that the herd had consisted of two toothless old scrubs. "Fenton Dunbar and his herd of Ayrshires" became for Judd a byword signifying any form of pretense or braggadocio. When he suspected Kevin of boastfulness, he would say, "That reminds me of Fenton Dunbar and his herd of Ayrshires," and laugh dryly while Kevin hid his head in shame.

Kevin knew that his mother often lied. In a cowboy film shown at the Orange Hall there had appeared an actor named Clay Dunbar. He had kept a saloon full of ruffians at bay, and when one of the outlaws reached for a pistol, Clay had shot it out of his hand. "Anybody else wanta try that?" he had drawled. And Mary had told Kevin that this Clay Dunbar was her cousin. "The last time I was visiting Aunt Elvira in Boston, Clay was home from Hollywood on vacation, and..." The story had gone on and on. Clay had shown her his $200 shirts and his $500 pistols and she had ridden on his palomino stallion, Playboy, and...Kevin had lain in bed, his knees drawn up into the old shirt that he wore as a nightdress, and she had stroked his ear lobes as she talked, the lamp on the floor throwing a halo around her face. He had enjoyed listening to her. But he had known that was all lies. All lies! And despite the pleasure he took from her story, he had despised her for lying to him.

Grandmother O'Brien sometimes told him stories about his mother. These were simple little stories, narrated without comment, but Kevin did not fail to observe the derision in her face and voice. She told him, for example, of how Mary and her brother, Leonard, had once, long ago, boarded the train at Ginsonville and bought tickets, at ten cents each, for Lockhartville. During the three-mile ride, they had enacted an elaborate pantomime in which they had posed as travellers who had ridden a great distance: they had leaned back in their seats, feigned weariness, and chattered loudly of tickets and time tables. Kevin could not understand why his grandmother obviously thought this act idiotic. It was the kind of thing that he himself would have liked to have done.

Mary played games with her son, something no other Lockhartville mother would have dreamt of doing. Wearing an old red shirt of Judd's and a pair of rinsewater-coloured jeans, she wrestled with him in the dooryard. Grappling one another, they rolled over thistles and couch grass and miniature rose bushes, the sky reeling above them. Kevin struggled until he was blinded by sweat; he gripped her wrists so hard that he left bruises. They butted and kneed and strangled one another. And, in the end, she always overpowered him. He never deliberately surrendered to her; he fought until strength and breath failed. But when she defeated him, he was glad. It was ecstasy to lie helpless, the weight of her body pouring through her arms and hands and onto his flattened shoulders. Silently, he rejoiced that he was in her power, that she could do what she liked with him.

But, paradoxically, he wanted her to defeat him only in play, only when his will was in abeyance. When she challenged his active will, he hated her. His defeat in the wrestling was good only because he knew it was merely a game. During their real quarrels he wanted to destroy her.

It seemed to him that she understood this; at times she appeared to take a brutal pleasure in breaking him. In return, he poured all of his energy into defiance.

A trivial question would arise. Perhaps it was raining and he started to go outdoors and she told him that he could not go, that he would catch a cold if he went. He argued. She issued commands. He whined. She threatened to tell his father. The initial argument was forgotten. What remained was a naked conflict of wills. It was at such times that they screamed and belaboured one another while Grandmother O'Brien looked on, a grim smile fixed on her yellowing lips.

Grandmother O'Brien also managed to rebuke Mary for wrestling in the dooryard. She said nothing, but when Mary returned to the kitchen, she always found that Martha had done some little job during her absence...she had washed the dinner dishes or polished the stove or mixed biscuits.

"You didn't have to do that!" Mary would say, her perspiring cheeks yellow with anger.

Martha would clutch her hot brick and stare at Mary in shammed astonishment.

"Why, child, I was jist tryin' tuh help out," she would say.

That night, when Judd got home from work, Martha would mention, with seeming casualness, the work that she had done that afternoon.

"I hope yuh like them biscuits, Judd. I ain't as good a cook as I usta be, mebbe. Seems as how whatever I cook tastes jist like I feel, and I been feelin' mighty poorly, lately."

Judd would look up from his food.

"Eh? You made the biscuits, Mother?"

"Oh, I try tuh make myself useful, Judd. The pain's been somethin' terrible tuhday, but I do try tuh make myself useful."

"Mary coulda done it jist as well as not."

"Oh, I know that, Judd! She told me I shouldn'ta done it. But I do try tuh make myself useful around the place."

And Martha would smile and look across at Mary while Kevin scowled, hating the cruelty and triumph he saw in her wrinkled, walnut-coloured face.

Mary's best friend and most frequent visitor was June Larlee. Kevin knew that his father detested her. Judd hinted that she had been guilty of monstrous sins. "My God, Mary! She's got herself in trouble twice and she ain't eighteen yet!" Mary's answer was always the same: "Hush, Judd! Think what you're saying in front of Scampi!" So Kevin, although he devoted a great deal of thought to the matter, did not discover what her mysterious trouble had been.

It was Sunday morning. Wearing tight red shorts and a loose blouse, June sprawled on the cot in the O'Brien kitchen and smoked cigarettes. She reminded Kevin of the simpering, near-naked women in the pictures nailed to the walls of Kaye Dunbar's camp. Watching her cross her legs, which he considered disgustingly fat and hairy, he was both intrigued and repelled by her abundant, adult flesh.

As they often did, Mary and June were talking in riddles. This was a favourite trick of theirs, one that infuriated Kevin.

"I saw you-know-who in Larchmont the other night," June said, puffing at her cigarette.

Mary shot a teasing little glance at Kevin.

"Little pitchers have big ears," she warned.

Kevin sat at the table, pretending to study his Sunday School lessons. Something wicked shaped his face.

"All I said was that I saw you-know-who the other night in Larchmont," June giggled. "You remember that certain person in Larchmont, don't you?"

Mary exhaled and screwed her face into an expression of melodramatic disbelief.

"Oh, no! Not him again!"

"You bet!" June's voice lowered. "And he was asking about you."

"He wasn't!"

"He was!"

"I don't believe it!"

"All right, don't you believe it, then. But it's true. 'How's Mary-Mary-Quite-Contrary-How-Does-Your-Garden-Grow?' he said."

Mary giggled. "That must have been him, all right. It couldn't have been anybody else."

"Didn't I tell you? Why don't you believe me when I tell you things?"

Kevin thought these conversations, with their groans, sighs, giggles, and head-shakings, unutterably pretentious and silly.

"Well, I'm an old married woman now," Mary said.

"Woe is me!" June snickered.

Mary smiled and shrugged. "Little pitchers have big ears," she said again.

"I've got somethin' else I want to tell you later."

"Oh, yes." Mary turned to Kevin. "Isn't it time you started to Sunday School, sweetikins?"

He stood up sulkily. He knew she wanted him to go so that she could be alone with June.

"Yeah," he muttered.

"That's a good boy, Scampi," June said, winking at him.

He hated the smug, teasing insolence in her grin. He hoped she would die in agony and burn forever in the deepest pit of hell.

Seven

The Minard farm covered a hillside on the northern side of the creek. The Minard brothers, reputed to be among the richest men in Connaught County, were old, and their wizened wind-burned faces were rendered forbidding by the blue-black and sallow blotches of great age. Zuriel, the elder, ruled his younger brother like a father. Watching them Kevin thought of the patriarch Abraham and his nephew, Lot, whose stories he had read in the Bible. The brothers were known as "old bachelors" and their sister, Sarah, who kept house for them, was called an "old maid." Sarah's hands were wrinkled and red, like the claws of a chicken, and her hair had thinned until she possessed only a scattering of stark-white wisps.

The previous summer, Judd had helped the Minard brothers with their haying. The mill usually closed down during the haying season, to allow the mill hands to help out on neighbouring farms. In afternoons when heat waves vibrated in the air like live electric wires, Kevin had galloped across the spike-sharp hay stubble, carrying a rum bottle full of cold buttermilk to quench his father's thirst. He loved the sensation of standing by the clattering hay rake to pass the bottle to his father. It thrilled him to see how his father teamed the great, pungent-smelling Clydesdales with one hand and levered the rake up and down with the other. His nostrils tingled to the hot, sweet smell of the curing hay. And he had made friends with Zuriel, Reuben, and Sarah. He liked the gentle formality of the men, the little, excited-hen movements of Sarah. He had kept going back to the Minard farm long after his father had ceased to work there. Through the winter and spring he had paid many visits to the whitewashed old three-storey farm house with is maze of sheds and porches.

Zuriel and Reuben seldom uttered a complete sentence. They spoke in grunts and gestures and monosyllables. But they seemed strangely flattered by his interest in their hens, cows, pigs, horses, and sheep. When he reached out to pat old Bess, the leader of the Clydesdale team, and murmured into her huge, comically expectant ears, the brothers nodded and smiled, as though the words of endearment he whispered to her had been addressed to them.

But the farm possessed a lure greater than that offered by the animals and the outbuildings. Kevin had never seen a room like the Minard parlour.

Miss Sarah made him wash his muddy feet before entering the house. He sat on a bench in the porch that she called her laundry room and scrubbed his feet in a gleaming white basin. Then he could come into the kitchen and, if Miss Sarah was in a good mood, into the parlour as well.

Miss Sarah had learned that he liked books, and the parlour contained dozens of them, stacked on the shelves of a shining, varnished book case. Often, he spent an hour or more alone in the room, lying on his belly on the soft, maroon carpet and paging through stiff-backed, leather-bound volumes. In the past year he had read *The Sermons of DeWitt Talmadge*, *The Life of Frances E. Willard*, *The Prisoner of Zenda*, *The Little Shepherd of Kingdom Come*, and — both of these last three times each — *The Life of Lord Nelson* and *A History of the United States* written in

1901. But he would have been captivated by the room had it not contained a single book. For to him it seemed the height of grandeur and luxury. It was such a room as he would build in his palace when he became King of Nicaragua, such an office as he would use when he was elected to parliament, such a study as he would possess when he became the wealthiest and most famous doctor in Canada.

The parlour was dark, with the darkness of old, varnished things, and with the darkness of shadows. The floor-length, tasselled window curtains were kept closed because, so Miss Sarah said, the sunlight would warp the furniture and fade the carpet. The darkness of the walls, the darkness of chairs and tables glowed with incredible black luminosity. Everything in the room was odorous with age, redolent of soaps and polishes. And there was another fragrance, ambiguous and haunting, that reminded him vaguely of the scent of dead flowers pressed between the pages of a Bible.

The room drew him as a magnet draws a jack-knife blade. But he did not wholly like it. Sometimes when the six-foot-high clock standing between the curtained windows struck the hour, he started up as though he had heard the snarl of a werewolf or the wail of a banshee. And sometimes when he lay reading he stopped abruptly and looked over his shoulder, as though he had felt a hot breath on the back of his neck.

Something in the dark, shining, airless room troubled him and made him uneasy. He could not give his uneasiness a name, but it was a little, just a little, like the uneasiness he had felt on the one or two occasions that he had passed a graveyard, alone and at night.

One day after school, he clambered over the pole gate at the foot of the Minard lane. The poles in this section of the fence were not nailed to posts but lay between frames built like miniature ladders. When cattle or horses were to be driven up the lane, the poles were lifted from their rungs and slid to one side. Kevin preferred to climb over them.

He ran up the hill. Beyond the fences, on either side of the lane, flocks of sheep were grazing, their fleeces the colour of dirty white shirts. They blatted at him as he ran by kicking up red dust, the old ram blatting first, then all the ewes echoing him. Kevin was not fond of sheep. He disliked their sour, vomity odour and their stupid, trusting eyes. Whenever he looked at them, he wondered why God had compared men to sheep. Horses would have been so much better...

With a hop and a jump and a windmill of arms he was in the Minard's back dooryard.

In the front dooryard, the grass was trimmed regularly with a lawn mower, the only lawn mower that Kevin had ever seen. The gravelled walk leading to the front door was lined with little flower beds in which Miss Sarah had planted butterfly-coloured, velvety pansies. Purple dahlias, which Kevin imagined to be flowers from some exotic land like Nepal or Peru, grew on either side of the front door.

The front dooryard belonged to the house. The back dooryard belong to the farm. Here there were weeds and thistles and discarded tools and odds and ends of harness, and if Kevin did not watch his step he was likely to step in hen dung or cow manure. Breathing hard from his run up the hill, he went to the back door.

Miss Sarah was in the kitchen, white-aproned, her cheeks flushed from the heat of the stove. The air was sweet with the scent of sugar, nuts, raisins, and flour.

"Good day, laddie."

"Hiyuh, Miss Sarah."

"Planning to do a little reading today?"

She smiled at him, absently wiping her flour-covered palms on her apron.

"Yeah, if it's all right."

"Yes, if I may," she corrected him.

"Yes, if I may," he parroted obediently.

"That's ever so much nicer. Well, run along. I'm much too busy to talk to you."

"Gee, thanks."

"Just a minute, haven't you forgotten something?"

"Huh? Oh, gosh, yes!"

He ran back to the porch and washed his feet.

When he re-entered the kitchen, she gave him a strange look. In trying to adapt himself to his parents' unpredictable moods, he had acquired the habit of studying faces and of giving names to the expressions he saw in them. He could not think of a name for the way in which Miss Sarah looked at him. Her eyes held something of the slavish gentleness he had seen in the eyes of sheep, yet there was something else... something almost like hunger.

"It isn't nice to stare, Kevin."

"Oh, I'm sorry. I didn't know I was starin'."

"Ing," she smiled.

"— staring."

"It doesn't matter. Run along with you, now."

He tiptoed down a dark, carpeted hallway, turned a dark-shining brass knob, and entered the parlour.

He was rereading *A History of the United States*. The final chapter said that the Spanish-American War had been one of the most crucial conflicts in the history of the world. William McKinley, the nation's war leader, would be remembered as one of the greatest of presidents, fit to be numbered with Washington, Jefferson, Lincoln, and Grant, the book said. Kevin was not sure that he agreed with this. He had a soft spot for William Jennings Bryan. There was something fine about that speech of his. "You shall not press down upon the head of labour, this crown of thorns! You shall not crucify mankind upon a cross of gold!" He studied the pictures... pictures of the battles of San Juan Hill and Manila Bay. He wished that generals still rode horseback. He would like to be General Kevin O'Brien, on a grey charger like Traveller, the war horse of General Lee. Flipping pages, he turned back to the picture of the battles of Gettysburg and Antietam and Bull Run. He looked at General Pickett, on foot, hat in hand, reporting to a mounted General Lee. "General, my noble divisions are swept away," the caption read. A cold shiver of joy rippled up Kevin's spine and into his scalp. He closed his eyes and saw General Kevin O'Brien in a grey tunic and an orange sash. "Now, gentlemen, give them the bayonet!" "Don't cheer, boys, the poor devils are dying!" "Damn the torpedoes, full speed ahead!" "We have met the enemy and they are ours!" "Have lost a cheek and ear but can lick all hell yet!"

From his shirt pocket he extracted a pencil stub and a scrap of paper. Shaping the letters with care and tenderness, he wrote:

Kevin Kaye O'Brien, born Atlanta, Georgia, January 25, 1833, the son of Colonel and Mrs. Judd O'Brien. Graduated from West Point Military Academy, 1851. Lieutenant, United States Army, 1851. Served with great distinction against Plains Indians. Captain, United States Cavalry at outbreak of Civil War. Major, Confederate States Cavalry, 1861. Colonel, 1862. Brigadier-General, 1863. Major General, 1864. Fled to Mexico at close of war. Became Field Marshal in Mexican Army. Returned to United States, 1880. Elected Senator from Georgia, 1882. Democratic candidate for president of the United States in

He stopped to reread what he had written. He decided that it sounded almost as good as the brief biographies of presidents printed in the book.

Suddenly, a hand touched his shoulder. For an instant, he froze in fear. Then he turned. Miss Sarah was bending over him.

"Hi," he said, rolling over and sitting up. She stared at him and he was bewildered by the morbid, fixed interest he saw in her face.

She ran her hands through his rum-coloured hair. Her fingers were as dry and rough as dead twigs. And she was trembling.

"Been having a good time with the books, laddie?"

The words came with an effort. He wondered if she were sick, if perhaps she might topple over, sprawl on the floor beside him and die.

"Yeah. I been readin'," he stammered.

She sat down in one of the cushioned, throne-like, black-shining chairs, her chickeny hands clasped in her lap.

"Come here for a moment, I want to see you, Kevin."

He got to his feet and went over to her chair. In the semi-darkness, she looked a little like Queen Victoria, as shown in a picture hanging behind the teacher's desk at school. But, no, she was too sad and thin. The Witch of Endor would have looked like this, had she been pictured in the Bible. He wished the parlour were not so musty and dark.

"You're a very pretty boy," she said.

Only his mother ever said such things to him. He did not know how to answer. "Mebbe, I better be goin' now," he mumbled.

She reached out quickly and held him. "No, please! Just stay a moment. I want to look at you."

He thrust his hands into the pockets of his shorts. Miss Sarah held him at arm's length, staring at him. He had never seen such starvation and loss as he saw now in her eyes.

71

"A long time ago I dreamt of having a boy like you, Kevin." She paused, then repeated his name, "Kevin," her lips shaping it like an endearment. "A boy with a fine, slim body and proud, dreaming eyes. When I was young — oh, almost as young as you! — I dreamt that the boy would come and take me away and we would go hand-in-hand over the fields until we came to the sea, and then we would board a ship with white sails and we would sail across the ocean until we came to a country where the sun shone twelve months of the year and where the air always smelled of flowers..." She stopped. Then in a different voice, she said, "Oh, I'm talking foolishness, laddie!"

"Mebbe, I better go now."

He felt as if he had blundered into a room and surprised her there, naked.

"No, don't go! Don't go!"

She touched his hair again, and his face and throat. Her flesh felt dead. It was as though a corpse had reached out and touched him. "You're so pretty," she crooned. "So pretty, Kevin." Her hands slid down his body. "You're so pretty! You're trembling, Kevin. Are you afraid?"

"No," he lied. "No, I'm not afraid."

"Do you know who I am, Kevin?"

Her voice had been soft, caressing. Now it became shrill and cruel.

"Huh? Sure, you're Miss Sarah. You're..."

"No, Kevin. I am death."

Her leer was so horrible that for one insane moment he imagined that she was telling the literal truth. Sarah Minard's body had been stolen by the Angel of Death! Then he shook himself and giggled.

"You're teasin' me," he said.

Her voice was hateful, brutal, grating. "No, it is true. I am death.

I was born dead. I was dead when I grew up. I am dead now. Zuriel and Reuben are dead also. We are entombed here together, three living corpses. Do you understand that?"

"No, Miss Sarah."

Her fingers were in his hair again, this time her nails raked his scalp.

"Do you know how men make an ox?"

She leapt from one weird subject to another. He could not follow her.

"Do you know how men make an ox?" she repeated harshly.

"Yeah, I guess so. I guess I do."

"They turn it into a living corpse. Almost everyone in Lockhartville is a living corpse. Not only Zuriel and Reuben and I, but all of the farmers and all of the men in the mill, and all of their wives — living corpses, all of them! All!"

"Please, Miss Sarah, I wanta go home."

He tried to pull away from her. Her fingers pinched his flesh like pliers. He knew that in another moment he would be weeping.

"Wait! One more thing! They'll come for you! Some night when you're asleep in bed, they'll come for you, and they'll make you a living corpse like all the rest of us! They will! You wait and see! They'll come with knives and ropes and they'll drag you out of bed and they'll..."

"No!"

He yanked himself free and ran to the door. She hid her face in her hands and made strange sounds. He did not know if she was laughing or crying.

He ran all the way to the pole gate at the foot of the lane. This time he did not see the sheep or the fields or the fences. He was blinded by the memory of an old woman sobbing or snickering in a dusky parlour.

He did not go to the Minard farm again. But, many times, during the remainder of that year, he awoke whimpering from nightmares of men with knives and ropes...

Eight

Three men strolled into the O'Brien dooryard. Kevin knew from the way in which they stopped in the yard, without coming to the door, and from the shy furtiveness of their gestures, that they were in search of liquor.

All the mill hands drank and all their wives hated liquor. The two sexes maintained an uneasy truce through a kind of tacit etiquette. It was in obedience to this etiquette that Judd went outdoors to greet the visitors, while Mary, eyeing them hatefully from the kitchen window, pretended not to have seen them.

The trio wore overalls and ragged cotton shirts, and their cloth caps were pushed far back on their heads. Todd Anthony had moist, reddish eyes and at the end of every sentence emitted a mirthless, cawing laugh. The mill hands called him the Crow behind his back. Eben Stingle, the ox teamster, came from another county, and spoke with a strange accent, slurring his *r*'s. Angus Northrup sported a grey moustache stained yellow with tobacco juice. He was the sawyer, the best-paid man in the mill, and the other mill hands treated him with a touch of deference, a hint of respect.

"Mighty hot day, eh, Judd?" Angus Northrup said. Since he was the sawyer, the other men silently granted him the prerogative of beginning the conversation. "Don't look as if it's gonna git any cooler neither."

"Yeah," Judd agreed. "It sure is hot enough."

Patiently, the others added their comments on the weather, on their work. The spruce logs sawn the previous week had been scrub stock. Hod Rankine had been a fool to buy them. They were foul things to handle and almost impossible to sell.

Then, casually, came the real point of their visit. "Wouldn't know where a man could git a drink would yuh, Judd?" Angus Northrup asked.

Judd scratched his head. Kevin detected something spiteful in the way his father delayed his answer.

"Don't know as I would," he said, at last.

"We're kinda dry," Todd Anthony laughed, rubbing one reddish eye with a dirty finger.

"Yeah," Judd sympathized.

He pulled out his chewing tobacco and gnawed off a chew. Most of the mill hands chewed tobacco; there wasn't time to roll cigarettes in the mill.

"Fact is we're so damn dry we're crackin'," Angus Northrup quipped.

He cast a glance at the others. They laughed. The mill hands always laughed at the sawyer's jokes.

"Eh? Well, I don't know, boys. I don't know. I don't know," Judd said thoughtfully.

The men made no move to leave. As yet they did not know if Judd's denial were genuine or merely formal. In Lockhartville, men took their time about giving away liquor. The men who had something to drink played with the thirsty ones, as Judd was playing now. Everyone accepted this without resentment.

"We been lookin' all over Lockhartville. Place is dry as a bone," Eben put in.

"So dry a man gits dust in his throat jist talkin' about it," the sawyer agreed.

He looked around again. Again the others laughed.

"Madge Harker ain't got nothin'?" Judd asked, his eyebrows raised in feigned disbelief.

"Nope. Sold ever'thin' out dance night," Eben replied.

Judd spat juice the colour of cow's urine on the ground at his feet.

"Well, I'll tell yuh now..." he drawled.

"Yeah?" the visitors pressed eagerly.

"Jist happens I got a little brew on in the barn. Don't know if it's ready yet, tuh tell the truth. Don't imagine it is. But, well, mebbe — I said, mebbe, now — we'll jist try it."

"Hot cripes!" Eben yelled.

"We won't fergit yuh, boy," the sawyer grinned.

Kevin saw that his father rather resented their presumption. "I said *mebbe* we'd try it," Judd reminded them gruffly.

"Sure, Juddie, sure."

Together, the men started toward the barn. Kevin, screwing up his courage, followed them.

The day was hot. Nodules of sweat rolled down inside Kevin's shirt, tickling his chest. Sweat glistened like oil on his arms and legs.

The barn was divided into three sections: the cow stable, the hayloft, and the store room. It was the store room that they entered now.

The room was as hot as the inside of an oven. A tart, herbal aroma rose from the sacks containing hen feed and merged with the soporific odour of hay and straw. A shutter, held in place by three wooden buttons, ran half the length of the wall, facing the stable. Through this shutter, Judd could push great forkfuls of hay into the mangers. Today, since it was summer, the shutter would not be opened. The cows were grazing on the heath.

As they always did when he came into the store room, Kevin's eyes gravitated to the strap, hanging from its wooden peg. Hastily, he grimaced and looked away.

Judd went to the corner and kicked away a pile of jute sacks, uncovering the old barrel churn in which he had made his brew. The men jostled one another, edging closer.

The lid was lifted off, its underside clammy. The room filled with the gas of the brew. Kevin could not understand why the men liked this drink. The stink sickened him. But he watched curiously as they licked their lips and laughed nervously to conceal their impatience.

Kevin squatted by the door, where the air was freshest and cleanest, and studied them. Judd dipped a mug into the churn, took an experimental sip and grunted. "Guess mebbe, it'll do till somethin' better comes along," he grinned. He was no longer playing with them. Now he seemed to take pleasure in extending his hospitality. "Drink up, boys," he invited.

The mug passed from hand to hand. Each man bolted his drink and passed on the mug quickly. They gasped, grunted, sighed, and wiped their lips. The mug circulated almost continuously.

This brew had been made from yeast, oranges, and molasses. Spears of hay and straw had fallen into the churn. The men scooped these out of the mug with their thumbs before they drank.

Kevin kept as quiet as possible. The men knew he was there. But as long as he did nothing to attract their attention, they would pretend not to notice him. When he intruded into the affairs of men, his father called him "Mister Big Breeches." And he did not want to be sent away.

Judd's cheeks reddened, his eyes became feverish.

"Damn good beer," Todd Anthony said.

"A real life-saver," Eben agreed.

"Allus said that Judd O'Brien was a Good Samaritan," Angus laughed.

The others guffawed. They were relaxing now, shaking off their sobriety and their formal manners.

Their voices became louder. The words poured out of them in torrents. Each man fought for a chance to say his piece. They laughed boisterously, slapping their denim-clad thighs, jostling and interrupting one another. But Kevin detected the underlying malice in their fellowship. They told spiteful little jokes at one another's expense, and when one man was held up to ridicule he sat in glum silence while the others hooted. In every joke there was a suggestion of cruelty.

After the fourth round of drinks, Judd burst into song:

> *Here's a cuckoo! There's a cuckoo!*
> *Here's a cuckaroo!*
> *Here's a cuckoo! There's a cuckoo!*
> *There's a cuckaroo!*

He always sang this song in the earliest, happiest phase of his drunkenness. His neck beet red, his breath coming in great gasps, he roared out the song, while his visitors tapped their toes against the floor and laughed.

> *Here's a cuckoo! There's a cuckoo!*
> *Here's a cuckaroo!*
> *Here's a cuckoo! There's a cuckoo!*
> *There's a cuckaroo!*

Kevin had heard this song often. So far as he knew, no one but his father ever sang it, and these were the only words that it had.

"Ya-ha-ha-ha-whooo!" Eben Stingle yelled. "Gimme another shot of that cripeless stuff and I'll step dance, by cripes!"

They drank again, spilling the thick, muck-brown liquid down their necks. Eben catapulted into the centre of the floor and danced like a war-painted Indian. The others clapped their hands and roared encouragement.

"Ya-ha-ha-ha-whoooo!"

The ox teamster kicked up hay seeds and shreds of straw. The floor boards on which Kevin sat bounced in rhythm to Eben's gum-rubbered feet.

"Ya-ha-ha-ha-whooo!"

Eben's eyes were shut, his mouth open, his nostrils flaring like a stallion's. The frenzy of his dance rather frightened Kevin. It did not seem to be a dance at all. Kevin had endured nightmares in which he ran desperately without gaining an inch of ground. Eben's dance reminded him of such unpleasant dreams.

"Ya-ha-ha-ha-whoooo!"

Exhausted, Eben sank down on a block of straw. The mug was passed from hand to hand again.

"Who's man enough to wrist-wrestle with me?" Todd Anthony shouted.

"I guess I'm yer man," Angus Northrup said, rising.

The pair knelt on either side of a block of straw, elbows pressed, right hands clasped, their arms forming an inverted V.

Ignoring the contest, Judd broke into song again:

> *As I was leaving old Ireland*
> *All in that month of June,*
> *The birds were singing merrily.*
> *All nature seemed in tune —*

"Too damn mournful!" Eben roared. "Sing somethin' cheerful, Juddie! Fer cripes' sake, sing somethin' cheerful!"

Judd quaffed beer, gasped and blinked. Rhythmically, he clapped his hands.

> *Oh, saddle up my fastest horse,*
> *My grey is not so speedy —*
> *And I'll ride all night,*
> *And I'll ride all day —*
> *Till I overtake my lady,*
> *Till I overtake my ladeee!*

A stranger would not have believed that this ruddy, roaring singer was the taciturn, tight-lipped Judd O'Brien who worked at Hod Rankine's saw mill. But Kevin had seen the transformation so many times that it no longer surprised him.

Meanwhile, Todd Anthony was forcing down Angus Northrup's arm. Sure of victory, the red-eyed man leered into the sawyer's wet, contorted face. Angus grunted and cursed, the muscles in his freckled arm rippling like the great belt that drove the slab saw.

"Had enough?"

"Uhhhh." The sound was part sigh, part groan.

"Had enough?"

"Uhhhh."

"Had enough?"

"Uhhhh."

"Damn it! I can break yer wrist, Angus. Had enough?"

"Uhhhh."

"He ain't had enough till yuh can make him put his arm down," Judd interjected.

"Had enough?"

"Uhhhh."

With a thud, Angus's arm struck the wood-hard straw.

"Phewwwww," Todd whistled, shaking his head wryly.

Angus massaged his arm. "Go tuh hell," he growled.

"Huh?"

"Go tuh hell," the sawyer repeated dully.

"Listen, mister —"

"HERE!" Eben shouted. "HERE! Let's all have another cripeless beer, eh? Come over here and have a drink, Toddie!"

"Shut up fer a second!" Todd snapped.

His fists hung close to his hips, like the hands of a gunfighter. He turned back to Angus.

"What was it yuh said tuh me, mister?"

Eben seized Todd's arm and tugged him toward the churn. "Come on now, Toddie. Come on now, Toddie." He might have been coaxing an obstinate puppy. "Come on now, Toddie."

All the way back to the churn, Todd kept looking over his shoulder at the sawyer. Angus continued to kneel by the straw, and he was still rubbing his defeated arm.

Experience told Kevin that before the day ended, these men would fight. Fist fighting was one of the essential rituals in the world of men.

"Sing somethin', Juddie," Eben begged.

My name is Howard Carey,
Near Grand Falls I was born,
In a cozy little cottage
On the banks of the St. John —

"Too cripeless sad!" Eben howled. "Sing somethin' cheerful, Juddie!"

Here's a cuckoo! There's a cuckoo!
Here's a cuckaroo!

Here's a cuckoo! There's a cuckoo!
There's a cuckaroo!

"Damn it, man, but yuh make a lot of noise." Angus North-rup growled, masking his annoyance in a grin. Judd swung on him, glowering.

"A man can make as damn much noise as he damn well wants tuh when he's in his own damn barn drinkin' his own goddamn beer!"

"HERE NOW!" Eben yelled. "Let Juddie sing! Come on now, Juddie! Love tuh hear yuh sing. Jist love tuh hear yuh sing, Juddie, boy!"

"Yeah," Judd growled. "Yeah."

"Sure," Angus agreed. "I didn't mean nothin' Judd. Allus did love tuh hear yuh, sing. Sing somethin' else, Juddie."

"But don't sing nothin' that's too cripeless mournful!" Eben said.

Judd gulped brew and tossed the mug to the sawyer.

"No hard feelin's," he said. "No hard feelin's."

"No, Juddie. No hard feelin's."

"I'd hate tuh think this beer of mine had stirred up hard feelin's between any of the boys."

"No, Juddie. There ain't no hard feelin's."

"Are yuh sure, Angus? Are yuh sure?"

"Yeah, I'm sure, Juddie. No hard feelin's."

"I'm glad tuh hear that, Angus. I wouldn't want any hard feelin's. I ain't that kind of a feller, Angus. I don't hold no hard feelin's."

"No, nor me, Juddie. I never held no hard feelin's against a man in my whole life."

"Are yuh sure, Angus?"

"Yeah, I'm sure as sure, Juddie. No hard feelin's a-tall."

"Shake on it?"

"Put'er there, Juddie!"

The two men shook hands.

"Sing somethin'," Eben cried. "Sing somethin' for cripes' sake!"

Here's a cuckoo! There's a cuckoo!
Here's a cuckaroo!
Here's a cuckaroo! There's a cuckoo!
There's a cuckaroo!

While Judd sang, Eben resumed his dance. As he gambolled and capered he blew his cheeks full of air, then slapped his face with his palm, as though his mouth were a drum.

"Ya-ha-ha-ha-whoooooo!"

"Anybody wanta jump through the broom?" Todd shouted.

"Ain't got no broom."

"Get me a fork, then. Anythin'll do."

While Judd sang and Eben danced, Todd fetched a fork. He grasped the tip of the handle with one hand and the base, just above the tines, with the other. The fork and his arms made a trapeze level with his knees, bending slightly; he jumped over the handle and laughed triumphantly, holding the fork behind him.

"Anybody else able tuh do that?"

"Nobody else is crazy enough tuh try," Angus jeered.

"Huh? Yuh sayin' I'm crazy?" Todd's red eyes gleamed.

"No, he ain't sayin' yer crazy, Toddie!" Eben yelled. "Come on now, let's all have another drink! Ya-ha-ha-ha-whooooo!"

Here's a cuckoo! There's a cuckoo!
There's a cuckaroo!
Here's a cuckoo! There's a cuckoo!
There's a cuckaroo!

"Ya-ha-ha-ha-whooooo!" Eben screamed. "Cripes! Ya-ha-ha-ha-whoooooooooooo!"

After two hours in the barn, Judd went away with the men. When he returned, it was supper time. He staggered into the kitchen, roaring with drunken laughter, and dumped an armful of groceries on the table.

Grabbing Mary by the shoulders, he spun her around and rubbed her cheek with his unshaven chin. This was as close as he ever came to kissing her.

"Hel-oh-ah-Mar!" he roared.

She laughed and pushed him away.

"Oh, you big silly!" she chided him.

He jerked a bottle from under the bib of his overalls, screwed off the cap and drank noisily.

There was girl in our town,
In our town did dwell,
She loved her husband dearly
But another man twice as well!

"Kevin!" he thundered. "Kevin!"

Kevin approached him, grinning nervously. And Judd exploded with laughter and grabbed the seat of Kevin's shorts and swung him high in the air. Such romping was as close as he ever came to a caress.

Kevin squirmed and kicked, but he did not really want to get away. He enjoyed the sense of helplessness he felt in his father's arms.

Judd threw him on the floor and knelt beside him, wrestling with him, tickling the backs of his knees and his armpits. He jerked up Kevin's shirt and poked his navel with a finger, rolled him over and smacked the seat of his pants, pinched his ear lobes and mussed his hair, grasped his ankles and stood him on his head, until Kevin was giggling hysterically, his eyes blurred and dilated with excitement.

"Fight me now! Fight me!" Judd ordered.

Kevin stood up. Judd knelt, facing him.

They boxed. Judd caught most of Kevin's blow on his palms. His own fist opened just before it landed and he slapped Kevin's cheeks and ears briskly with his open hand.

"That's enough!" Judd cried. "I give up! Yuh beat me!"

He squatted on the floor and drank from his bottle.

Kevin laughed. His face was still stinging from the force of Judd's slaps. But he was happy.

> *Here's a cuckoo! There's a cuckoo!*
> *There's a cuckaroo!*
> *Here's a cuckoo! There's a cuckoo!*
> *There's a cuckaroo!*

Judd had bought bologna, canned pineapple, peanut butter, marmalade, oranges, and the canned clams that he liked to eat cold and raw when he was drunk.

Supper was a feast. Kevin chewed slowly, extracting the last drop of flavour from the moist peanut butter, rolling the shreds of syrupy pineapple pulp on his tongue. At certain seasons, the O'Briens went weeks without tasting any food other than bread, milk, eggs, and potatoes.

Judd, who claimed to have no taste for such delicacies, ate clams and drank black tea out of a tin mug, blowing on it to cool it. He was proud of the food piled on his table, Kevin knew, and basked in the excitement of his wife and son as though their hunger were a kind of tribute.

Nine

Judd got drunk on weekdays only when the mill shut down because of rain or a failure in the machinery. On most nights, he ate supper, worked for an hour or two in the garden or in the barn, then dozed on the cot until Mary called him to bed. But on rare occasions, after the kerosene lamps were lit, he sat at the kitchen table and made pictures, while Kevin leaned across his arm, his chin resting in his palms, and watched. From time to time, Mary left her chair to glance at Judd's handiwork and laugh. Gripping the lead pencil as though it were an axe handle, pressing it down so hard he tore through the paper, Judd drew preposterous fat horses with melancholy eyes and great, dropping bellies. As he sketched, his forehead wrinkled in concentration and he chewed at his lips and moistened his pencil with his tongue. Kevin watched, eyes narrowed, lips drawn back from his teeth.

"Now, this here's a mule," Judd explained, "Bet yuh ain't never seen a mule, eh?"

"Jist in pictures, I guess."

"Yeah. Well, this here's a mule."

Judd dampened the graphite with saliva and sketched a beast with long, triangular ears.

"Drove a team of mules when I was Out West," Judd explained. "Stubbornest damn things yuh ever seen."

He pencilled a harness on the mule. Over the years, Kevin had heard his father speak often, but always briefly, of his experience Out West. Like many Lockhartville men, Judd had gone on a harvest excursion to Saskatchewan in his youth. When they reminisced about their days on the wheat harvest, most of the men claimed they wished they had not come home. "If I'da knowed then what I know now," Judd would say. "I'da never come back. That's a big country — Out West." To Kevin, the Out West spoken of by his father was as exotic as the lands depicted on pink and blue maps in the back of the Bible.

Now Judd swept up his sketches and wadded them in his fists.

"Guess that's enough foolishness for tonight," he said shortly.

He removed the chimney from the lamp, touched the paper to the wick, and carried the flaming sheets to the stove, where he tossed them into the fire box.

"Judd!" Mary cried. "You'll burn the house down!"

"Eh? Jist gittin' rid of some damn foolishness."

He lay down on the cot. Five minutes later, he was snoring. Kevin knew that his father would have died rather than have any man in Lockhartville know that he had amused himself by making pictures. Such games were for children and idiots.

In other evenings, Grandmother O'Brien sat under the kerosene lamp and read aloud from the Bible.

All the mill people held the Bible in superstitious respect. So it was with Judd. When his mother read, he threw his cigarette in the stove; he would have considered smoking during a Bible reading the most egregious vulgarity. He lay on the cot with his hands under his head, eyes open, listening.

Kevin sat on the arm of his mother's rocking chair. Putting her hands under the armrest, Mary took his hand. They held hands slyly, unknown to Judd and Martha, who would have snorted in disgust had they observed the gesture. From time to time, his mother gave him a little intimate, confiding smile. He breathed the familiar lilac and wintergreen fragrance of her perfume, felt the rich warmth of her body. And Grandmother O'Brien read:

And as for thy nativity, in the day thou wast born, thy navel string was not cut, neither was thou washed in water to supple thee, nor wast salted at all, nor swaddled at all. None eye pitied thee, to have compassion upon thee; but thou wast cast out in the open field, to the loathing of thy person in the day that thou wast born...

Kevin shuddered and his mother's grip on his fingers tightened. Martha seemed to read less with piety than with grim satisfaction. Under the book resting in her lap lay her hot, wool-wrapped brick.

And as I passed by thee and saw thee polluted in thine own blood, I said unto thee that wast in thy blood, Live; yes, I said unto thee that was in thy blood, Live. I have caused thee to multiply as the bud of the field, and thou hast increased and waxen great, and thou art come to excellent ornaments: thy breasts are fashioned and thine hair is grown, whereas thou wast naked and bare...

Grandmother O'Brien loathed nakedness, Kevin knew. "Devilish," he had heard her say. "Ain't no other name for it but clear sheer devilish! Them young girls runnin' around in them bathin' suits — why, they might jist as well leave their backsides bare and be done with it. That June Larlee! Ugh! They oughta be whipped, all of 'em. They oughta be whipped good and proper. Naked! Devilish, I call it. Devilish!" And her eyes would burn with scorn and rage.

Now, when I passed by thee, and looked upon thee, behold thy time was the time of love and I spread my skirt over thee and covered thy nakedness; yes, I swore unto thee and entered into a covenant with thee, saith the Lord God, and thou becamest mine . . .

Later that night, Kevin awoke to the sound of his grandmother singing:

There is a fountain filled with blood,
Drawn from Emmanuel's veins,
And sinners plunged beneath that flood
Lose all their guilty stains.

And, lying there in the dark, Kevin remembered a time, long ago, when he had gone hunting with his father.

He was six years old, and for weeks his father had promised to take him hunting.

When the day finally came, Kevin was almost beside himself with excitement.

He was then very small and he danced and chattered until his father told him that unless he was quiet, he would not be allowed to go. His antics would frighten away the deer, his father said.

Terrified of being left home, Kevin fell silent and walked on tiptoe. He looked on admiringly as his father dismantled the .22 calibre rifle and hid the parts under his overalls bib.

"Season don't open for another month. Never know when yuh might run intuh a warden," Judd explained.

In this long-ago time, Kevin did not know what a "season" might be, and he suspected that a "warden" might be some ferocious species of beast. But he had learnt not to ask questions of his father, who usually responded by shaking his head in disgust and reprimanding him for his stupidity.

They tramped across the heath and down the abandoned logging road. As they walked on, they came to taller trees, spruce and balsam fir, and the shadows around them thickened. Kevin alternately walked and trotted, keeping up to his father, who never slowed his pace for him.

At intervals, the road was lost in huge puddles of muddy water, clouds of blackflies and mosquitoes humming above them. Judd waded the puddles with Kevin perched on his shoulders, his legs scratched by the denim of his father's smock, his father's horny hands gripping his knees.

Once across the puddle, Judd stopped quickly and dropped him and Kevin walked again, secretly disappointed, wishing his father would carry him all the way. He would have loved to have ridden mile after mile on his father's back, swaying in time to his stride. But he knew this wish was babyish. So he buried it, and felt ashamed.

"Yuh gittin' tired?" Judd asked suspiciously.

"Gosh, no," Kevin answered quickly, afraid of being sent home.

They walked until Kevin was convinced that he had trudged for a hundred miles.

He panted like a collie, and when he tried to hurry, a stitch of pain scalded his side.

"Yuh gittin' tired?" Judd demanded again.

"Gosh, no," Kevin answered. "I ain't tired."

"Then don't make so damn much noise," his father admonished him.

They came out of the woods at the edge of a field in which the grass grew as high as Kevin's waist and where there were innumerable daisies like white and gold stars.

"We'll stop here for a spell," Judd announced.

Kevin threw himself down and lay on his back, looking at the quivering grass that bent forward as if to cover him. The clouds hung low, swollen into shifting shapes like huge white faces and ships and fish as big as the world, and he wondered how tall he would have to be before he could reach out and touch the sky with his fingers.

His father spread his smock on the ground, squatted on it, and began to re-assemble the gun. Kevin rolled over on his belly and leaned on his elbow to watch him. When he had finished, he sat back with the rifle across his knees and waited.

"There gonna be a deer come out here?" Kevin asked eagerly.

"Mebbe. Gotta wait and see."

"Gosh!"

He turned and looked in the direction his father was facing. But he could not see above the grass without standing up, and he was very tired.

He rolled over on his back and broke off a daisy. He nibbled a white petal and found it flavourless, then chewed up the golden eye, enjoying its bittersweet pulp, licking at the grains stuck to the backs of his teeth, and wondering how many daisies he would have to eat every day if he were a cow...

He was halfway to his feet before he awoke.

Judd had fired once and was swearing as he reloaded.

"Where? Where? Where?" Kevin cried.

His father threw up the gun barrel and fired again.

The gun cracked and Kevin jumped back in fear.

"Got him! Got him by God!" Judd yelled.

Kevin whirled around and around, frantic because he could not see the deer.

"Where, Daddy, where?" he insisted.

Judd bounded across the field and Kevin ran after him, yelling.

At the centre of the field, Judd stopped.

Kevin ran faster, his heart hammering.

Then he saw the deer.

"Oh!" he cried.

He stopped.

The buck lay sprawled on its belly, one foreleg bent under its body, the other stretched out in the grass and daisies.

"Oh!" he repeated, stunned.

Judd ran forward and straddled the deer's shoulders.

The buck tried to rise, then fell back.

Judd drew a knife.

Kevin giggled. His father looked funny on the deer's back.

Judd bent low, reached under the white throat.

"Oh!" Kevin said. "Oh."

His father's free hand grasped the antlers, jerked the head back.

Kevin's own head went back. His mouth dropped open. His eyes widened, staring.

Red blood gushed out.

"Oh," Kevin groaned. "Oh."

He smelled the blood, hot, saline, sickening.

It seemed to pour from his mouth and nostrils.

"Please, Daddy," he whimpered. "Please."

The earth under his feet was a sea of blood.

Blood. Blood. Blood. Blood.

He put his hands to his throat, as though to staunch a wound.

"Oh, Daddy," he whispered. "Oh, Daddy."

His father carried him home. He floated through a ghost-ridden void and saw only black blobs moving with terrible purposefulness through the shadows. Twice he emerged into semi-consciousness, while his father held him up and he retched.

His mother had undressed him.

Naked, wrapped in a blanket, he lay in her arms.

She rocked him gently, whispered into his hair.

"Baby," she whispered. "Bay-bee. Sweet bay-bee. Sweet Scampi ... Sweet Scampi baby ... Sweetest, sweetest baby ... bay-bee ... bay-beee ... bay-beeee ..."

He tried to draw closer to her warmth, wishing he could crawl into her body and sleep there forever.

Ten

Isabel DuBois was the daughter of a French-Canadian who had come to Lockhartville that summer to work as tally man at the mill. She was in Grade VI, and everything about her — the colour of her hair, her swift, unpredictable movements — reminded Kevin of a squirrel. Because she spoke with a quaint, liquid accent, he thought her as alluringly alien as the purple dahlias beside the front door of the Minard house. And because Riff Wingate, Harold Winthrop, and the others twitted and baited her, he came to feel a deep confraternity with her — even though they had hardly ever spoken to one another.

Riff sat in the seat behind Isabel. In class, when Miss Roache was writing on the blackboard and had her back turned to the room, Riff would bare his yellow-snag-toothed grin and lift his leg until the toe of his sneaker slid under Isabel's skirt and nudged her thigh. The squirrel-haired girl, her eyes flaming, would turn and hit at him with her ruler. Hearing the children giggle, Miss Roache would whirl and demand to know who was responsible for the disturbance. Not a boy or a girl would blink an eye.

At recess each morning, when the children were let out of the class room for fifteen minutes, Harold, Riff, Av, and Alton would corner Isabel between the school and the woodshed.

"Oh, God, yuh look sweet tuhday, Frenchie!" Riff would leer. "Don't Frenchie look sweet, this mornin', fellers? Don't she look sweet, eh? Don't she, eh?"

Isabel would stamp her feet and claw at Riff's face and curse him: Kevin had never heard such oaths and obscenities pour from the mouth of a girl. Her profanity shocked him. But he envied her ability to defy her tormenters. In similar circumstances, he became as dumb and will-less as a stone.

"What colour panties yuh got on tuhday, Frenchie?"

"Oh, didn't yuh know, Riff? Frenchie don't wear no panties. She don't wear no panties a-tall. Didn't yuh know that?"

"Shut your big mouths, you bastards!"

"Aw, come on, Frenchie. Let's see if yuh're wearin' panties, eh? Let's see, eh?"

"Make her show yuh, Riff!"

And Riff, dodging and weaving to evade Isabel's flailing fists, would grab the hem of her skirt and yank it up around her hips. Watching, Kevin blushed and trembled with anger — though he felt a quick little shock of excitement in his stomach as he got a momentary glimpse of her yellow underpants and uncovered flesh.

"I'll tell Miss Roache on you, you big fool, you! You wait and see if I don't!" Isabel would shriek.

"What duh yuh think, fellers, had we better take Frenchie's panties down, eh?"

"Go ahead, Riff! I dare yuh! I dare yuh, Riff!"

And Isabel would back away, cursing them at the top of her voice.

"Watch 'er, Riff! She's gittin' away, boy!"

And the bell would clang and they would scramble back into the school house, the bigger boys cackling and squirming with excitement.

A dozen times a day, Harold or Riff pinched Isabel's rump or pulled her squirrel-coloured hair. Sometimes, at recess or noon hour, they teased her until she wept.

Kevin wished he could tell Isabel that she had one friend in school. He would have liked to have gone to her and told her that he understood her rage and anguish, that he too was the butt of taunts and ridicule. But he was too shy.

When he grew up, Kevin told himself, he would be like the Scarlet Pimpernel or Prince Florizel of Bohemia. He would wear a black, red-silk-lined cape and carry a sword-cane, and he would go all over the world punishing bullies and rescuing the weak and despised. Someday — twenty or twenty-five years from now — his black limousine, driven by a Hindu chauffeur, would turn into the yard in front of a miserable shack on the Lockhartville road. By that time the fame of the Black Avenger would have spread to the four corners of the world. Riff Wingate, a dirt-grubbing, sawdust-covered mill hand, would come from the shack to greet him.

"It's the Black Avenger!" And while Riff — poor humble peasant — knelt in the mud at his feet, Kevin would sweep off his hat and throw back his cloak.

"Do you know me, peasant?"

"Yes, sir, begging your pardon, sir, you are the Black Avenger!"

And Kevin would laugh sardonically and light a fabulously expensive Armenian cigarette.

"Ach, peasant! I am not only the Black Avenger! I am Kevin O'Brien. Do you remember me?"

And Riff would grovel like a whipped cur.

"Please, sir, let me live, sir! Have mercy, sir! Don't kill me. Let me live. Oh, please, please, sir!"

And the Black Avenger — Kevin O'Brien — would raise his sword-cane and—

When the day came that he finally intervened, no one was more surprised than he.

It was a few minutes before the noon bell. Half a dozen boys, led by Riff and Harold, had dragged Isabel into the woodshed. Kevin followed them.

Riff held one of her wrists, Harold the other. The younger boys, Alton Stacey, Av Farmer, Dink Anthony, and Jess Allen, shoved and capered, their eyes spiteful and intent. Had they noticed Kevin, they might have pushed him outside. But they were too engrossed in the scene before them.

"Gawd-a-mighty, yer a hell-cat, Frenchie!" Riff snickered.

She kicked at his shins, lunged forward, and tried to sink her teeth in his arm.

"Nobody's gonna hurt yuh, Frenchie!" Harold grinned. "Jist be a good girl. Ain't nobody gonna hurt yuh!"

"Oh, go poke your pimply face down a toilet hole!" the girl retorted.

"All we're gonna do is take yer little panties down, Frenchie," Av Farmer shrilled.

"Go to hell!"

"Okay, Av. Git tuh work, boy," Riff ordered.

While Riff and Harold tightened their grips and the others moved closer, Av stepped forward and reached down for Isabel's skirt.

"Hey! Hold 'er feet, somebody!"

"You dirty bastard! You sonovabitch!"

To his own amazement, Kevin found himself pushing between Dink Anthony and Jess Allen.

"You leave her alone!" he heard himself saying.

Eight eyes stared in disbelief. Isabel ceased to struggle. Av straightened and turned. For a long moment, the boys were too astounded to move or speak.

Then: "What the hell yuh sayin' there, Key-von?" Av Farmer growled.

The power that had made Kevin intervene had deserted him. He did not know what to say or do next.

"Jist you leave her alone," he repeated meekly.

The six relaxed back into normalcy. There were a few scattered snickers.

"Who says so, eh? Who says so?" Av leered, laying his open hands on Kevin's chest and pushing. "Who says so, eh?"

"Say, who does that little snot-nosed runt think he is, anyway?"

This was Isabel's voice. Yes, she meant him! The withering contempt he saw in her eyes was like the slap of a frozen alder branch across the face.

"Oh, this ain't nobody, Frenchie — jist Key-von!" Riff sneered. They had released her wrists. But she did not attempt to move away.

"Tell him to get lost," Isabel snapped.

"Yuh heard what she said, Key-von! Git lost. Hit the grit, sonny boy. Yuh ain't wanted here."

"Get lost, you nosey little squirt," Isabel called. "Run home and tell your mother to change your didies!"

Kevin slowly back away.

Later, he consoled himself with the reflection that girls were crazy and that the French were a heathenish and perverse people. Frogs, Judd called them. After all, Isabel was only a frog. But each time she crossed the schoolyard, encircled by boys, he found his eyes following her...

Eleven

The manner in which objects grew as they approached fascinated Kevin. There was his father who, a moment ago, had appeared at the end of the gravelled road leading down from the mill. Kneeling in a chair facing the window, Kevin saw him first as a toy man, smaller than Kevin's littlest finger, hopping past the tiny lumber piles. But when he re-appeared, after vanishing behind a clump of matchstick alders, he was as long as Kevin's entire hand.

"Daddy's comin'," he announced, half-turning.

His mother worked over the stove, wisps of hair caught in the sweat on her forehead. Even in the hottest weather, mill men like Judd O'Brien wanted hot meals when they came home from work.

She was hot and tired. "Don't he always come home when the whistle blows?" she snapped.

"What?"

"Don't he always come home when the whistle blows?"

She banged pots together, hating the adhesive heat.

"Gosh, yes. I mean, sure he does."

He turned back to the window. The top rung of the chair bit into his belly, his face flattened against the hot, sticky glass.

Now, turning into the lane, passing the lilac hedge, Judd grew as long as Kevin's arm. The denim smock swung back and forth across his hips, a pendulum keeping time to his stride. Kevin loved the way the mill men carried their smocks, an arm thrown across the chest, the hand resting on the opposite shoulder, pinning the smock there, the other arm swinging free. All the men carried their smocks thus. It made Kevin think of the capes of Hussars.

The aroma of warmed-over beans, compounded of sweetness and fat, merged with the bitter steam of tea. His mother rattled the stove lids, angry with herself for hurrying.

Now his father stood in the dooryard, by the wagonshed. And he was longer than the legs that bent back under Kevin's denim shorts.

Kevin leapt from the chair, bounded across the room, threw open the screen door and ran across the yard to meet him.

Judd sat in the swing that hung in the wagonshed door. He had taken off his gum rubbers and was shaking clouds of aromatic sawdust out of them. Even on Sundays, when he lay resting on the cot, bits of yellow sawdust trickled from his hair.

"Hi!" Kevin said.

He shifted his weight from one foot to the other, waiting to see what his father's mood would be. Their every meeting began with this pause, this moment of waiting.

One of the swallows that nested beneath a horseshoe nailed to a high beam in the wagonshed darted past Kevin's head.

Judd had rolled down the cuffs of the jeans that he wore under his overalls and was rubbing the sawdust away with his thumb. Kevin never looked at these thumbs without thinking of hooves.

"Hot day," Judd commented.

"Yeah," Kevin agreed eagerly.

It was all right. He felt sure of himself now. There were times, especially at the end of hot days at the mill, when his father stared at him sullenly and refused to speak.

Judd bent down and ran his hands briskly through his hair, scratching out showers of spruce and pine dust.

He grunted. "That feels a damn sight better," he said.

Kevin did not speak. Even during his father's relaxed moods, he was terrified of saying the wrong thing. When he was not sure of what he was expected to say, he kept silent. Their conversations were punctuated by gaps of tense, expectant silence.

Judd stood up, shaking himself.

"Guess we'd better git somethin' tuh eat," he said.

They followed the footpath along the wagonshed to the house. Kevin tried to imitate the solemnity and assurance of his father's tread. His consciousness adapted itself to his father's presence, changing. Once he had caught a field mouse and imprisoned it briefly in his closed hand. He remembered the small animal's strange movements, its furious thrusts against his clutching fingers alternating with moments of tremulous peace in the soft centre of his palm. A frantic surge — then quiet. The sequence was repeated over and over. When with his father, he felt this astonishing rhythm of frenzy and peace repeated in his own breast.

His mother had filled their plates with beans and fried potatoes. Bread, butter, and tea completed the meal. And already she had fetched the kerosene lamps from the pantry and placed them on the table, next to the sink, their freshly scrubbed chimneys gleaming.

"Well, Mar," Judd grunted.

"Hi, Judd. Pretty hot day at the mill."

"Hot enough."

Judd threw his smock and overalls on a chair by the door and rolled up his shirt sleeves. Tiny bits of sawdust were caught in the reddish hair on his arms. He washed in cold water, head low, eyes shut, panting and spluttering.

Kevin enjoyed watching his father wash. It was much more

exciting to watch him shave, but that ritual he performed only on Sunday mornings. Kevin could almost tell the day of the week by the length of his father's whiskers. This being Friday night, the whiskers were at their longest: a thick, reddish-brown moustache and beard.

The man and the boy would have eaten in silence if the woman had not prodded them. Sometimes she spoke because their silence made her nervous and lonesome and sometimes simply because their quiet annoyed her.

"Scampi made a hundred in his test today," she said.

Judd ate with his face only inches from his plate, his shoulders rounded almost protectively over his food. He did not look at her when she spoke.

"He did, eh?"

Kevin's ear lobes burned. He was beginning to be embarrassed by his mother's pet name. And, before his father, he was ashamed of his successes at school, sensing that the man despised such things. He had heard him say, scornfully, that if a calf were taken to school and kept there for twenty years it would still be a calf when it left. Judd himself had left school in Grade V, and when he said that a man acted like a college boy he meant that he was both a weakling and a fool.

"Yes," Mary said. "He made a hundred in history."

"Huh."

"Aren't you proud of him?" she insisted.

Kevin wished she would let the matter drop. He hated her nagging moods, the times when she would not let well enough alone.

"It ain't nothin'," he interjected.

"Git me some more beans will yuh, Mar?" Judd asked, not as though he were trying to change the subject but as if he had already forgotten what the subject involved and had allowed it to slip out of his mind because, after all, it did not concern him.

Without speaking, she rose and refilled his plate. Kevin hoped she would not speak of the test again. At the same time he felt hurt that his father had dismissed the matter so indifferently. In his father's presence, he tacitly agreed that school work was a childish thing that deserved no share in the conversations of adults. But that afternoon he had run almost a mile, coming home from school, to wave his test paper under his mother's eyes. The memory of that triumph remained. In spite of himself, he wished that his father would condescend to share in it.

"June Larlee was in today," Mary said.

"Eh?"

Judd had not been listening. When he ate, all his attention was concentrated on his food. He ate with his whole body, like a healthy animal.

"I said June Larlee was in today."

"Oh."

"She said mebbe you and me'd like to go with her and Larry Hutchinson over to the dance in Larchmont tonight."

He scowled, picking his teeth with a fingernail.

"She did, eh."

"I said to stop in when she was going by. Mebbe we'd go. Anyway I'd talk it over with you, I said."

He rose abruptly and crossed to the cot where he sat down and unlaced his rubbers.

"A man works all day in the mill he don't feel much like kickin' up his heels at a dance, Mar."

He removed his rubbers, kicked them under the cot, and lay down, grunting.

"But it's just this once, Judd. You can get cleaned up in no time and I'll press your suit and Grammie can stay with Scampi and —"

He shut his eyes, cutting her off, pushing her out of his consciousness.

Kevin stopped eating. His belly twisted into its familiar, quivering knot.

"Please, Judd."

He did not answer. Perhaps he did not hear her. His ability to detach himself was always his best, most unanswerable argument. He had cut her off as surely as if he had gone into another room and slammed the door in her face.

In a few minutes, he fell asleep. Kevin and Mary walked on tiptoe and talked in whispers to keep from wakening him. Through the window, Kevin saw the outlines of the barn and the wagonshed softening in the purple twilight.

Twelve

There were times, Kevin's mother said, when a person had to dance or die. Once or twice, she had given him lessons in dancing.

"Come on now, Scampi," she cried, taking his hands in hers. "I'm going to teach you to waltz!"

Embarrassed, he tried half-heartedly to pull away. But she would not let him go.

"Now, come on, Scampi! I'll teach you!"

Surrendering to her, beginning to enjoy himself, he brought his feet together, then swung them apart, as she directed. They danced through the house, in and out of his parents' bedroom, across the hall, into his room and back again to the kitchen. She did not let him stop until they were both of them giggling and breathless.

And through it all, she hummed a wordless little tune. This was the music, she said, and he must learn to feel it in his shoulders and hips and legs. At dances, the music was provided by guitars, fiddles, and mandolins. Once she had attended a dance where a blind man had played an accordion and a mouth organ at the same time.

"Oh, Scampi, you'll learn in no time at all. You really will! Someday you'll dance just like your uncle Kaye!" She smiled. "Kaye goes out into the middle of the floor and step dances. He kicks off his boots and dances in his socks! Oh, you should see him, Scampi. All of my people — every one of them — were dancers..." Her voice trailed away.

Grandmother O'Brien said that dancing was sinful. Salome, dancing before Herod the King, had demanded the head of John the Baptist. John the Baptist, Grandmother O'Brien said, had founded the Baptist Church. Ever since his death, the Baptist Church had condemned dancing.

"There ain't no greater wickedness, boy," she said darkly. "Men and women pressin' belly tuh belly and hoppin' up and down tuh devilish music! Terrible, bad, wicked things come of dancin', boy. Why, the devil hisself sometimes shows up at dances!"

"Gee whiz!"

"Yes, the devil hisself! It's the God's truth, boy. Why, I remember my own mother tellin' me about a time right here in this very settlement. There was a girl lived here, a girl name of Hutchinson, I do believe — and that girl loved dancin'. Rain or shine, she never missed a dance. Well, boy, one night there was a dance in the school house and about half-way through the evenin' a stranger walked in. He was black as a gypsy, Mother said, and his suit was as black as coal. And that girl that loved dancin' so much shared every dance with him! Nobody had ever seen anybody dance the way them two danced that night! They waltzed and they jigged and they clogged. They danced long after everybody else stopped dancin' — and still that stranger wouldn't let her stop. He made that girl dance until her feet bled and the blood ran down ontuh the floor! Well, boy, some of the men had a mind tuh stop it — and, yuh know what? — they was froze in their chairs! Yessir, they was froze in their chairs! They couldn't wiggle a finger. And the stranger and the girl kept a-dancin'. The fiddler laid his fiddle down — and, glory! That fiddle kept a-fiddlin' all by itself on a chair! There weren't no human hand nowhere near that fiddle bow but it kept a-playin'. Why, Mother said she never in her life heard a fiddler play like that fiddle played. And that stranger kept that girl a-dancin' until daybreak! After he left the people got up and looked at that girl and yuh know what they found, boy? Yuh know what they found?" Her voice became a high, quivering whisper. "Well, boy, they found two terrible big burns on her back where the stranger's hands had touched her, and — listen tuh this, boy! — there was a smell of brimstone in the room!"

Kevin thought of his mother dancing belly to belly with a gypsy-faced man in a coal black suit. The thought made him look over his shoulder and shiver.

For Mary went to dances now. June Larlee would come for her, and as his mother led him to bed, Kevin would look back and see June slouching in the chair by the window, making a ribbon of her chewing gum and running it in and out of her mouth. Sometimes, she would pull up her dress and scratch at her legs where her tight rubber garters had made them itch.

"'Nighty-night, Scampi," she would call. And his hatred for her would rise in his throat like gall.

In putting him to bed before she left for a dance, Mary gave him even more caresses and endearments than usual. But he knew it was a sham.

She was abandoning him. Every kiss was a swindle and a betrayal. A million kisses would not have assuaged his anger and hurt. Stroking his cheek as she sat in the chair by his pillow, she sang to him:

> *I see a fireplace, a cosy room...*
> *A little nest that nestles where the roses bloom.*

Just Mollie and me, and baby makes three,
Are hurried to my blue heaven...

He wished he could contract a mortal illness — some horrible, incurable disease like the leprosy mentioned in the Bible. She would be sorry then! He saw himself on his deathbed. A doctor in a white smock stood at the foot of the bed. His parents knelt on the floor, gazing tearfully at his face; on his cheeks there was an angelic pallor like that on the cheeks of Eva St. Clair. It was dusk, and the room smelled of flowers.

The doctor wiped a tear from his eye.

"Mrs. O'Brien, be brave; your son is dying."

Mary buried her face in his quilts and wailed.

"Oh, no, doctor! No! No! No! It isn't true! Say it isn't true, doctor! Please, say it isn't true!"

"Alas," said the doctor, blowing his nose and again wiping his eyes. "Alas, it is too true."

"Oh, Scampi," she moaned. "Oh, I'm so sorry, Scampi! I'm so sorry for the terrible way I left you alone and went to dances. If you get better I promise I won't ever do it again. I promise, Scampi!"

Sobbing piteously, she pleaded with him.

A gentle smile touched his death-white lips as he whispered —

"What's wrong, Scamper?"

"Huh?"

"You were a million miles away."

"Oh, I guess I'm just sleepy," he said sulkily.

"Oh, my! You look fierce, Scamp. You aren't mad at me are you, sweetikins?"

"No. I ain't mad."

She was a fool. He wished she would go away.

"That's my baby." She bent down to kiss him.

"Ummmmmmmmmmmm-eh!" He turned away his head.

Taking the lamp, she started toward the door.

"Goodnight, sweetikins!"

"'Night."

Purposely, he closed his eyes before she left the room, spurning her.

And she didn't even notice that I didn't want her to go! he reflected. The big fool! A fat lot she cares for me! Sweetikins — horse chestnuts. The big fool!

He lay in the dark and listened, hearing first the small, comforting sounds of her moving about in the kitchen and, a little later, the harsh, conclusive sounds of her steps on the porch.

She was singing again. Her voice came faintly from the dooryard, fading into silence as she and June walked away from the house:

> *Put me in your pocket*
> *And I'll go along with you,*
> *No more will I be lonesome*
> *And no more will I be blue...*

"Oh, Mummy. Oh, Mummy... please don't leave me," he whispered.

Thirteen

In almost every night of waiting for his mother — and when she was away from home, there was not a moment in which he was not waiting for her to return — Kevin crawled out of bed and stumbled, stupid with sleep, through the darkness to his father. Until Mary got home, Judd lay on the cot in the kitchen, on the straw-filled tick, with an old coat under his head, an army blanket pulled over his shoulders. No words were exchanged when Kevin climbed up beside him. The kerosene lamp, with its wick turned low, glowed like a single red coal. The green mill-wood, smouldering in the stove, crackled and sizzled. Wind wailed on the telephone wires and moaned in the rose bushes under the northern window. The smell of Judd's body was compounded of sweat, tobacco, sawdust, and leather. It made Kevin think of the sharp, good odour of ploughed earth, the aroma of onions and horse droppings.

Kevin lay still, fearful of annoying his father. The man's body was adamant, impenetrable. It was like rocky earth in comparison with the yielding, creek-water body of his mother. The Bible said that man had been created from the dust of the earth and that woman had been made from man's bone. Kevin wondered if this could be a mistake. Surely, his father had been created from stone, chiselled from a boulder like those that stood in the west pasture, and his mother — his mother had sprung from water, risen from the white foam.

He stirred only when the ache in his calves became unbearable. Each time he moved, the man beside him grunted. So he postponed the moment of moving until immobility became torture. Yet even this was preferable to the loneliness of his own room.

His eyes were open, and the darkness in the corners, by the woodbox, under the sink, beneath the table, might have been the shadows of vampires and werewolves. At times like this, he believed in malevolent, occult things. The vampire pushed away the lid of its coffin and rose from the grave — a black Christ, an Antichrist, rising from its sepulchre. Werewolves could be identified by the hair growing on the palms of their hands. The thought made his own hand itch. Secretly, he rubbed his knuckles against his palm...

A vampire could not be seen in a mirror. And vampires and werewolves could be killed only with silver bullets. But if one made the sign of the cross and cried, "In the name of the Father and of the Son and of the Holy Ghost!" these monstrosities would cower and disappear. He shaped the words soundlessly, so that his father would not hear. "In the name of the Father and of the Son and of the Holy Ghost." But if he came face to face with a vampire his lips might be paralyzed with fear!

Were there vampires in the Lockhartville cemetery? Was one of these monsters even now placing hairy palms against the inside of a coffin lid? Was something with red, dripping fangs even now crouching under the window?

In spite of himself, he found his eyes turning toward the window. No! He did not wish to look! But his head moved with a will of its own. In another second he would be looking at the glass and then he would see —

"What in hell's the matter with yuh, Kev?"

"Huh?"

"What in hell's the matter with yuh? Why in hell can't yuh lay still for a minute?"

"Oh, I'm sorry. Nothin's the matter," Kevin whispered.

He closed his eyes.

But what of the thing in the cellar that drinks so much blood?

From where had this thought come? It was as though something evil and invisible were whispering at his ear.

But what of the thing in the cellar that drinks so much blood?

He put his hands over his ears. But he could not shut out the whisper.

But what of the thing in the cellar that drinks so much blood?

In an attempt to exorcise the voice, he began a mental catalogue of all the sane, substantial things in this room.

On the shelf between the pantry door and the door to the living room: an alarm clock, a box of household matches, three cuds of chewing tobacco, scissors, spools of white and black thread, a bottle of iodine, and a jar of the salve that his mother rubbed on his chest and throat when he had a cold.

But what of the thing in the cellar that drinks so much blood?

On the green frame of the pantry door: shamrock-shaped tin tags from chewing tobacco, shaping the letter K. Long ago, his father had driven the tags into the wood with a hammer. On the shelf above the cot: mail-order catalogues, the wooden box in which his father kept bills and lawyers' letters, felt inner-soles for Judd's gum rubbers, a stack of love story magazines, school books, his water colours, a broken cap pistol.

But what of the thing in the cellar that drinks so much blood?

On the shelf above the woodbox: three of the bricks which his grandmother heated and held against her belly, a jar of stove polish and a sooty-black rag, his father's leather work mitts, a hunting knife, a jar of shingle nails, a claw hammer.

But what of the thing in the cellar that drinks so much blood?

In the cabinet over the sink: yellow, ammoniac laundry soap, white, lily-scented toilet soap, his father's shaving brush and razor, pills for toothache and earache, ointments for cuts, Epsom salts, sulphur, witch hazel.

But what of the thing in the cellar that drinks so much blood?

On the pole hanging over the stove: towels, dish cloths, face cloths, all made from rags or flour bags, a pair of his denim shorts and one of his father's cotton shirts which his mother had washed that day...

He awoke with a jerk. He did not know if he had slept for only a second or for hours. Knowing that his father never slept during these nights of waiting, he felt rebuked. He listened to the sounds of cars passing, watched their headlights flash across the walls.

On dance nights, many cars passed. Nearing the house, the sad night-sound of their motors rose in a crescendo of desolation and loss. Passing the lilac hedge, the sound subsided, as though the cars were being driven into a bottomless valley. Soon, there was only a hum, no louder than that of a mosquito. Then, there was no sound at all. Each time a car neared the house, Judd's head rose a fraction of an inch from the pillow. When the car did not stop, his head sank down again.

Silently, Kevin counted the cars. One. Two. Three. Four. Five. Six. Seven. Eight. Nine. Ten. Each number was the undulating whine of a motor, a golden ghost of light streaking across ceiling and walls. Twenty... thirty... thirty-five... thirty-nine, forty...

In some of the cars, men were singing. In others, voices were raised in anger. Sometimes — not often — words were distinguishable.

Oh, there's a love-knot in my lariat!
And I'm dreamin' of my little prairie pet.

"Damn rat! Damn friggin' pig. Damn stinkin' louse!"

When I grow too old to dream
I'll have you to remember!

"I told the sonovabitch! I told the goddamn stinkin' bastard!"

Sweet Adeline, my Adeline!
Each night, dear heart, for you I pine...

"Keep your hands to yourself, you stinkin' —"
The songs were lively but sad, almost wistful.

They were the whistle of a locomotive in the night, the wind under the eaves, the wail of the telephone wires. The threats and curses were the speech of men who feared nothing, men who swaggered unafraid through the vampire-ridden night. Here were Harold Winthrop, Hod Rankin, and Av Farmer, grown to manhood. And Kevin both despised and envied them. Someday he would be a king and a vampire, while these men would never be anything more than turnip-heads and slab-carriers. And yet, if they could have chosen between his dream of kingship and their electric muscles and roaring bravado —

A car stopped. Thrusting Kevin aside, Judd rose and went to the window facing the road.

"Good night, beautiful!"

"Oh, you big silly!"

The first voice was the teasing, intimate voice of a man. The second voice, giddy with laughter, was that of Mary.

Judd doubled his fist and brought it down hard on his palm. "Ha," he ejaculated, the sound midway between triumph and despair.

Kevin sat up. He decided to steal back to his room before his mother entered the kitchen.

"Stay there!"

"Huh?"

"Stay there, I told yuh!"

"Gee, sure, Daddy."

Shivering, he drew the army blanket around his shoulders like a shawl.

The car hiccoughed into gear. He heard his mother's footsteps, running up the path. She sounded as if she were walking on something breakable. Had he been blind he would have known her by her steps.

Judd went to the table and turned up the lamp. Kevin blinked in the sudden rush of brightness.

Mary threw open the door and swept into the room. Her hair was dishevelled, her body skittish with excitement.

Then she froze.

"Scampi! Why aren't you in bed?"

Her words were like a slap.

"Gee, Mummy," he stammered. "Gee whiz."

Shoeless, his father stood in the centre of the floor. There was something evil in his eyes.

"He's waitin' fer yuh, same as he allus does," he grated harshly.

Mary flung her coat on a chair. "There isn't any need for him to stay up! That's all your idea! You want to shame me! You want to make him ashamed of his mother!"

"If yuh ain't ashamed now, there ain't nothin' I'n do tuh shame yuh," Judd said.

He emitted a terrible, unreal snicker.

"Come on, Scampi! You come to bed where you belong, right this minute!"

She seized his wrist and wrenched him to his feet.

"Gee, Mummy…"

"You come to bed!"

She led him back to his room, walking so fast that he had difficulty in keeping his footing. Her fingers were a vise, burning his wrist. The floor was cold and gritty under his bare feet.

Fourteen

"Don't you want Mummy to be happy, Scampi?"

"Gee, sure, I want yuh tuh be happy."

"Sometimes, I don't believe anyone wants me to be happy. It seems like everybody in the world wanted to make Mary Dunbar O'Brien unhappy. Even you, Scampi! You don't want Mummy to go to dances. But going to dances makes Mummy happy. Don't you understand, Scamper?"

"Sure. I understand."

"No. No. You don't understand at all. You're only a little boy. I shouldn't even ask you to understand. I should stay home, if you want me to. I should stay in this old house all the time and rot. I should stay in it until I'm an old, old, old woman. That's what you want me to do, Scamper?"

"No! Gosh, no, Mummy!"

"Yes, it is. You don't even want me to go to a dance!"

"Gosh, no, I never said I didn't want yuh tuh go tuh dances, Mummy."

"You didn't say it, mebbe. But I know you don't want me to. As soon as I get out of the house you go running to your father. He doesn't want me to go either. He wants me to sit in the kitchen until I rot. And as soon as I get out of the house you go running to him. You do that every time, Scampi!"

"It don't mean nothin'."

"Yes, it does! It means a whole lot. It means you like your father more than you like me. That's what it means."

"No, it don't!"

"Yes, it does!"

"No, it don't!"

"Do you really and truly love me, Scamper?"

"Gosh, you know I do!"

"Tell me that you love me, Scamp."

"I love you, Mummy."

"Say it again."

"I love you, Mummy."

"— Again."

"I love you, Mummy."

"— And again."

"I love you, Mummy."

"Oh! I could never get tired of hearing you say that, Scampi! Never! Never! Never! Some people have to be loved or they'll die. Mummy's like that. Mummy wants you to love her to pieces, Scampi."

"Gee."

"Let me tell you something, Scampi. I don't know how to say it. But I want you to remember it. I don't want you ever to forget it. Will you promise me you won't forget?"

"Sure."

"Cross your heart and hope to die?"

"Cross my heart and hope to die."

"Well, then, Scampi, listen: Mummy loves you. But when you really love somebody, you have to keep giving them parts of yourself. I don't know how to explain it. But it's as if you had to cut off a finger or tear off a piece of your heart and give it to the person you love. And you have to keep doing that — you have to keep giving pieces of yourself, day after day. That means you have

122

to be awfully strong to love. And Mummy isn't always strong. And Mummy isn't always brave. Sometimes, she's too scared and weak to cut off a part of herself, even a little part. Because it hurts, Scampi. It hurts to give away a part of yourself, even when you're giving it to someone you love."

"Gosh."

"But I want you to remember that Mummy loves you. Don't ever forget that, Scampi."

"I won't forget."

"Sometimes I feel as if I wasn't any older than you. Isn't that silly? I was sixteen when you were born, Scampi. Sixteen! But I guess that seems grown up to you. It seemed grown up to me, too. But it isn't, not really. I was just a baby. And I guess I've never had time to grow up. I guess mebbe that being grown up means getting used to being unhappy. I can't get used to it, Scampi. I want to dance and sing and wear pretty dresses and play!"

"Gee, sure, Mummy."

"And you want me to be happy?"

"Gee, sure."

"Oh! That's my sweetikins. That's my sugar-baby! Tell me that you love me, Scampi. Tell me again!"

"I love you! I love you! I love you!"

And another time: "You should hear the music, Scampi! It makes you want to dance and dance and dance."

"Yeah."

"You're not mad at me for wanting to dance, are you, Scampi?"

"No."

"Of course, it isn't just the dancing. It's being with people — real living, breathing people."

"Yeah."

"It's wonderful to be alive, Scampi. You don't know how wonderful it is until you've been dead. Sometimes I think that I've been dead for years and years. I work in this old house and I'm dead. I don't feel anything. Then I go into the hall and hear the violins and see the people dancing and, all of a sudden, I'm alive again! It's like rising from the dead, Scampi!"

"Gee whiz!"

"Do you know that most people are dead? Did you ever think of that? Lockhartville is full of dead people. The old women cook and clean and scrub and make pickles. And all the time, they're dead. And the men are dead, too. When I get away from Lockhartville, I feel like somebody who's risen from the dead! You don't know what a terrible, wonderful feeling it is, Scamp!"

"Gosh!"

"Oh! When I look at their faces I want to yell, You're dead! You're dead! You're dead! That's what I feel like doing, Scampi!"

"Gee, Mummy."

"Yes! That's what I want to do! I wish they'd all fall over and I wish somebody would come and take them away and bury them! Because they're dead! Dead! Dead!"

"Gosh!"

"And sometimes I'm dead, too. But when I hear the music I come alive again! It's a terrible thing to be dead, Scampi. There isn't anything worse than being dead."

Fifteen

Every evening, Judd worked in the garden. The only fertile land he possessed was a narrow strip between the heath where he pastured his cows and the swamp where they drank. But, slaving every night, after his eleven hours of drudgery in the mill, Judd made this soil yield all of the vegetables that his family ate.

Kevin loved the smell of the manure-seasoned earth, the fragrance of ripe peas and squash, the feel of the soft corn stalks and abrasive turnip tops on his feet and legs — but he hated to work with his father. The man attacked the land as though it were an obdurate and intractable beast. When he plunged his fork into a hill of early potatoes, his grunt was almost a snarl. And when the yield was meagre, he cursed soil, seed, and weather as though they had joined in a conspiracy to thwart him.

"Damn potatoes ain't no bigger'n walnuts," he spat, kicking the tubers viciously, as though they were living things, capable of feeling pain.

Kevin picked string beans, plopping them into a bucket hanging from his elbow. From time to time, he ate one of the raw, yellow-green pods, savouring its grassy sweetness. At long intervals, Judd straightened to roll a cigarette or to wipe the sweat from his eyes, his leathery palms leaving streaks of reddish dirt on his forehead.

And Judd did not fail to notice when Kevin slowed or stopped.

"Better sharpen up there, Kev. We ain't got all night, boy." Or, "If yuh can't do no better'n that, mebbe yuh better go back tuh the house an' stay with yer mother."

Kevin scowled and flushed. For a little while, he worked with furious haste. Then, "Look what yer doin' there, Kev. Yer only gittin' about half of them beans, boy."

No, his father would not admit that he could do anything right. He was either too fast or too slow, too clumsy or too weak. This work that he would have enjoyed had he been free to do it in his own way became grinding drudgery when he did it under his father's supervision.

Leaving the garden at nightfall, they were both of them exhausted and sulky, hating the work and one another.

Moreover, Judd's outbursts of rage were becoming more frequent and more capricious. Kevin knew when to expect a strapping. And there were the incidents involving the orange-haired cat and the runaway cow...

Judd kept two cows. One of them — a red, swaybacked, sad-eyed creature that he had bought while he was drunk — hated the barn and vaulted over fences whenever Judd tried to drive her from the pasture.

The animal's perversity drove Judd into fits of rage that both terrified and amused Kevin. When she bounded over the fence, scrambled out of the ditch, and trotted down the road, her doleful face turned sideways, her aspect one of melancholy triumph, Kevin swayed between tears and laughter, and when Judd bellowed, broke off an alder switch, and took after her, Kevin first shrank back in fear, then slapped his hands over his mouth and giggled.

The cow had run away almost every night during the summer. The climax came one evening after Judd had come home and found Mary getting ready to go to another dance.

As usual, the cow jumped the fence and started down the road.

"Come back, yuh sad-faced bitch!" Judd howled, running after her.

Kevin always laughed when he saw a grown man running.

"Come back, yuh swaybacked fool!"

Brandishing his alder switch, Judd stumbled and fell to his knees. He rose, brushing himself and swearing incoherently.

"Come back, yuh dirty bitch!"

The cow ran faster.

Judd roared at Kevin.

"Hey! What the hell's wrong with yuh, boy? Head her off! Head her off, damn it!"

Quickly, Kevin crawled under a barbed wire fence and galloped across the garden to the road.

"Head her off! Head her off there!"

He clambered over the pole fence lining the road and leapt the ditch. He stopped, about twenty feet in front of the cow.

"Head her off! Head her off!"

The cow halted and stared stupidly at Kevin.

"Go on, now! Get back there!"

He was pleading with her.

"Go back to the barn! Go back to the barn, you old fool."

Running back and forth across the road, he kept her from getting away. Judd caught up to her, struck her with the switch, and turned her back toward the gate.

She tossed her head once, as though in defiance, then slumped in defeat.

"Open the gate, boy! Wake up there and open the gate!"

Kevin scampered to the gate and struggled with the stiff, heavy bolt. When it slid back, letting the gate swing open, he sighed with relief.

The cow swung through the gate, entered the dooryard, and made for the barn, Judd trotting beside her, still wielding the switch.

"Took yuh long enough tuh git that damn gate open!" he barked as he ran by, puffing.

Spiritlessly, Kevin followed his father to the barn.

The cows were stanchioned. Having already forgotten her adventure, the red cow chewed her cud complacently.

The thing that happened next, Kevin never forgot. For Judd grabbed a pitchfork and, exerting every ounce of his strength, drove its three tines into the cow's side.

Kevin moaned as though the fork had gored him. The cow bellowed and tried to free herself from her stanchion.

"Yuh dirty bitch!"

Judd tore out the tines. Thick, dark blood spurted from the wounds. Smelling the blood, the other cow bellowed in terror. Her head almost touching the floor, the swaybacked cow was choking herself in her efforts to escape from her stanchion.

"I'll kill yuh, yuh bitch!"

Judd drove the tines home again. Kevin clapped his hands to his chest as if he had been speared. "Oh, please, Daddy... Oh, please, God," he whimpered.

The cow, gushing blood in black jets, sank to her knees. Blood soaked into the straw on the floor. Her stable mate kicked and jerked wildly, trying to escape from the hot, salt stink of blood.

"That'll learn yuh, yuh whore. Yuh whore!"

The bloody fork still in his hands, Judd turned toward Kevin. For one insane moment, Kevin believed that the man was about to impale him.

"No, Daddy! Don't kill me!" he screamed.

Babbling, his lips frothing, he backed toward the door.

His father threw the fork aside, seized his shoulders, and shook him until his teeth rattled.

"Don't be a damn fool, Kev! Don't be a damn fool!"

With a terrible, sobbing shriek, Kevin wrenched himself free and ran from the cow stable.

"Come back here, boy! Don't be a damn fool!" he heard Judd roaring behind him.

The other incident, that involving the orange-haired cat, took place one Sunday afternoon, about two weeks later.

Judd, Mary, and Kevin went picking blueberries on the heath. Judd picked berries, as he did everything, with glum determination. By the time that Kevin and Mary had each gathered a quart, he would have filled a five-gallon lard pail to overflowing.

The day was cloudless, porous, serene. Kevin and Mary picked side by side, a little apart from Judd. She wore jeans and one of Judd's shirts and her hair was bound with a yellow kerchief, but even now, in the open field, he could smell the lilacs and wintergreen of her perfume.

They laughed together about the way in which the tiny mouths of the berries tickled their fingers.

"They're tryin' tuh kiss you," he told her, shyly.

She laughed, and the sound was like the music of little silver bells.

"Oh, you say sweet things sometimes, Scamper. You really do."

She threw him a little sly, teasing, almost wistful smile.

His knees were stained where he had knelt on them, crushing the rich, juicy berries. He and his mother had eaten berries until their lips, teeth, and tongues were purple-black. He could taste the berries in every fibre of his body. From time to time, he stopped and rubbed a berry between his fingers until all its blue dust was wiped away and it turned shining black.

A sudden thought struck him.

"Do yuh know who yuh remind me of today, Mummy?"

"Who, sweetikins?"

"Ruth — Ruth in the Bible — gleanin' in Boaz's corn field. That's who yuh remind me of."

"Oh, you *are* sweet, Scampi! You really are!"

He searched for words.

"I guess Ruth wasn't a princess, not really. But seein' you pickin' berries here is like seein' a princess — one that's been driven outta her own country so she's had tuh go and pick blueberries, and ... I guess I don't know how tuh say it."

"Oh, you have a fine way of saying things, Scamp. And you know something?" Her voice sank to a whisper, and she leaned closer.

"No. What?"

"That's how I think of myself, sometimes. I think that mebbe I'm really a — oh, a Romanian or a Hungarian princess — and when I was a little small girl, too little to remember anything about it, I —"

He stopped listening. He was sorry that he had spoken. Something in her responses — some nuance of tone or phrasing or gesture — had made the idea seem false and silly. His mother never knew when to stop, he reflected resentfully.

"Hey — yuh fellers can talk when yuh git home. We're up here tuh pick berries!"

Judd laughed, but Kevin detected a note of annoyance in his voice. Perhaps he had overheard their talk of princesses ...

"Golly, we'll be eatin' blueberries for months, Scamp!"

"Yeah."

"Blueberry pies, blueberry muffins, blueberry shortcake,

stewed blueberries — ugh! Well, I guess it's better than it will be in March when we'll be eating potatoes — and potatoes — and potatoes — and potatoes — and potatoes!"

"Yeah."

"Oh, Scampi, it's terrible to be poor, isn't it?"

"I guess so, yeah."

"Come on you fellers! Yuh expect me tuh pick all the berries myself?"

Kevin and Mary bent to their work, winking at one another.

An hour later, they returned, hot and tired, to the house. Judd threw open the door and Kevin and Mary followed him into the kitchen.

The orange-haired cat — a pet of Mary's, which she coddled as though it were an ailing baby — crouched in the centre of the room, playing with a string of sausage, as though the meat were a mouse. As the door opened, the cat looked up in almost human surprise.

"Eh! Ha!"

Judd kicked. The animal skidded across the floor, squealing, its claws screeching as it fought for footing on the slippery linoleum.

"Damn cheat! I ain't never had no use fer a damn cheat!"

Judd thumped his blueberry pail down on the table. He advanced on the cat cringing against the wall. There was fear in its eyes, but it continued to stare hungrily at the meat.

"Shut that damn door!"

Dead-faced, Mary shut the door.

Stunned by Judd's kick or petrified with terror, the cat did not try to run. It pressed against the wall, as though trying to crawl into the wood. Its back curved like a hoop as Judd seized its neck.

"Scratch me, will yuh, yuh cheat! Scratch me, will yuh, yuh cheatin' bitch!"

He carried the quivering, fear-crazed beast to the door.

"Kev! Fetch my hand-axe!"

Kevin stared wildly.

"Yuh hear me? Fetch my hand-axe!"

"Judd!"

Mary's cheeks were like chalk. She swayed, as though, she might faint.

Judd gave her a look that was almost a leer.

"Fetch me that hand-axe! Yuh hear me!"

Mary stiffened, collecting herself.

"You'd better do it, Scampi," she said wearily.

Kevin went to the woodbox and got the hatchet. Holding it in limp, trembling fingers, he followed his father.

Judd ran to the wagonshed.

"Hurry up, boy! This damn cheat's tryin' tuh scratch me!"

Inside, he tore the hatchet from Kevin's hand and thrust the cat down on the chopping block—

Kevin closed his eyes.

"Yuh goddamn cheatin' whore!"

There was a dull thud. The cat screamed. Kevin had never heard such a sound as came from the throat of this cat. It bore no resemblance to the yelp of a cat in pain! This scream was almost a strangled laugh.

Not until he turned did he open his eyes. Then he ran, weeping, to the house. His mother stood on the doorstep, her arms outstretched...

Sixteen

Kevin had learned that there were two kinds of fear. There was daytime fear — his fear of his father and of all strong, unpitying daytime things — and there was nighttime fear, the queasy horror he felt when he imagined a creature in a black cloak creeping toward his bed under cover of the wailing darkness.

The presence of his grandmother O'Brien sometimes filled him with a vague, unsettling dread, akin to that nighttime fear. For years, Martha O'Brien had fought against death. Her struggle was as frantic and squalid as that of a hen in the clutches of a fox. And, like the hen, she was doomed to defeat. Death had infiltrated her body. Death peered from her ice-blue eyes. And when she emitted a lusty cackle it seemed to be death that laughed.

Yet Kevin was drawing closer to her. For she hated the bright, dancing world of the flesh. And it was this world that was taking his mother away from him.

One night when his grandmother and he were alone together, she spoke of the sins that had been committed by June Larlee. She spoke in dark hints and sly conundrums, but he grasped the central fact: June's sins had their origin in her opulent flesh.

"Yes, the flesh, laddie!" Grandmother O'Brien said, her dentures, with their clay-coloured gums, rattling in her mouth. "The sins of the flesh!"

And he thought of June in her tight red shorts. His grandmother said that June was like unto Jezebel, the harlot of Ahab, whose bones had been licked by the dogs. In his mind's eye, June's thighs were like the bristled wick-white fat of pork. Shuddering — yet not without a thrill of cruel joy — he imagined June being pushed closer and closer to the edge of a precipice while the white-fanged hounds howled in the courtyard below her...

"Eh, yes, laddie — when God was on the earth, women like her was stoned — stoned to death, laddie. Can't yuh see that sinful white flesh of hers turnin' black under the stones!"

And Martha O'Brien laughed.

The picture inside Kevin's mind changed. He saw June Larlee on her knees, shielding her face with her arms and whimpering piteously... Surrounding her were robed men with fiery eyes and waist-length beards, and the names of these men were the names of books in the Bible: Isaiah, Jeremiah, Haggai, Ezekiel, Malachi, Joshua. They hurled stones at her, and as the stones sank in her flesh, she screamed — she screamed as the orange-haired cat had screamed under Judd's hatchet. And Kevin bit his lips and groaned, hating himself for having such a dream.

"— And she does terrible, bad wicked things with men, laddie — things so bad I can't tell yuh about 'em. My tongue would burn up in my mouth if I tried tuh tell yuh about such wickedness, laddie..."

He wondered what June and the men did to one another. Something his grandmother had said made him think that, perhaps, they drank of one another's blood. In any case, it was a diabolical, obscene thing that they did. In the days when God had lived upon the earth, men and women who did this thing were smitten with leprosy and they walked over the world in white shrouds, like ghosts, crying, "Unclean! Unclean!"

The thought of uncleanliness made him imagine that perhaps June and the men ate of — but he squelched the thought. It sickened him. He almost retched when he tried to conceive of what the lepers might have meant when they cried, "Unclean! Unclean!"

His grandmother opened the Bible and read:

And I saw in the right hand of him that sat on the throne, a book written within and on the back side, sealed with seven seals. And I saw a strong angel proclaiming with a loud voice, Who is worthy to open the book and to loose the seals thereof? And no man in heaven, nor in earth, neither under the earth, was able to open the book, neither to look therein ...

And the fifth angel sounded and I saw a star fall from heaven unto earth, and to him was given the key of the bottomless pit. And he opened the bottomless pit; and there arose a smoke out of the pit, as the smoke of a great furnace; and the sun and air were darkened by reason of the smoke of the pit...

Kevin's detestation of June and his uneasy awareness of the flesh were heightened and intensified by June's teasing. As summer drifted into fall, her visits became more frequent. Twice she burst into the kitchen on Saturday nights while his mother was bathing him. And each time she made many little snide, giggling remarks about his nakedness.

"You don't have to be scared of me, Scamp. I've seen naked men before, haven't I, Mar?"

And, "Golly, Scamp, you look just like a bantam rooster with all his feathers pulled out!"

And, "Gee, Mar, I'd like to have myself a little play-toy like Scamper to keep me company when I get tired of the big boys!"

And, "Nobody'd have to look at him twice to see he wasn't a girl, would they, Mar?"

Each such remark was followed by a wink and a giggle. Kevin sensed that June found his nakedness not only comical but exciting. And, to his further discomfiture, Mary laughed with her.

"Oh, don't be silly, June!" she said.

But she flushed a little and laughed, and Kevin knew that she considered June's teasing amusing. For the first time in his life, he felt ashamed of his body.

And, a few days later, his shame became an almost superstitious dread.

Late one afternoon he went to Kaye Dunbar's cabin on the creek road.

As he always did, he flung open the door without knocking.

Kaye and a naked woman lay on his straw-filled bunk.

Blushing to the roots of his hair, Kevin whirled and ran back to the road.

"Hey, wait a minute, Namesake!" Kaye yelled after him.

But he did not stop. And behind him he heard the lewd, mocking laughter of June Larlee.

Seventeen

But, one Sunday in October, his path, for a while at least, turned in a new direction.

Mary liked to dress him for Sunday School. She had somehow persuaded Judd to give her the money with which to buy him what she called a "darling little suit." And every Sunday morning she dressed him in black leather shoes, wool knee stockings, flannel shorts, a starched white shirt and bow tie, and a blue blazer. Getting him into these clothes involved innumerable small adjustments: she flicked tons of imaginary lint from his blazer, knotted and reknotted his tie until it almost choked him, straightened his collar and stockings again and again. And when she finished, she stood back and looked him up and down admiringly.

"Oh, Scamper, you're beautiful!" she gloated.

He knew that she was treating him as though he were a doll. These chafing clothes were his doll's suit. Bitterly, he thought of the dolls he had seen whose clothes were stapled to their bodies; he felt as though tacks had been driven through cloth and leather and into his scalded neck, itching legs, and contorted feet. Nothing irked him more than to be made a plaything; he detested the grinning adults who poked and jabbed him and asked him inane riddles. When his mother told him that he was beautiful, he knew she meant that he was as beautiful as a doll — and he hated it.

Coming to the first turn in the road, he sat down by the ditch and took off his shoes and stockings. The rest of the way, he walked barefoot. The soft mud was like a cooling ointment.

He came to the field in which the mill oxen and horses were pastured on Sundays. The horses grazed at one end of the field, the oxen at the other. Kevin could not recall ever having seen them come near one another. The horses ignored the oxen and the oxen did not seem to know that the horses existed; the indifference of the horses sprang from pride, that of the oxen from stupidity. He stood for a moment by the fence, watching them. In the polished October sunlight, the yellow bodies of the oxen called up visions of smoke-coloured fall sunsets. Despite their bulk and power, they looked old and despondent. He remembered the strange, frightening words of Miss Sarah Minard. An ox was a living corpse. Almost everybody in Lockhartville was a living corpse, she had said. And it was true that there was an uncanny, indefinable resemblance between these resting oxen and men let off from their work at the mill. The oxen did not appear to know that they were no longer yoked to the log-boat. Plodding across the rusting grass, they seemed to drag an unseen burden behind them. And it was the same with the men: even on Sunday they did not really interrupt their work. Kevin had seen Judd, lying on the cot, raise his arms and fling them about as if he were throwing boards down the rollers in his sleep.

The horses were better. Men spoke of breaking horses, but, in reality, a horse was never wholly broken until it was killed. He called to the old marble-eyed sawdust horse, and she trotted across the field and reached her head, with its blunt, tobacco-coloured teeth and great, moist nostrils, over the fence.

"Hiyuh, old girl," he said.

She snorted and tossed her head. Suddenly, he felt sad; he wished he dared open the pasture gate and let the horses run away. The oxen, he decided disgustedly, would stay where they were even if the fence were torn down. But the horses — even this old, swaybacked nag, given the chance, would run into the woods like a deer.

"You're nice," he told her. "You're real nice."

She looked at him as though she understood perfectly, as though she could answer him with words of her own, if she wished to. He wondered what horses thought, if their eyes saw the same world as his. Judd had told him once that in a horse's eyes a man looked twenty feet tall. He wondered if this were so.

"Nice old girl," he crooned, "nice old girl."

Abruptly, she turned and trotted away. He was a little annoyed with her. He had imagined that she liked him, enjoyed having him talk to her. Her sudden withdrawal rather hurt him.

"Oh, go on then, you big fool!" he laughed.

And he tossed a pebble between her hooves, so that she threw her head in the air, stared at him for a moment, and then walked lazily away.

The bank was so steep that he had to run down it and clamber out of the ditch on his hands and knees. He brushed off dust and dead leaves and continued on his way.

The mill was silent and motionless. It made him think of a dark, brooding prison. Judd had been fourteen, only three years older than he, when he had first gone to work in the mill. For as long as Kevin could remember he had known, dimly, that the mill was waiting for him. The mere thought of this place of pulsating, shrieking power was sufficient to dispel all but his deepest and most desperate dreams.

Walking through the mire where the road had been churned into muddy soup by wagons, log-boats, and lumber trucks, he visualized himself three years hence: an ox labouring at a slab saw or on a sawdust cart. Perhaps Miss Minard had been right — maybe men would come for him with ropes and knives. He thrust the thought away and walked faster.

A dead raccoon lay by the roadside. As he came near, the ravens that had covered the corpse as flies will cover a lump of sugar, flew up and hovered above him. They made no sound at all.

The raccoon's body was like a piece of fur torn from a coat to stanch a wound. It was almost impossible to imagine that this little heap of bloody rags had ever been a living creature.

Turning his eyes away, he hastened past it.

Ten minutes later, he reached the church. The building was almost a replica of the school house: square, tin-roofed, and whitewashed. Kevin much preferred the appearance of the Anglican church, which had bells and a steeple. But his grandmother O'Brien said that the Anglicans were almost as wicked as the Catholics.

Before entering the church, he hid himself in an alder thicket, washed his feet in a puddle, dried them with his handkerchief, and donned his shoes and stockings. Then, automatically adjusting his consciousness so that he changed from the person he was when he was alone to the person he was when with other people, he went into the building. He was greeted by organ music and the voices of children singing:

> What a friend we have in Jesus,
> All our sins and griefs to bear.
> What a privilege to carry
> Everything to God in prayer!

The children, grouped according to their ages, sat in little clusters in various parts of the room. The smell of the church, the aroma of furniture polish and old, musty books, reminded Kevin of the Minard parlour. Embarrassed by his lateness, imagining that every eye was focused on him, he stumbled awkwardly to his own class, a dozen boys and girls sitting in the pew normally reserved for the choir. The teacher, Mrs. Cranston, nodded to him as he sat down. Her smile was as jarringly sweet as homemade fudge candy.

Oh, what peace we often forfeit,
Oh, what needless pain we bear.
All because we will not carry
Everything to God in prayer.

"Hiyuh, Key-von," Av Farmer whispered.

"Hi."

"Didjer mother change yer didies a-fore she let yuh out this mornin', Key-von?"

"Now, now, Avard and Kevin," said Mrs. Cranston sweetly. "We don't talk with our friends in Sunday School, you know. We wait until Sunday School is over and then we can talk all we want to. I'm sure that all of us understand that, don't we?"

"Yes, ma'am," Av grinned.

"And what about you, Kevin?"

"Yes, ma'am."

Mrs. Cranston was the wife of the foreman of a railway section gang. Like all the Sunday School teachers, she belonged to the higher of Lockhartville's two economic and social classes. "The High Muck-a-mucks," Judd called them. "The rich," Grandmother O'Brien said. Kevin had heard his mother say, enviously, that Mrs. Cranston entertained at bridge parties and that she wore an evening gown when she went to lodge meetings in Larchmont.

Kevin knew that Mrs. Cranston pitied him, and he hated her for it.

"This morning," she smiled, "our lesson has to do with worldly things. Now I'm sure that all of us know what *worldly* means —"

The girls sat in the front pew, the boys in the back. The girls wore little pink or blue or orange bonnets and their beribboned pigtails hung down over the back of the seat. Av Farmer and some of the other boys made a game of jerking the pigtails during class. Kevin thought this unspeakably silly and refused to admit that he would have done it himself had he dared to. Out of the corner of his eye, he saw Av Farmer slip off one of the rubber garters that held up the long cinnamon-coloured stockings that he, like most of the other boys in the class, wore with his knee pants. Av leered slyly and Kevin kept watching him. But, after a few minutes, his attention wandered...

"— 'Come ye out from among them,' the Bible tells us. Now I'm sure that all of us know what that means. It means —"

THWACK! The elastic garter hit Kevin's bare knee like the sting of a hornet. He flung himself back in surprise and pain. Av choked back a laugh.

"Now, Kevin, I'm sure there's no need for any of us to jump about like that," Mrs. Cranston chided him patiently.

"No, ma'am," he blushed.

"That's fine, Kevin. Now all of us will sit quietly in our seats until we finish our lesson and then we can run and skip and hop about as much as we please!"

The hot fudge syrup of her laughter was so sweet that Kevin wondered if it ever made her teeth ache.

"— Now I'm sure that all of us know that drinking is a worldly thing, drinking liquor, that is. God tells us in His Word that wine is a mocker, strong drink is raging, and he —"

THWACK! The garter stung Kevin's knee again. This time he did not jump. He sat very still, hoping that Av would think he had felt no pain.

"— Smoking, as all of us know, is another worldly thing. I hope that none of us think it's smart to smoke cigarettes without our mummies and daddies knowing about it. Because God knows what we do, even when our mummies and daddies don't, and —"

Av's fingers closed on the soft flesh under Kevin's knee like the jaws of a dog. Kevin gritted his teeth and pressed his spine hard against the back of the pew. As it always was at such times, his will was impotent, cataleptic. It was as though he had been injected with a paralyzing drug. He would not summon even the will to lift his hand in an attempt to push Av's wrist away.

"— Now, just as our mummies and daddies have to punish us when we're naughty, so God has to punish us if we're bad, and I'm sure that all of us —"

Mrs. Cranston's sweet, idiotic voice droned on. Pain burnt Kevin's leg like pincers of fire.

"— to accept our Lord Jesus as our own personal saviour. Now, those of you who haven't done that yet — well, you're really missing out on something, I can tell you! To know that the Lord Jesus Christ is your own personal saviour is better than eating the biggest ice cream cone in the world. Why, it's better than —"

Av dug his fingernails into Kevin's flesh, piercing the skin. Kevin's initial anger was replaced by self-pitying bewilderment. He wished he could find the voice to ask Av why he was doing this thing to him. He wished he could say, Look, here, Avard Farmer, I've never done anything to you, have I? Then, why —

"Now, we'll all stand up and sing — and we'll smile as we sing, and sing good and loud, because —"

The rest of Mrs. Cranston's words were lost in the noise of the children getting to their feet. With a great sigh of relief, Kevin felt Av release his leg.

> *Softly and tenderly, Jesus is calling,*
> *Calling, O sinner, come home!*
> *Come home! Come home!*
> *Ye who are wearrry, come hommmme!*

The wistful, melancholy tune of the hymn brought tears to Kevin's eyes. THWACK! Av's garter bit him beneath the chin.

A little giddy with their sudden release from restraint, yet subdued by the atmosphere of the church and the presence of their teachers, the children chattered in throaty whispers as they pushed each other toward the door. Hoping to elude Av, Kevin loped down the steps and out of the doors.

"Don't yuh know it ain't nice tuh run when yer leavin' the church, Key-von?"

Av grasped his collar. The boys nearby rocked on their heels and laughed. This was an old game and one they never found wearisome.

Kevin blinked. The knuckles of the hand clutching his Sunday School papers whitened.

"I wasn't runnin'," he mumbled inanely.

Av steered him around the corner of the church, past burdocks and thistles. The others followed, grinning like the cats in a motion picture cartoon.

"What yuh doin', Key-von, callin' me a liar?"

"No, I ain't callin' yuh a liar, Av."

Almost tenderly, Av led him into the graveyard. They crossed it and halted beside a barn that had once, long ago, sheltered the horses of those who drove buggies to church. The building was now abandoned, odorous with decay.

"Yuh gonna say yer sorry fer callin' me a liar, Key-von?"

He pushed Kevin against the barn wall and leered into his face. Kevin felt the sharp edges of the shingles against his back.

"Answer a man when he speaks tuh yuh, Key-von."

"Gosh, no, I didn't call yuh a liar, Av."

"Don't yuh tell me what yuh did or didn't do, sonny. I say yuh called me a liar. And I say yer gonna apologize."

"I'm sorry I called yuh a liar, then," Kevin said dully.

For no reason that Kevin could understand, the other boys laughed. They formed a half-circle behind Av, dancing with eagerness, their lips drawn back from their teeth. Illogically, Kevin noticed the pigeons at the other end of the graveyard: silver and steel-blue, their heads bobbing as though they pecked at grain, falling like invisible manna from the air.

Av giggled. "Yuh know somethin', Key-von? I think yer a snotty-nosed little pimp. Don't yuh think that's jist about what yuh are, Key-von?"

"You tell 'im, Av," Alton Stacey yelled.

Kevin noticed that an empty rum bottle lay on the grave nearest the road. No doubt a drunken automobile driver had thrown it there during the night. Or perhaps some mourner had brought rum instead of flowers? He tried to concentrate on other things — things like the weathervane on the church roof — anything that would take his mind away from his tormenters.

"Don't yuh agree that yer a snotty-nosed little pimp, Key-von?"

Av shook him, banging the back of his head against the wall.

"Don't yuh agree with me, Key-von?"

"Yeah," Kevin moaned.

The boys howled.

"Say it, Key-von. Say it!"

"Say what?"

"Say: Key-von O'Brien is a snotty-nosed little pimp."

145

Kevin took a deep breath. He concentrated desperately on the jittery, mud-coloured sparrows near the windowless rear wall of the church. From the other end of the world, the steps of the church, he heard Mrs. Cranston and another teacher laughing.

"Say it!" the boys whooped. "Say it!"

Humiliation was like a bottomless well.

"Kevin O'Brien is a snotty-nosed pimp," Kevin repeated.

Some of the boys laughed so hard they threw themselves on the ground. The universe reverberated with laughter.

Av licked his lips. The hands, gripping Kevin's shoulders, were moist with sweat.

"Say: Key-von O'Brien is a stinkin' stuck-up lantern-jawed bastard."

"Kevin O'Brien is a stinkin' stuck-up lantern-jawed bastard."

"Say: Key-von O'Brien's mother still has tuh change his dirty didies."

"Kevin O'Brien's mother still has to change his dirty didies."

He gave the responses quickly, almost eagerly, wanting to hasten this liturgy of humiliation to its end.

"Say: Key-von O'Brien ain't never been weaned yet."

"Kevin O'Brien ain't never been weaned yet."

The boys whooped, their eyes bright and pitiless.

"Put yer thumb in yer mouth, baby."

Like a robot, Kevin thrust his thumb into his mouth. He vowed that when they let him go, he would find a rope and hang himself.

"Now say: Key-von O'Brien's mother is the biggest old whore in Lockhartville."

There was a moment of silence. Even Av seemed a little shocked by what he had said.

Then: "Make 'im say it, Av! Make 'im say it!"

"Ever'body knows it's true! Make him say it!"

"Make 'im say it, Av! Make 'im say it!"

At this instant, Kevin's mind was engulfed by a great cataract of light. For a moment, he believed that a falling star had landed in the churchyard, almost at his feet. Then the darkness surged up around him and the earth under his feet rocked like a teeter-totter. With a wail of despair, he tore himself free of his impotence and struck Av's Adam's apple with all the strength in his fist.

Clutching his throat and gurgling, Av fell back. He stared at Kevin in disbelief.

"Why, yuh little bastard," he said. "Why, yuh little bastard."

"Don't you say anythin' about my mother," Kevin croaked through dead dry lips.

Av stepped forward. "I said once she was a whore and I'n say it again, Key-von. Yuh wanta try and stop me?"

Accustomed to Kevin's stupified meekness, Av half-turned his head and winked at Alton Stacey. As he did so, Kevin lunged forward and kicked — Av roared in pain and rage. "Fight fair, damn yuh, yuh yeller little bastard!"

Almost casually, he drove his fist into Kevin's face. Pain rose like sheets of searing red-gold flame, blinding him. He fell to his knees and, as he fell, Av kicked him in the chest.

"Come on, give it tuh 'im, Av!"

"Come on, Av!"

"Paste the yeller little bastard, Av!"

In his conscious mind, Kevin believed that anyone in the world, no matter how weak, could thrash him. He believed, as he had always believed, that he was an anemic poltroon. But that didn't matter now. All that mattered was that he strike out until, at last, he was downed and killed. Av would kill him — he was certain of that. And he wanted to die. He babbled meaningless syllables through froth-dampened lips.

As he staggered to his feet, Av struck him again. Again he fell. The other boy was stronger than he, tougher, the winner of a hundred schoolyard battles. Rising, Kevin aimed a kick at Av's groin. Av caught his ankle and sent him spinning—

He did not know how many times Av knocked him down. But each time he staggered to his feet, his mouth full of the jungle-taste of blood, and each time he leapt upon Av, butting, striking, kicking, scratching, and biting. From a great distance, he heard a boy yelling, "God, looka that crazy look he's got on his mug!" But his fists, feet, and teeth found Av's body. Av's cheek might have been clawed by a cat and blood trickled from his nostrils.

Av pounded him to his knees and brought both fists down on his neck. Again, Kevin dragged himself to his feet. He was weeping now, howling, the tears blinding him, but once more he fell upon Av.

"Give it tuh the sonovabitch, Av!"

"Let 'im have it, Av!"

And now Kevin was so frenzied with insanity that some of the boys fell back. He did not attempt to guard his face or body. Even had he been sane, he would not have known how. Not one of Av's blows missed — and each time Av struck, Kevin went to the ground.

Time and again, Av knocked Kevin to his knees or sent him sprawling on his back. The skin was torn from his palms, blood gushed from his nostrils and dribbled from his mouth. All his consciousness was permeated with pain.

But he got up. And Av, whose injuries were comparatively slight, was baffled. In one of the flashes of awareness that cut like lightning across the blind madness of his frenzy, Kevin saw in Av's eyes the slow darkening of fear. The small spark of reason still flickering in his mind recognized this fear and was amazed by it. But the murderous, insane part of his mind did not care. Prone on his belly in the grass, he grabbed Av's ankles, tripping him. Av fell and, like a cat, Kevin leapt upon him.

They rolled in the dirt, wrestling. Wrenching his hands free, Kevin seized Av's throat. Av struck out at his face, kneed his belly, grasped his wrists, and tried to jerk his hands away. But Kevin would not let go. He choked Av until the boy's face reddened, until his eyes became as weird as those of a trapped and dying animal, until he ceased to struggle but only stirred weakly, his arms and legs trembling spasmodically.

"Git up, Av! Git up and paste him!"

Then, unbelieving, Kevin heard this, "Give it tuh 'im, Kev! Make 'im say he's had enough."

Straddling Av, Kevin released his hold on his throat. Methodically, with the terrible impatience of the homicidal insane, he pounded his fallen adversary's face. The head jerked from side to side. But Av did not try to dodge. He lay helpless, moaning, as Kevin beat him. Pausing a moment, Kevin saw a stone lying near Av's head. With a sly, spine-chilling grin, he reached out his hand for it —

"He's had enough, Kev!"

This was Alton Stacey, standing over him. Slowly, the light returned to Kevin's mind. The barn, the grass, the church, the sky emerged from the darkness. He saw the boys, standing silent and awed, looked down at Av's smashed and whimpering face.

Shaking like one naked in an unbearable cold, Kevin got unsteadily to his feet. Dear God, don't let me faint, he prayed. Dear God, don't let me faint.

"He ain't said he's had enough yet, Kev," one of the bystanders cried eagerly.

"Shut up," Alton Stacey said. "Jist shut yer mouth."

Av raised himself to a sitting position and looked around him. Seeing Kevin, he started back in fear.

"Yuh leave me alone," he whined. "Yuh jist leave me alone."

"Yuh had enough, Av?" Alton asked.

Av did not answer. Oh, please God, Kevin prayed, I don't

want to have to fight him again. Please God. He had sunk back into his old paralysis. Had Av risen now and attacked him, he would have stood with his hands by his sides and taken whatever was meted out to him. For he was not brave. His fury had sprung from a source beyond bravery, a source beyond his understanding. A falling star had struck the earth at his feet —

"Yuh had enough, Av?" Alton insisted.

Kevin was amazed by Alton's grin. The girl-faced boy seemed amused by the defeat of his friend. Suddenly, Kevin realized that his school mates did not care who was the tormenter and who the tormented. Had he bullied Av, they would have laughed and wriggled exactly as they had laughed and wriggled when Av had bullied him —

"Hit 'im again fer luck, Kev," somebody yelled.

"Yuh had enough, Av?"

"Yeah," Av muttered through thick lips. "Yeah, I've had enough."

Thank you, God, Kevin prayed silently, thank you.

He looked down at his ruined clothes: at his blazer and shorts, torn, muddy, grass-stained, and bloody. Dismayed, he wondered what his mother would say when she saw his clothes...

Eighteen

At recess, next day, Riff Wingate and Harold Winthrop herded Kevin and Av into the woodshed. Riff pinched the muscle of Kevin's arm and whistled in mock admiration. "I hear tell yer one helluva fighter, Key-von," he snickered.

Kevin grinned sheepishly. A dark, secret part of him was coyly proud of his victory. But he did not like Riff's sneer and the eyes that glinted like sharp pebbles under rippling creek water.

"Yessir, I hear yuh licked the livin' bejaysus outta Avie boy, yesterday. Is that right, Key-von?"

The others — Dink Anthony, Jess Allen, Alton Stacey, and Harold Winthrop — nudged one another and winked. Av Farmer glared at the toes of his sneakers.

"— Is that right, Key-von?"

"I don't know." Kevin blinked and shuffled his feet in the bark, chips, and sawdust covering the dirt floor. The onlookers seated themselves on the chopping block, on the saw horse, on the tiers of crocodile-barked, dry maple logs.

Riff laughed soundlessly and slapped his thigh. "He don't know! Hear that, fellers! Joe Louis here licked Av half tuh death and he don't even remember doin' it! Man, that Key-von is jist like a grizzly bear!" Riff stepped away from Kevin, shielding his face with his hands and feigning fear. "Say, Avie boy, do *you* happen tuh remember it?"

151

"He's lucky tuh be alive tuh remember it!" Dink Anthony tittered. At times such as this, Dink, an alder-thin boy in ragged overalls who spent hours jack-knifing obscene symbols into the wood of his desk, alternately giggled and licked his lips like a famished dog.

Av did not look up. "Go tuh hell," he muttered.

Lazily, Riff reached out and slapped Av's face.

"Hey! Whatja do that fer?"

Riff smiled gently. "I thought mebbe yuh was talkin' tuh me, Avie boy," he said.

Av massaged his cheek. His eyes were moist and luminous with self-pity.

"I wasn't talkin' tuh you, Riff. I was talkin' tuh Blabbermouth Anthony there," he complained.

For an instant, Kevin enjoyed Av's pain. He half-hoped Riff would slap him again. Then he felt only pity and shame.

"Now, Key-von, you and Avie boy is gonna fight again," Riff announced. "Yer gonna show us how yuh beat him yesterday. That okay with you, Key-von?"

Oh, please God, no.

"— That okay with you, Key-von?"

Please God. Please.

"Speak up, feller! That okay with you?"

"No. I don't wanta!"

Kevin tried to edge away, but Riff grabbed his arm. "What's yer hurry, Key-von? What's yer hurry, eh?" He turned toward Av. "What about you, Avie boy? Yuh ready tuh fight Key-von again?"

Av buried his fists in the pockets of his shorts and kicked at a chip. "We fought once," he mumbled. "There ain't no need fer us tuh fight again."

Riff snorted. "My Gawd, Avie boy, ain't yuh never heard of

a return match? Why, prize fighters is allus havin' return matches. This here is gonna be a return match between you and Key-von."

"Billy Conn and Joe Louis!" Dink Anthony howled, running his tongue over his lips hungrily.

"Eh? Yeah. Billy Conn Farmer and Joe Louis O'Brien. Harold there is gonna manage Billy Conn Farmer and I'm gonna manage Joe Louis O'Brien. Ain't that worth fightin' fer, Avie boy?" Riff looked at Harold and winked. Harold scratched excitedly at the ripe pimples under his chin. "Bring yer prize fighter over here, will yuh, Harold boy?"

Harold laid hold of Av's shoulders and, despite his protests, thrust him forward. Kevin and Av, their knees, chests, and chins almost touching, stood in the centre of a tight circle of grinning faces. Av looked as tragic as a young bull whose horns had been sawed off. His eyes were dark with bewilderment and shame. Suddenly, Kevin felt a great rush of pity for the other boy. He would almost have preferred to face the old Av — the fox-eyed, arrogant tormenter.

He is just as scared as I am, Kevin thought wonderingly. He is every bit as scared as I am.

"Fight!"

"Fight!"

"Fight! Fight! Fight!"

"I guess we're gonna have tuh manage 'em, Riff."

"I guess yer right, Harold boy."

Harold stepped behind Av, while Riff stationed himself behind Kevin. The two fifteen-year-olds seized the wrists of the smaller boys and, "Now, fight!"

Kevin's limp arm was lifted and driven into Av's face. Then Av's dangling hands were brought down on Kevin's head like a club. The onlookers roared.

"Now a right tuh the jaw!"

Kevin's lax, imprisoned hand struck Av's jaw.

"— And now an upper-cut!"

Harold jerked up Av's hand and drove it against Kevin's chin. The smaller boys were rag dolls being manipulated in a violent, ludicrous pantomime. Then Riff forced Kevin to slap his own face —

"Whoa! Whoa, there Key-von! Yer supposed tuh be hittin' the other feller. What yuh wanta do, knock yerself out, boy?"

Laughter was like the bellowing of cattle in a burning barn.

"— And a left tuh the jaw!"

Ho! Ho! Hee! Ho! Hee! Ho!

"— And a right tuh the chin!"

Ho! Ho! Ho! Haw! Haw! Haw!

"— And a left tuh the ear!"

"Now, fight! Fight, damn it! FIGHT!"

"Hey, Riff, I jist thoughta somethin'."

"What's that, Harold boy?"

"Well, if they ain't a-gonna fight, don't yuh think mebbe they oughta kiss and make up?"

"Damn good idea, Harold boy."

"Come on now, Key-von, let's see you and Avie boy kiss and make up. Come on now —"

With Riff holding Kevin's neck and Harold grasping Av's, their faces were shoved together —

"Ain't that sweet! Ain't it sweet tuh see them two little fellers kissin' like that!"

Kevin's teeth rattled against Av's.

Ho! Hee! Ho! Haw! Hee! Ho!

Then the bell rang. Five minutes later, seated in class, Kevin's mouth was still full of the salty, fear-scented taste of the kiss...

*

When Kevin started home that afternoon, he saw that Av was following him. His first impulse was to run.

"Hey, Kevin! I wanta talk tuh yuh!"

He stopped and waited for Av to catch up to him.

Av's eyes were sly and he made little nervous movements with his head and hands.

"Look, I mean..." The voice trailed away. "Well, I mean... Look, damn it all tuh hell. I'm sorry I called yer old lady... bad names."

Kevin flushed in embarrassment. He knew that it had been painful for Av to make this apology. He almost wept for sympathy with him.

"It's all right," he stammered. "It don't matter none."

"No, yuh licked me and I had it comin', I guess."

They walked for a while in uneasy silence, watching one another out of the corners of their eyes.

"Riff Wingate is a bastard," Av declared murderously. "Some day I'm gonna stick a knife in him."

"Yeah."

"Didja see how Stacey and Anthony and Allen howled their goddamn heads off this mornin' — didja see that, eh?"

"Uh-huh, I saw it."

"Well, I guess me and you couldn't fight Riff and Harold. The big, overgrown sons-a-bitches would knock hell outta us. But what duh yuh say we knock the livin' Jesus outta Anthony and Allen tomorrow?"

They had come to the mill. In the thunder and roar of the engines, they had to shout to make each other hear. Inside the mill, Kevin knew, the men learned to read lips...

"Yuh beat me and if yuh can beat me yuh can beat Anthony.

He's got a yeller streak a mile wide down his back. And I'd jist love tuh give that Jess Allen a mouthful of fist. What duh yuh say, eh?"

The splitter saw screamed. Some men — Judd O'Brien was one of them — could identify the variety of wood being sawed from the sound of the saw's scream. Steel tearing maple made a different sound than steel tearing spruce...

"Oh, gosh! I mean it wasn't them that made us fight, Av!"

"But they laughed! Yuh hear 'em laughin'."

Again the splitter saw screamed. The men in the millyard ran to and fro like the members of a bucket brigade. Eben Stingle cracked his black whip over the drooping heads of his yellow oxen. The old mare tugged at the scarlet sawdust cart, a boy scarcely older than Kevin driving her. The boy whipped her with the reins as she staggered up a great yellow-green hill of sawdust. The top of this hill, Kevin knew, was a desert: a desert where sand-coloured cones of sawdust rose like dunes. He watched the scarlet cart reach the top and disappear...

"Yeah, I heard 'em laughin'."

And they had laughed so many times before! *They used to laugh when you tormented me. Don't you remember, Av?* But Kevin was shy and it was hard to find the right words, so he said nothing...

"Yuh gonna do it?"

The edger saws blatted like a slaughtered sheep.

"— Yuh gonna do it?"

"Gonna do what?"

"You know! Are yuh gonna do what we was talkin' about? Are yuh gonna fight 'em?"

Kevin sighed. Here on the shoulder of the road, sawdust and mud had mingled, creating something that looked and felt like black clay. The scarlet cart pushing her, the old mare staggered crazily down the sawdust hill, the boy with the reins laughing and yelling at her ...

"No. I guess not, Av. I guess I ain't gonna fight."

Av spat on the black clay.

"I guess we ain't got nothin' tuh talk about then," he grunted.

"I guess not, Av."

"Well, so long, Key-von."

Av whirled and stalked away, his back erect and unforgiving. Walking backwards, Kevin watched until he vanished behind a clump of spruce. He felt — knowing the feeling to be foolish — that he had somehow betrayed a friend.

Nineteen

But, in the spring, Kevin had begun to read the Bible, and now the Book altered the very geography of his world.

Squatting in the field behind the hen house with the cool, black, faintly odorous volume on his knees, he read of how God created the heavens and the earth and of how the earth was without form, and void, while darkness was upon the face of the deep. Looking out over the heath, over the alders and maple saplings and young spruce nodding in the breeze, he tried to imagine how it had been on that first day. The sun had risen for the first time, a tumbling red-gold splendour in the east, and God had walked across the new, loam-pungent earth, grass and flowers and shrubs springing full-grown from the prints of His feet. God *had walked through this very field.* The very ground on which Kevin sat might once have been touched by the sandalled feet of God!

Grandmother O'Brien often spoke of the ancient time when God had lived among men. She would say that such and such a thing had happened in the days when God was still on earth. And the Bible told of how He had walked in the garden in the cool of the evening. Kevin imagined Him walking down the rows of vegetables, the skirts of his robe swishing against potato and turnip tops, His ankles brushing against sun-coloured pumpkins and green-gold squash.

Prone on his belly in the tall grass by the lilac hedge, he read of how God had created Adam, and of how He had put Adam to sleep and taken out his rib and made a woman. And he remembered that his grandmother had assured him that even to this day men had one rib fewer than women.

God had created woman so that man might have a helpmeet. But, sometimes, men did wicked things with women. The hot blood pulsated in Kevin's veins as he remembered Kaye Dunbar and June Larlee lying together on Kaye's bunk. How had they escaped from the wrath of God? Why had God not struck them dead?

Several times since that day when he ran from Kaye's cabin with June Larlee's laughter seering his ear drums like the wail of a banshee, he had met his uncle. But now there was an invisible wall between them. They were like two houseflies facing one another from opposite sides of a sheet of window glass. The barrier could be neither seen nor penetrated. They neither of them spoke of that day, but once or twice Kevin had caught his uncle giving him a strange look, half-mocking and half-pitying, that showed that he remembered...

And when, one night near the end of October, Kaye went jacklighting deer, tripped on a windfall, and shot off his big toe, Kevin was convinced that this was God's way of punishing him.

For God was a jealous god and quick to punish. The serpent had tempted Eve and she, in turn, had led Adam into sin. They had eaten of the forbidden fruit of the tree of the knowledge of good and evil, and God had driven them from Eden and stationed angels with flaming swords at the gates to see that they did not get back in.

But, after eating of the fruit, Adam and Eve had known that they were naked, and they had sewn fig leaves together and made themselves aprons. Why were they naked? Grandmother O'Brien said that nakedness was a great sin. And she was wise in the ways of God. Excitement stirring like a live thing in his belly, Kevin thought about nakedness...

He had seen Kaye naked. The man took off all his clothes when he swam. But Kaye's body, aside from its muscles and scars and hairiness, was not very different from his own. He had never seen his father naked. When Judd went to bed, he removed only his trousers, socks, and shoes. And Kevin knew that it annoyed and embarrassed him to be surprised in his shirt and underwear. On the few occasions when he had gone into a room and found Judd pulling on his trousers, the man had flushed and told him to get the hell out of there. Recalling the fate of Ham, the son of Noah, who had looked upon the nakedness of his father, Kevin blanched and shuddered. God had turned Ham's skin black. Judd seldom spoke of the Bible, but once he had told Kevin that Ham, when God cursed him, stood on all fours, like a dog. As a result, the palms and soles of Negroes were white, even to this day.

He wondered about the nakedness of women. He had seen June Larlee naked, but only for an instant. It was as though the darkness had been broken by a lightning flash. In that flash, he had caught a momentary glimpse of a white, palpitant mound of living flesh.

Surely, he had committed no sin in looking upon June Larlee's nakedness?

But there was his mother. Unlike June Larlee, Mary never wore shorts; both Judd and his mother said it was disgraceful for grown women to dress like little boys. Kevin had seen her only in fragrant flannelette pajamas. In these she was more fully clothed than in a frock. But the pajamas suggested something secret and intimate, something almost as private as nakedness.

Hastily, he turned his mind away from his mother and to less terrible sins. There was Isabel Dubois, who had called him a snot-nosed runt because he had tried to keep the other boys from shaming her. And there was Nancy Harker, the daughter of Madge Harker, the bootlegger. A poplar-limbed, golden-skinned girl of about his own age. The boys who teased Isabel became almost diffident in the presence of Nancy. And once on the way home from school she had asked him (not teasingly, but as though it were the most casual question imaginable) if he liked girls. He wished now that he had — but it was a sin to make such a wish. A hellfire sin. For wishing such things, boys were thrown into a lake of never-ending fire. He thought of moths that hurled themselves down the chimneys of the kerosene lamps, of how the heat of the burning wick baked their frenziedly whirring wings. And he thought of the high-pitched whistling that sometimes came from the stove. Judd said that this was the sound of insects roasting in their burrows inside the wood...

And one afternoon, alone in the kitchen, Kevin lifted the lid of the stove and held his hand over the flame until the heat rasped his palm like sandpaper. This was what it was like in hell! *Oh, please God, forgive me,* he prayed. *I won't think any more about sinful things. I promise I won't, God!* And he rubbed the tears from the corners of his eyes and set the lid back in place.

For the answers to some questions, the questions that were not so much weighted down with darkness and sin, he went to his grandmother. He asked her, for example, if Lot's wife, who had turned to salt when she looked back at Sodom, still stood upon the plains of Zoar.

And Grandmother O'Brien tightened her grip on the hot brick that lay against her waist and answered, "Yes, laddie, she's still a-standin' there, right where she was when the Lord turned her tuh salt! Why, I'n remember when I was a little wee tiny girl, there was an old sea captain came tuh our house. He'd sailed on every one of them seven seas, laddie. And I'n remember how he told mother and father about seein' Lot's wife — he seed her fer hisself, seed her with his own eyes. Right there on the plains of Zoar. She was still a-standin' there, jist like a statue made outta salt. An' yuh know what that sea captain done, laddie? Yuh know what he done?" Her voice sank to an awed whisper. "Why he broke off one o' her fingers! An' he had that there finger right there in his pocket! He showed it tuh us right there in the kitchen. I'n remember it jist as if it was yesterday. A woman's finger that had turned tuh salt!"

"Gee whiz," Kevin breathed. "Gosh!"

"O'course I expeck she's growed another finger by now, laddie. I expeck when somebody breaks a piece off of her, the Lord makes another piece grow right back on."

"Holy mackerel!" Kevin whistled.

And he promised himself that when he became a man he would take a ship to Zoar and look upon the woman whom God's wrath had turned to salt.

At night, in the firelight-coloured seclusion of near-sleep, he saw the moon stand still on Gibeon and the sun in the valley of Ajalon. He saw the gleaming war chariots of the Amorites and heard the wall-shattering trumpets of Joshua. Swords flashed, spears rattled, lances hissed through the air. Fire and brimstone rained upon Sodom and hailstones smote the land from Azekah to Makkedah...

The creek became the River Jordan and beyond Jordan lay the lands of the Amorites. There dwelt Sihon, the King of Heshbon, and Og, the King of Bashan, who dwelt in Ashteroth, great ogres in leopard skins whose beards were frothed with their hatred of the Most High God.

In the sawdust desert behind the mill were the lands of the

Hittites, the Perizzites, the Hivites, and the Jebusites. And beyond the cedared hills was the valley in which the swordsmen of Joshua ambushed and slaughtered the sons of Ai.

The grain field across the road was the field of Boaz in which Ruth had gleaned. And the swamp at the foot of the garden was the land of the Moabites. There Ehud, the son of Gera, the Benjaminite, slew Eglon, the King of Moab, a man so fat that when he was slain the fat of his belly closed over the hilt of the sword and hid it.

The north fence was the border of Abel-meholah. The great stone on the heath was Hebron. The barn was Jerusalem. The easternmost section of the heath was the valley of Rephaim and the alders were the mulberry trees in which the wind had sounded on the day that David, King of Israel, slew the hosts of the Philistines.

In this secret world, Kevin found somewhat the same sense of power and security as he obtained from his mother. And, unlike his mother, the God of Abraham and of Isaac and of Jacob never abandoned him.

"I think you brood too much. It isn't good for you," Mary said. She sounded resentful — almost jealous.

"I ain't broodin'," he growled.

His voice was sullen. Since she had started going away in the evenings, her slightest criticism infuriated him. He felt that she no longer had any right to criticize him.

"Don't sauce, Scampi. I've got enough troubles without having you sauce me."

"I ain't sassin'," he retorted.

They were in the kitchen, and Grandmother O'Brien was watching and listening. Her mouth might have been full of vinegar or sour milk, but Kevin knew that this was one of the ways she had of smiling.

Mary stamped her foot like a petulant child.

"You *were* saucing me! Don't you tell me that you weren't!"

"All right! Have it yer own way! I was sassin' yuh!"

This was how their quarrels were ignited and spread. It was like a grass fire: a single match was dropped in the dry spears and, within seconds, the flames were roaring across the field with the speed of the wind.

"Oh, Scampi! You treat me so awful sometimes! I do everything in the world for you and I don't get a bit of thanks for it! You aren't the least bit grateful for all the things I do for you —"

"I ain't never asked yuh tuh do anythin' fer me."

"Oh, yes you have! You've come bawling to me a thousand million times, Scampi! Whenever the least little thing bothers you, you come running to me and you —"

"I won't come runnin' no more!"

He clenched his fists. Her taunts were a breach of trust. He hated her for betraying him.

"Oh, yes, you will! You'll come bawling to me. Oh, Mummy, you'll be whining. Oh, Mummy —" She imitated his terror-stricken whimpering. Her eyes were spiteful and pitiless. "Oh, Mummy, you'll be whining, and you'll want me to treat you just as though you were a tiny little baby and you'll —"

"It's allus *you* that wants me tuh act like a baby! It ain't me! It's you!"

"Me! Why, I wish you were a man! I wish you were big enough to go out and work for your living. Then I could put on my coat and walk out of here. I —" Her voice died. She bit her lip and glanced at Grandmother O'Brien. The old woman emitted a rattling, chuckling cough.

Kevin spun and ran to his room.

Throwing himself on the bed, he buried his face in the

pillows and wept, his body jerking with the convulsive force of his sobbing.

After a long time, someone entered the room. He did not look up. This was his mother. She had come to comfort him. For as long as he could remember, their quarrels had ended with her voice in his ear, her soft, warm hands on his body. For a little while, he would pretend that he was still angry. She would stroke his ear lobes and the small of his back... Her breath would tickle his ear. And he would pout and refuse to respond to her pleading, lie stiff under her caresses. Then, when he felt that he had punished her sufficiently or when he could no longer restrain himself, he would turn and throw his arms around her neck and they would kiss, and —

"It don't do no good tuh bawl," a harsh voice chided.

He lifted his head. Through a bubbling fog of tears, he saw his grandmother standing over him.

"It don't do no good tuh bawl," she grated again. In her voice, sadness mingled with satisfaction.

Burying his face again, he sobbed until his throat burned as though boiling water had been poured into his mouth and nostrils.

Twenty

David was Kevin's favourite among the prophets, kings, and judges of Israel. He re-enacted the story of David until it seemed to him that he was not assuming the role of another, but repeating scenes from his own dimly remembered past.

As Kevin-David, he played the harp until the evil spirit departed from Saul. And as Kevin-David he went down into the valley of Elah to face the champion of the Philistines, Goliath of Gath, whose height was six cubits and a span and whose coat weighed five thousand shekels of bronze, and there he slew him with a stone from his shepherd's sling and smote off the head with his own sword, and when he returned from slaying the Philistine, the women came out of the cities with instruments of music and sang, *Saul has slain his thousands and Kevin-David his ten thousands.*

As Kevin-David, he fled from Saul to Achish, King of Gath, and there he pretended to be mad until he could escape to the Cave of Adullam, where four hundred men came and asked him to be captain over them...

Then came all the tribes of Israel to David unto Hebron and spake, saying, O Behold, we are thy bone and thy flesh. Also in time past when Saul was king over us, thou wast he that leddest out and broughtest in Israel, and thou shalt be a captain over

Israel. So all the elders of Israel came to the king of Hebron and King David made a league with them in Hebron before the Lord and they anointed David King over Israel.

The hen house was Gath, and the wagonshed was Perez-uzzah, where Uzzah was smitten when he touched the Ark of the Covenant. The east fence was Helam, where the king gathered together the men of Israel and slew the men of seven hundred chariots of the Syrians, and forty thousand horsemen, and smote Shobach, the captain of the host, who died there. And around him, Kevin summoned an invisible army led by the captains of David, among whom there were Abishai, the brother of Joab and the son of Zerulah, who lifted up his spear against three hundred, and Benaiah, the son of Jehoida, who went down into a pit and slew a lion in a time of snow.

And while Kevin-David led the armies of Israel into battle with the hosts of Bethrehob, Zobah, and Maacah, winter descended upon Lockhartville.

Judd hated winter. When the first snow fell, the lambent, star-shaped flakes melting the moment they touched the unfrozen earth, he stood at the window, shaking his fist and muttering with bitter sarcasm, "Snow, you bastard, snow! Snow, damn yuh, snow!" A few days later, the mill shut down and he, with most of the other mill hands, went to Larchmont and got drunk. This was November and Judd would be without a steady job until the mill re-opened in May...

One stony grey afternoon, Kevin helped his father bank the house. Now he wore wool breeches, tied with leather laces below his knees, flannel underwear that might have been made from rosethorns and thistles, two pairs of wool stockings, and a toque drawn over his ears. These clothes chafed like a straightjacket. And the wind, raking his cheeks and the strip of bare flesh between the cuffs of his mackinaw and his mittens, burnt like a dull knife.

Judd had wheel-barrowed slabs from the mill and, with these, built a box four feet high around the base of the house. Then, with a grub-hoe, he broke up a patch of frozen turf near the heath fence, and he and Kevin carried the sods and loose gravel to the box in shovels. The earth was almost odourless, but Kevin could smell the faint, yet unmistakable, scent of impending snow.

Judd worked like a machine, concentrating only on the shovelful of dirt in his hands. But this was not Kevin's way. He was depressed by the thought of all the hundreds of shovelsful of dirt that would have to be poured into the box before the task was finished. Two hours from now he would still be shovelling! When he emptied his shovel into the box it did not seem to make any difference at all in the level of the dirt. He tried to increase his load and, to his chagrin, more than half of it spilled away before he got back to the house. He moved faster, broke into a run, and again much of his load was lost. He dumped every load in the same spot, seeking to fill at least one small section of the box. Then he spread dirt from one corner of the house to the other, trying to do all of it at once. And all of these experiments his father watched with amusement and scorn.

"Take yer time, boy. We got all day," he said. Or, "Be careful there, boy. Yer spillin' more on the ground than yer puttin' around the house."

And Kevin almost wept in vexation and self-pity.

At last, he pretended that he was helping to build a wall for a fort. Yes, with the beginning of winter, the Amalekites began raiding villages. He was building a redoubt, against the lances and fire-arrows of the heathen.

He cast aside his coat of mail and his helmet of bronze and

stood the sword of Goliath the Philistine against a mulberry tree —

"Look! The king himself is working at the wall!"

"Yes! He is setting an example to the people! He is giving them courage!"

"The great king himself is not ashamed to soil his hands with this lowly labour!"

"Surely, there is none like unto him in all Israel!"

"— What in Gawd's name are yuh doin', boy? Talking tuh yerself?"

Kevin was overcome with confusion.

"Gosh, no, I never said nothin'," he croaked.

"Sounded tuh me as if yuh was mumblin' tuh yerself."

"No. I never said nothin'. Honest I didn't."

"Well, it don't matter none, I guess. But remember this, boy, nobody never got no work done by standin' around an' dreamin'."

"Yessir. I'll remember."

An hour later, Judd cut spruce and fir boughs, spread them atop the dirt and tied them down with haywire. The first flakes of snow were melting on Kevin's cheeks.

"I guess there ain't nothin' more fer yuh to do here," Judd said. "Yuh might as well go tuh the barn and start the milkin'."

"Yessir."

Only recently had Judd begun to trust Kevin with the milking. And even now he did not trust him wholly: he was constantly scolding him for leaving milk in the cows. "If yuh don't git all the milk, the cow will go dry. Remember that, boy," Judd warned him.

"Yessir."

He fetched the pails and the lantern from the house. It was dark now, the pertinacious, immuring dusk of winter. As he went in the cow stable, a gust of wind caught the door and sent it crashing shut behind him. He pulled off his mittens with his teeth, fastened the latch made of a length of haywire and a rivet, and went over to the cows.

The odour of the barn and the tawny-saffron glimmer of the lantern seemed to belong together. If smells had had colours, the smell of the cow stable would have been the colour of the lantern. He set the lantern on an overturned pail and kicked a milking stool, made from an old kitchen chair, under the red cow. She lifted her head and looked at him with mild curiosity, then turned back to her hay. The crunching jaws of the two animals made placid sounds. On a little mound of straw near the door to the feed room, an orange cat — half-brother to the cat that Judd had killed for stealing — lay purring. The wind bayed poignantly under the eaves and, somewhere on the roof, clacked a loose shingle.

His fingers began their rhythm: in and out, up and down, in and out, up and down, massaging X's of sweet milk into the pail, the sound changing as the pail filled. The walls were insulated with straw, stuffed behind unbarked slabs and secured with cardboard, but a draught from beneath the door chilled Kevin's ankles. He rested his cheek against the cow's warm, leather-and-manure-scented side. Scenting the milk, the orange cat rose, stretching, and came to arch its back against his feet...

Earlier, Judd had rented a team and a wagon from a neighbouring farmer and hauled twenty loads of millwood to the back yard. Every afternoon when he got home from school, Kevin took the bucksaw from its nails in the wagonshed and worked till supper, sawing the fourteen-foot-long staves into stovewood lengths. And, every day, as soon as he finished his mid-day meal, Judd hurried to the yard and sawed and split rock maple logs until the wail of the whistle summoned him back to the mill.

The millwood was burnt by day and the rock maple by night. The house was old and decayed, and the glacial winds burst through its walls like torrents of icy water churning through a broken dam. There were two stoves, one in the living room and one in the kitchen, and, from late November till March, Judd kept both fires burning day and night. In these months, Judd slept, fully clothed, on the cot in the kitchen so that he could rise hourly and stoke the fires without waking Mary. Once or twice in each winter, he overslept and allowed the fires to go out. On such nights, water froze in a crystalline mass in the bucket by the sink, twelve feet from the couch on which Judd slept.

And it was in winter that the rodents became most numerous and bold. Often, in the evening while Judd lay on the cot and Kevin and Mary read or played checkers at the table, a mouse, attracted by the heat, crawled from behind the woodbox and scuttled across the room. Bellowing curses, Judd sprang to his feet, swooped on the broom and bounded after it. Kevin wanted to laugh at the incongruity of the spluttering, red-faced man stalking the timorous little animal, but the peeling, orange strap in the barn had taught it was dangerous to express amusement during his father's rages. The broom cracked against the floor with a report like a pistol shot, and the mouse darted into hiding beneath the cot. Judd sank to his knees and swung the broom handle under the cot like a boom. Worn-out shoes and un-matched rubbers were swept into the centre of the floor. Almost incoherent with fury Judd kicked the cot away... The mouse had disappeared. Tremulous and livid with anger and frustration, Judd replaced broom, shoes, rubbers, and cot and lay down, still muttering profanities. Within half an hour, the same mouse, or another, dashed from beneath the sink — and Judd again sprang for the broom.

He set traps and kept the orange cat in the house. There was rarely a morning on which the trap did not contain the broken, obscenely greasy corpse of a mouse. And, many times, the cat sprang on Judd's chest in the night and caterwauled until he awoke and examined his trophy. In winter, Kevin slept on a cot in the living room, to be nearer the fire, and he was sometimes wakened by the sound of his father's voice, crooning to the cat. "Nice old kitty," Judd murmured in a stroking tone. "You is jist the best little old mouser in the world, ain't you, kitty?" He spoke to him in the throaty, slurring croak in which some women address babies, and, Kevin knew, he would have been appalled had he known that anyone other than the cat was listening...

But, despite brooms, cots, and traps, the mice waxed fat and multiplied, until they reminded Kevin of one of the plagues with which God had chastened the hardened heart of Pharaoh. They played havoc with the vegetables in the cellar, polluting a bushel for every pound they ate; they gnawed their way into the pantry and left hideous, disgusting messes in flour bag and bread box; they shredded mail-order catalogues, love story magazines, and school books; and, to her tearful despair, they tunnelled into Mary's closet and chewed unpatchable holes in her best dress.

Rats were few, and for this Kevin praised God, for they filled him with abject terror. Running across the floor of the kitchen attic, a rat made as much racket as a full-grown man. Hearing the animals, one would have imagined them to be as big as dogs. Their feet shook the slats in the ceiling.

This sound nettled Judd to frenzy, also. He would pound the ceiling with a broom handle until the rat fell silent. Staring at the ceiling with wild eyes, his lips white and quivering, nausea gripping his stomach, Kevin sensed the ghoulish intensity of the rat waiting, with ears erect, in the darkness above him. Five minutes after Judd put aside the broom and lay down, the beast's Frankenstein-tread was heard again...

And there was the school house, heated by a pot-bellied iron stove to which the boys lugged maple and birch. The stove panted like a live thing and the children seated nearest were scorched by its heat. Their mouths and nostrils were parched by the moistureless air and their bodies, enveloped in flannel and wool, were parboiled in their own sweat. At the same time, the children farthest from the stove, those near the draughty door or the rattling windows, shivered until their teeth chattered, and acquired chilblains that itched their legs until they raked themselves raw with haywire in search of relief. The only seats in which it was possible to escape the extremes of heat and cold were those in the front row, facing Miss Roache's desk, and there she placed her favourites: the dainty, pertly aloof daughter of Hod Rankine, the mill owner; the plump, fawn-eyed son of Jeremy Upshaw, the township's representative on the County Council; and four others whose fathers, so Riff Wingate sneered, were members of Lockhartville's Board of School Trustees.

Kevin and his seatmate, Alton Stacey, huddled like frost-numbed sparrows in one of the bleakest and most aguish seats. They both of them knew better than to complain. Miss Roache punished such imprudence by transferring the offender to a desk fourteen inches from the stove. There stockings, breeches, skirts, and, sometimes, flesh were burned by the hot cinders that burst like shooting stars from the open grates.

Like many of the boys, Alton treated Kevin as an equal when the two of them were alone or in the presence of adults. These boys became mockers and bullies only when they gathered in groups and egged one another on with jeer and snigger. Taken singly, they were all of them rather passive and bashful.

And one afternoon in late November, Kevin and Alton showed their resentment by an act that, for a little while, gained Kevin admission to the school's aristocracy of scapegraces and daredevils.

Miss Roache was telling Grade VI about the Spanish Armada. Riff Wingate, who was loafing through his third year in the grade, had affixed a pin to a ruler and, while feigning an almost morbid interest in Miss Roache's words, was attempting to prick Isabel Dubois's leg. Pretending to work arithmetic exercises, which he detested, Kevin listened to Miss Roache. It was a habit of his to neglect his own lessons, if they bored him, and concentrate on the history and English lessons being given to Grades VI, VII, and VIII. "And we count our blessings that Queen Elizabeth did not enter into matrimony with King Philip of Spain," Miss Roache was saying. "Philip, when all is said and done, was a Catholic and —" Kevin's mind drifted away. Miss Roache, had she noticed him, would have said that he was woolgathering. He wondered what was wrong with being a Catholic. His mother's people, the Dunbars, were Catholics, although it had been years since any of them had gone to church. He wondered—

"My God, I'm cold," Alton whispered.

"Yeah."

"Yer fingers stiff?"

"A little."

"Mine are jist like —" Here Alton used an obscene smile that made Kevin blush. "Well, leastways, they're ready to break off most any time, they're so goddamn cold."

Kevin wished Alton would shut up. This talk made him colder. And, moreover, Miss Roache had a hardwood pointer which she used on whisperers —

"Look, yuh want some excitement?"

"Huh? What kinda excitement?"

Keeping his hands hidden under the desk, Alton drew a small red box from his pocket.

".22 rifle shells," the choirboy-faced lad explained, trying to leer but succeeding in attaining only a rather girlish grin.

Automatically, Kevin glanced at Miss Roache, but she had turned her back to them and was standing over Harold Winthrop's desk.

"What yuh gonna do with 'em?"

"Well, now, I thought I jist might shoot myself with 'em."

"I don't care, anyway," Kevin retorted resentfully, piqued by Alton's sarcasm.

"Can't yuh take a joke? We're gonna throw 'em right smack intuh that goddamn stove!"

Illogically, Kevin looked at the stove. The heat had tinted its sides scarlet, but in his corner of the room it was still Siberia.

"Who's gonna do it?"

"You and me — that's who!"

"Uh-ah! Not me! I ain't gonna have nothin' tuh do with it!"

SMACK!

Suddenly — from out of nowhere — Miss Roache's hardwood pointer swished through the air. Pain as adhesive as hot wax scalded Kevin's neck and shoulders.

"Now you just let me catch you whispering again and I'll *really* lick you!" Miss Roache snapped. With a tight-lipped little grin, she watched Kevin massage his shoulder. "You hear me?"

"Yes, ma'am."

"Well, make sure you remember!"

She stalked back to her desk. Av Farmer stuck out his tongue at Kevin and smirked. Jessica Rankine wriggled her nose in disdain. Jeremy Upshaw curled his lips with the ironic detachment of a man of the world. And the other boys and girls grimaced, half-flinching in fright and half-squirming in avidity.

"The old bitch," Kevin whispered. "The old bitch!"

"She'll hear yuh," Alton whispered warningly.

Not for worlds would Kevin have uttered such an epithet had he felt there was the remotest chance of Miss Roache hearing.

But he was pleased that Alton thought him a bold and reckless fellow. He clenched his fists and drew fierce breaths, the frosted vapour curling from his mouth like smoke. Ah, he was a fire-eater and a swashbuckler indeed! Had Miss Roache been a firing squad, he, Kevin the Dauntless, would have growled, "To hell with the blindfold!" and then —

Alton nudged him.

"We gonna do it?"

Kevin had forgotten the plot.

"Do what?"

"Put them shells in that there stove."

"Oh."

Alton gave him a searching, faintly contemptuous look.

"You yeller?"

Was he yellow? Yes, he was yellow. No! He was the boy who had dared call Miss Roache an old bitch to her face. Well, any-how, almost to her face. He was the —

"Tuhday is our day tuh bring in the wood, yuh know that?"

"Yeah."

"And there's too damn many of them things fer me tuh handle all by myself. Sooooo —"

"Yeah."

"Jess Allen is gonna git old Cock Roache tuh turn her back, and while she's got her back turned me and you is gonna git them shells intuh that there stove."

"What will they do?" Kevin quavered.

He envisioned an explosion, a smoking wreckage-strewn pit where there had once been a school.

"How the hell should I know what it'll do? Yuh scared or somethin'? Av Farmer said yuh would be too scared tuh do it."

Kevin drew a deep breath.

"No," he growled in what he imagined to be the accents of a buccaneer. "I ain't scared a nothin'!"

"Okay, then. Boy, I can't wait tuh see the look on old Cock Roache's mug when them shells start goin' off. Holy Jesus!"

Oh, Lord, I don't know how I got myself into this. But, please God, just get me out of this, and I'll never ask for anything else. Never. Never. Never. I promise I won't, God.

"We'll git licked," he stated flatly.

"Well, what the hell if we do? Yuh been licked a-fore, ain't yuh?"

"Yeah."

"And, anyway, how the hell is she gonna know who did it? Why, God, man, she'll be so goddamn scared she won't have time tuh worry about who done it. She'll think old Hitler is a-comin' down the chimney like Santa Claus!"

Thirty minutes later, Kevin and Alton were sent for firewood. They lay new birch logs on the coals, their wrists smarting with a sudden suffusion of heat. Then, as Alton had instructed him, Kevin spread his handful of cartridges atop the logs. In this way, the heat would not ignite them until the boys were back in their seats...

Though he had known it was coming, the first explosion made Kevin throw himself back in surprise. *Oh, please God*, he thought despairingly, *oh, please God.* He knew, with spine-chilling certainty, that in a few seconds he, and all of his classmates, would die. The stove bucked like a machine gun as the caps of the cartridges responded to the heat. With a shriek, Miss Roache sprang from her chair and sprinted like a deer to the door. "Oh, my God!" she wailed. "Oh, my *God!*" Helter skelter, the children followed her, the smaller boys sobbing as they were thrust aside by the bigger. *Oh, God what have I done?* Kevin moaned silently. *Oh dear Lord what have I done?* Surely, he would be tried for murder. And he would be hanged. They would put a black hood over his head and tie a knot under his left ear and —

"Let's git the hell outta here, Kev!"

This was the voice of Alton Stacey.

"We're gonna git killed!"

"Like hell! Don't be such a goddamn fool! Yuh think them shells is gonna git through an inch a iron? But it's gonna look damn funny if we're the only sons-a-bitches that stay in the goddamn school house!"

They jumped to their feet and ran out through the porch. The cold air slashed their faces like a whip.

Miss Roache stood amid a bevy of older girls. The wind swept dry snow from the ground and hurled it into their eyes; they squinted and hugged themselves against the cold. Kevin felt a quick little tremor of brutal joy as he observed that Jessica Rankine was blubbering, her face hidden in the folds of Miss Roache's skirt. *Go ahead and bawl, you stuck-up little* — But she looked so fragile and vulnerable, and she was so pretty in her little blue frock! Suddenly, he realized that he had done a mean and stupid thing.

The barrage ended, and there was silence inside the school. Miss Roache wiped her eyes with one hand and patted the back of Jessica Rankine's head with the other.

"School is dismissed. Go get your coats," she said in an absurd choked voice.

Then, chiselling each syllable out of rock, "Tomorrow, I'm going to find out which of you did this. *And when I do!* When I do I'm going to give you something you'll remember for the rest of your life!"

The bigger boys winked at one another. The smaller children sobbed harder.

Her face like chalk, Miss Roache marched into the porch and came out wearing her hat and coat. Jessica Rankine walked beside her, gripping her hand.

"Are you people deaf? I said that school was dismissed!"

The children hastened back into the school house and wriggled into their caps and mackinaws. *Tomorrow, she'll find out and she'll beat me to death. She'll kill me, and that's what I deserve. I'm a coward, and a fool and I could have been a murderer and* —

Then suddenly Riff Wingate was slapping his back. Kevin swung around to face him. The taller boy grinned, showing the stumps of a dozen moist, decaying teeth.

"Stacey jist told me! Never saw anythin' so funny in my life! Why, Kev, old Cock Roache damn near jumped outta her drawers!"

Harold Winthrop pumped Kevin's hand.

"God-a-mighty, Kev! I never saw anythin' like it in my whole life! I gotta hand it tuh yuh and Stacey, feller!"

Alton swaggered in the background, his choirboy face lighted by an angelic smile. "Don't you fellers fergit it was my idea!" he said.

"It don't make no difference whose idea it was. It was the goddamn funniest thing I ever saw in my life!" Riff chuckled. "Didja see old Cock Roache? Lord, she'da like tuh a-snapped the elastic in her pants!" He laughed and the others joined him with guffaw and leer.

"Yer a good man, Kev!" Harold interjected. "Yer a good man!" These words, although uttered always in a faintly derisive tone, were the highest compliment that could be bestowed by Riff and Harold. This was the Victoria Cross of the Lockhartville school-yard. "Yeah, yer a damn good man, Kev," Riff agreed.

For the first time in Kevin's school life, he had been accepted into the fraternity. For a moment, pride throbbed in his temples like fever. Yes — he was a tough hombre, a gamecock, a *good man*. Bathed in their approval, he strutted a little, conceived other diabolical schemes for disrupting the school. He thought of striding across to Dink Anthony. "What the hell are *you* laughin' at?" he would bark into Dink's peaked face. Who had given that lip-licking, giggling scarecrow the right to stand in this company of men?

Then this edifice of braggadocio collapsed like a pricked balloon. He could not deceive himself. He knew that what he and Alton had done was not an act of heroism, but a foolhardy and ignoble trick. Shamefaced, he pushed Riff Wingate's arm aside and shuffled toward the door...

Next day, Miss Roache thrashed Kevin and Alton with her hardwood pointer, and Kevin rose higher in the respect of Riff and Harold by standing erect and tight-lipped while his hands were beaten until his fingers were unable to close on a pencil. But, to his own mild amazement, he found he took no pleasure from their plaudits. "Yer a good man, Kev," they said again. And he was more bitterly ashamed than he had been during the times when they had abused and scorned him...

Later that same day, Alton Stacey, who had slobbered like a baby during the whipping, dragged a pleading Dink Anthony into the woodshed and beat him until blood trickled from his mouth.

And he showed Kevin Dink's blood on his yellowish-blue, hideously swollen hands.

"He's the sonovabitch that squealed on us," Alton explained. And he made a strange sound: half sob, half shout of exultation.

His mind dark with the strangeness of the world, Kevin turned away...

Twenty-One

As he walked home from school, the sky was radiant, rich, and soft. Early December sunlight sparkled on the patches of gravelly snow that lay like little islands of salt in the fields. Sparrows, the colour of frozen mud and dead grass and sluggish with cold, wobbled groggily across the road in front of him or stood still enough to be mistaken for rocks. When he stepped onto the prowed shadow of the house, he pretended that he was going aboard a raft.

He opened the storm door and closed it behind him. There was barely room enough for him to stand between the storm door and the door of the kitchen. It was like being enclosed in a long, narrow, vertical box. The knob of the inner door had broken and his father had made a latch from an old table knife, fencewire rivets, and a strand of rabbit wire. He lifted the latch and entered the kitchen —

The sudden uprush of heat was faintly nauseating. The room reeked of boiling turnips. He threw his books on the table, hung up his cap and mackinaw, and laid his wet mittens on the oven door. "Anybody home?" he called. He knew that his grandmother was visiting her daughter in Larchmont and that his father had gone to the woods to chop firewood. "Anybody home?" he called again.

"I'm in here, Scampi."

At the door to the living room, he stopped abruptly. A ruddy, moustached man in a blue serge suit sat on the old burlap-covered cot. Mary rose from her chair by the stove.

"Scampi, this is Mr. Masters — Mr. Ernie Masters."

She planted a kiss on his forehead. He hated the gesture. It sickened him to have strangers see her kiss him.

"Hello," he said coldly.

Ernie tapped the end of an unlighted cigarette against the back of his wrist and grinned.

"Your mother's told me a lot about you, Scampi," he said.

Here was a townsman. Neither a mill hand nor a farmer could have worn a serge suit as casually as this. On the rare occasions on which Judd could be induced to take his shiny old suit out of the newspapers in which he kept it wrapped, he behaved with the self-mocking embarrassment of a man forced to assume the garb of a woman. And when forced to wear a necktie, he clawed at his throat continually...

Mary ran her fingers through her red-brown hair. Kevin noted that she had put on her best frock and that she had painted a little red bow on her lips.

All during this conversation, she kept bobbing in and out of her chair.

"Yes, your mother has told me all kinds of things about you, Scampi. All nice things of course" — here Ernie chuckled indulgently. There was a long moment of silence in which the man continued to tap the cigarette against his wrist. Finally, Ernie spoke again. "How are you doing anyway, Scampi?" he asked irrelevantly.

My name is Kevin! Don't you know enough to call people by their right name? "All right, I guess."

"That's good. I'm glad to hear it." Ernie paused, appeared to search for further comments.

"Mr. Masters works in Larchmont, Scampi — in the bank in Larchmont. He's an old, old friend of Mummy's."

For no apparent reason, Ernie looked relieved. "Yep," he said eagerly. "I knew your mummy when you were just a glint in her eye, Scampi."

The man and the woman laughed uneasily.

Kevin wished he dared turn on his heel and go. But he was too shy for that. He pushed his hands into the pockets of his breeches and clenched his fists.

"Mr. Masters just dropped in for a little talk, Scampi."

"Uh-huh."

Ernie lit his cigarette with a little silvery lighter and ran a finger across his moustache. "Let's see now, how old are you, Scampi?" He inhaled and pretended to ponder the question seriously.

"He'll be twelve next month," Mary said.

"Twelve!" Ernie raised his eyebrows and pursed his lips as though Mary had announced that Kevin was one hundred years old. "Gee whillikers! The time sure does fly, doesn't it?"

Kevin said nothing.

"I told you I was getting to be an old woman, Ernie."

"You — old? Naw, you'll never be old, Mary," Ernie smiled gallantly.

"Your mother will never be old, will she, Scampi?"

Kevin half-shrugged. "I don't know. I guess she will be."

"Naw! Twenty years from now she won't be a day older than she is now. I'd bet my life on that, Scampi."

For a long time, no one said anything. Kevin knew instinctively that Judd would hate this man. Ernie was the type of person whom Judd dismissed as "big-feelin' bastards." Kevin watched him contemptuously as he ran his thumb and forefinger up and down the razor-sharp crease in his trousers.

"What you planning to be when you grow up, Scampi?"

I am going to be an Axeman and I will go all over the world cutting off the heads of persons who ask stupid questions. "I don't know," he muttered aloud.

"Oh, Scampi's going to do wonderful things when he grows up, aren't you, Scampi?"

"I don't know. I guess mebbe I'll work in the mill like my father." He said this rather defiantly. At the moment he was willing to pledge all the rest of his life to the mill as a gesture of spite against Ernie Masters.

"Oh, no! Scampi isn't ever going to work in the mill! Never! Never! Never! When he grows up, he's going to keep his hands all nice and pink and soft. He's going to work in an office, that's what he's going to do."

"Maybe you'll work in the bank someday, hey, Scamp?"

Ernie laughed, and Kevin detected a hint of mockery.

"No, I ain't never gonna work in any old bank," he declared sulkily.

Ernie guffawed. "Well, I can't say I blame you, fella! I can't say I blame you!"

Ernie got to his feet and crossed the room. He smelled of hair tonic, tobacco, and cologne. Cupping Kevin's chin in his hands, he made him look up, and the boy turned hard and cold under his touch.

Their eyes met and Kevin saw many things in Ernie's face. In his eyes there was a dark gleam of derisive tolerance; Kevin had observed this look in the faces of many men when they talked with boys. And he was familiar also with the mingling of playfulness and brutality in the grin and in the hands gripping his shoulders. Without saying a word, the man was telling him that he was doing him a great honour in treating him as an equal when, after all, he could break him like a dry twig any time he wished.

"Tell you what, Scamp," Ernie chuckled. "How about me giving you a bright, new, shiny silver dollar. Would you like that, boy?"

The boy read embarrassment and a hint of impatience in the man's voice.

Then Ernie released him and Kevin relaxed slightly. With almost morbid curiosity he followed the man's hands as he reached into his coat and drew out a wallet.

"There you are, Scamp — don't that look purty, hey?"

Taking Kevin's wrist, Ernie lifted his hand and pressed the coin into his hand. Dubiously, Kevin closed his fingers and felt its cold, rough surface. Never before had he possessed a dollar.

"Well now," Ernie drawled with the air of a man who had performed a difficult act creditably. "Well, now, I guess when a guy gets a dollar he just naturally wants to go somewhere and spend it."

Kevin looked at him without understanding. Ernie returned to the cot, tugging up the legs of his trousers so that he revealed red, yellow, and blue socks. Blinking, Kevin glanced at his mother. She smiled rather coyly. "I think what Mr. Masters means, Scamper, is that you probably want to take your money to the store so's you can buy something."

He knew that they wanted him to leave. Still holding the coin, he put his hands back in his pockets.

"Yeah, sure," he said.

He strove to sound sarcastic but succeeded only in sounding rather silly and sulky.

Rising quickly, she embraced him and kissed his cheek. Like Judas kissing Christ, he thought bitterly. As she drew away, he fingered the spot touched by her lips.

"Oh, my! You've got lipstick on your face, Scampi!" Her voice was eager and silly. She brushed at his face with a lilac-and-wintergreen-scented handkerchief. He stared at the floor, observing that she had donned the little blue slippers that she wore to dances.

"I guess I better go," he mumbled, wanting them to know that they had not deceived him. Perhaps, if Ernie knew that his trick had been detected, he would go away.

Gently, she steered him toward the door to the kitchen. "Supper will be ready by the time you get back, sweetikins."

"Uh-huh."

She turned her head and spoke to Ernie: "I'll be back in half a second."

"Yeah, sure, no hurry a-tall, Mar."

Kevin prayed fervently that God would send a thunderbolt from heaven and strike this man dead. He prayed that God would empower him to strike off his head as David had struck off the head of the giant Goliath. He prayed that —

She started to help him into his mackinaw. "I can do it myself," he muttered. "I don't need nobody tuh help me."

"Oh, sugar-baby, Mummy just loves to help you!" Quickly, she pressed her lips against his. Then, for only an instant, her giddy playfulness died and she looked at him sadly, almost pleadingly. "Oh, Scampi!" she cried.

For the first time today, she looked vulnerable. Grinning ghoulishly, he wiped his lips with the back of his hands.

"I'm goin' now," he said harshly.

She winced as though he had slapped her. Then she shrugged. "All right, Scampi."

He did not look at her again until his hand touched the latch. She stood by the door to the living room, slumping a little, her eyes plaintive and imploring.

But, less than a minute later, he stood on the doorstep and heard her and Ernie laughing together...

Though he plodded in the direction of Biff Mason's store, he was not really going anywhere in particular. The sun was a dying coal on the brick-coloured horizon, and the temperature had fallen until he seemed to walk on the floor of an ocean of icy water. The cold closed on his temples like an iron hand crushing his skull.

He thought of wandering into the fields, of becoming lost and freezing to death. Gloating, he imagined how his mother would wail and tear her hair when his rigid corpse was found and carried back to the house. Perhaps she would be driven to madness or suicide by her grief. Perhaps she would turn on Ernie Masters and kill him with a knife. He could almost see Ernie's look of anguish and astonishment as he looked down at the blade protruding from the blood-stained white of his shirt...

He had heard Judd say that in the last minutes before death a freezing man was bathed in an unnatural warmth. No, freezing would not be an unpleasant death. His corpse would be white and beautiful, and his mother would kneel by his coffin and moisten his face with her tears...

Passing under the overhanging limbs of silver-green cedars and golden-green hemlocks, he thought of running away. He would hitchhike to Bennington and hop a freight to Halifax or to Moncton or to Truro. In his mind's eye each of these towns was a metropolis like Rome or Jerusalem. And he had read the books of Horatio Alger. For a little while, like Phil the Fiddler or Paul the Matchboy, he would wander cold and famished through the streets.

Then a millionaire in a great, glittering automobile would stop... and pick him up... and take him home... and treat him as his own son. He would be enrolled in one of those schools where the boys wore uniforms and played football, and... someday, years hence... he would come back to Lockhartville as Sir Kevin O'Brien, the head of some great railroad or bank, and he would find his mother, a ragged, snag-toothed crone, living on bread and water in a tarpapered shack...

He stopped at a turn in the road, thinking of the silver dollar in his pocket and wondering what it would buy —

No, he could not spend this money! It was a bribe, like the thirty pieces of silver which had been paid to Judas for his betrayal of Christ. He would stalk back to the house and throw the vile coin in Ernie Masters's moustached face! Or, rather, he concluded lamely, that is what he would have done had he not been a coward...As it was, he would throw it away! The idea of such a sacrifice intoxicated him.

Jerking the silver dollar from his breeches pocket, Kevin sent it flying over a fence and into a field. For an instant, it cut a bright arc through the air. Then it was gone. Sighing and shaken, he congratulated himself. He had performed an act comparable to those recorded in the Word of God. He compared himself to Abraham who had been willing to give his son, Isaac, as a burnt offering unto the Lord. Then, remembering how God had sent a lamb as a substitute for Isaac, Kevin half-expected a million silver dollars to fall from the sky and lie like mounds of clean snow around his feet...

On a sudden impulse, he reached down and dug a stone out of the frozen earth. As his target, he chose a grey, skeleton-naked alder on the other side of the fence.

"This is for you, Ernie Masters!"

Leaping into the air, he threw — The stone struck the trunk of the alder and dead-grey limbs danced crazily.

"And this is for you, Ernie Masters!"

Pulling off his mittens, he clawed at the pebbles embedded in frozen mud. He heaved rocks at the tree until his nails were broken and bloody and his arms were numb.

"And this is for you, Ernie Masters!"

Exhausted at last, with the dusk closing around him, he sank to his knees.

"O God," he prayed aloud. "O God of Abraham and of Isaac and of Jacob, make me one of Thy mighty ones! Make me one of Thy kings and prophets, O God of Israel. Give me the faith to move mountains and the power to call down fire from heaven on the enemies of the Most High! Give me the staff of Moses and the sword of David! Oh God, make me like unto David and Isaiah and Jeremiah and Ezekiel and Solomon! Thy servant, Kevin, asks this, O God. Amen."

Then, still kneeling in the road, he covered his face with his hands and wept.

Twenty-Two

In mid-winter, the house was a match cupped in a man's hands in the perpetual night and storm. To Kevin, the weather seemed to possess will and sinister intelligence. Shivering under the weight of nightmare, he thought of the wind as a pack of howling wild dogs who threw their ice-encrusted bodies against doors, windows, and walls. From the kitchen window, he had seen such dogs drive a deer out of the woods and onto the heath. There, the fear-maddened, spindle-shanked beast had floundered in deep snow and the dogs had torn her flanks and belly and sunk their teeth into her throat...

Sometimes, in the evenings, a draught struck the lamp by the window and caused the flame to bend until it lay horizontal, then shrink back into the wick, so that it almost went out. And on several nights, Kevin awoke with the little moan of fear as a sheet of glass was knocked from its sash in an upstairs window and went crashing to the floor.

The wind slithered under doors, though Judd stuffed the cracks with rags and gunny sacks. In living room and kitchen, cold fastened on Kevin's ankles like invisible jaws. In the grip of the wind, the roof shingles rattled like his grandmother's laughter. And when he ventured outdoors, the wind seized and lifted him as though to tear him from the earth. He half-expected that someday he would be caught up like a kite, his coat-tails flying, and sent hurtling into the endless cold of the sky.

And there was snow: mountains and deserts of snow. The road became a canal between great banks of snow. And on stormy nights, snow sifted in through the cracks around the windows and lay in crystalline mounds on the sills.

When Kevin's ears were frost-bitten, Judd took the wash basin to the yard and scooped up snow. While Kevin bent over the sink, Judd held handfuls of snow against his ears, held it there till it melted in the warmth of his flesh as pain shot through his scalp, and he whimpered and squirmed in the man's hands. "Whinin' ain't a-gonna do no good, young feller," Judd growled and almost gleefully (or so it seemed to Kevin) he reached for another handful of snow...

Every morning, Judd rose from his cot before daylight, breakfasted on fried potatoes and warmed-over beans, and trudged into the woods with his axe across his shoulder. He was chopping firewood — illegally — on the crown lands south of the creek. It was almost certain that he would never be able to haul the wood home. There was no logging road to that part of the forest. In the spring, the cords of beech and maple that he had felled, sawed, and tiered would be left to rot. But he went forth every morning and came home exhausted every night. "It's foolishness, Judd," Mary told him impatiently. "You might just as well stay home where it's warm." But Judd always gave the same answer: "If a man ain't doin' anythin' I guess he might jist as well be dead."

In the evening, Judd lay on the cot in a stupor of weariness, and Mary and Kevin sat for hours without uttering a word for fear that some chance remark would strike the spark that would bring him to his feet in an explosion of rage. Usually, Kevin read the Bible while Mary perused romances containing heroes named Julian and Adrian and Anton and heroines named Cecily and Cynthia and Mifawny. All of the heroes were tall, dark, and handsome, and all of the heroines had honey-coloured hair.

And sometimes, Mary wrote letters to imaginary correspondents. Unknown to his mother, Kevin had read many of these letters. The bulk of them were addressed to an apparently rich, aristocratic, and understanding matron named Lady Astrid Villiers.

My Dear Lady Villiers:
In this desolate and frigid outpost, your letters are like a breath
of warm spring air. You are so wise and so familiar with the
ways of the world that there must be times when you weary
of the trials and tribulations of a silly little country girl like me.
But I do not think I could continue to bear my burden if I did
not know that there was in the world one person at least with a
capacity for understanding and sympathy.
Geoffrey, the man whom I met in Boston last summer
(Mary had never been in Boston) *wants me to run away*
with him to New York. But I have told him that my duty is
here with my little boy. I tremble to think of his fate in a cruel
world if left to the mercies of that being whom I once called
my husband and whom I am still forced to call by that title,
although he is no longer capable of inspiring the faintest spark
of affection in my suffering heart.
I have suffered so much, my dear Lady Astrid, yet I know
my duty. I must remain a prisoner in this dismal place to
which I have been consigned by a cruel fate. If it were not
for my little boy —

And so on, for eighteen pages, which Kevin read with mingled fascination and scorn.

Grandmother O'Brien continued to sit in the rocker under the clock shelf, the heated brick hugged against her pain. She ate her milk and cracker gruel and read her Bible and, as in the past, she sang:

> There is a fountain filled with blood,
> Drawn from Emmanuel's veins,
> And sinners plunged beneath that flood
> Lose all their guilty stains.

Though he was beginning to think of himself as a prophet of the Lord, one who would smite sinners with whips and swords and call down fire from heaven upon the habitations of iniquity, Kevin was still terrified of blood. At times it seemed to him that the world was not whirling through space but rather bobbing like a cork on a churning ocean of blood. There was the blood of deer and cats and fish and cattle. There was the blood of porcupines and raccoons and sparrows. There was the blood of Dink Anthony on Alton Stacey's hands. There was the blood of Av Farmer trickling from his nostrils and the corners of his mouth. There was the blood of Kevin O'Brien. And there was the blood of Christ.

He wondered what Christ had felt at the moment the nails were driven into His feet and hands. What had He thought as He felt the steel touching his skin, heard the swish of the hammer as the crucifier lifted it for the first stroke? In Kevin's imagination the hammer made a sound like that of the strap hissing through the air.

Perhaps, if he were a prophet, he too would be crucified! Men with faces like those of Riff Wingate and Harold Winthrop would scourge him and crown him with thorns. And, nailed to the tree, he would smile down pityingly at the mother kneeling beneath his feet.

A thought struck him like a thunderbolt! Perhaps he was Jesus born again! The Bible said that Jesus would return. And the Jesus pictured in the Bible had reddish-brown hair and blue-grey eyes like Kevin's. If he were a man and wore a beard — why, he would look exactly like the Christ in the Bible! But did not the Bible say that on His Second Coming Christ would fall from the sky with a shout? If that were so, then he could only be a prophet — a forerunner like John the Baptist. But, in any case, God would give him a sign in due time. And if he were to be crucified, God would give him the strength and courage to endure the nails.

"What are you thinking about, Scampi?"

Rather worriedly, his mother smiled at him across the lamp-lit table.

"Oh, I wasn't thinkin' about much of anythin'."

"A penny for your thoughts."

"I guess mebbe they wouldn't be worth it."

He was annoyed at her for trying to insinuate herself into his mind. *Why won't she leave me be? Why does she want to know every thing I think and feel?*

Shrugging, Mary turned back to her letter.

Immediately, his attitude changed. *Why won't she talk to me? Why does she want to waste her time writing silly old letters to people who aren't even real?*

Wearily, Judd rose from his cot and stoked the fire, banging stove lids and pokers.

"If it weren't fer me I guess yuh fellers would let yerself freeze tuh death," he growled.

Mary looked up from her writing and Kevin's eyes left his Bible. There was a tenseness, a waiting, until Judd returned to the cot and closed his eyes. Grandmother O'Brien smiled and embraced her brick...

Then came the soldiers and brake the legs of the first, and of the other which was crucified with him. But when they came to Jesus and saw that he was dead already they brake not his legs: But one of the soldiers with a spear pierced his side and forthwith came there out blood and water...

A week before Christmas, Judd sold the hens. Old Biff Mason had informed him that he would not extend credit for such luxuries as fruits, nuts, and candies. In repeating the storekeeper's words, Judd imitated his thin, querulous whine. "The way I've allus figgered it a man that cain't afford tuh pay fer what he gits oughta call hisself lucky if he'n have bread and potatoes on his table," Biff Mason had said. And Judd swore that when he found work again and paid the $200 he owed, he would drive his fist down Biff Mason's throat and tell him he could put his store on his back and carry it to hell.

So one night, the hens were thrust into gunny sacks and trucked away. Kevin watched and listened at a window, excited by the men running to and fro in the dark dooryard and moved to pity by the squawking terror of the hens. "I ain't never seed nor heard o' sich foolishness in all my born days," Grandmother O'Brien proclaimed from her rocker. "Goin' without eggs all the rest o' the winter jist so's yuh'n have a heathenish feast on one day o' the year!" And she turned her eyes toward heaven, as though to remind God that she accepted no responsibility for such sinful improvidence.

But the hen money was not spent on a feast. That same night, Judd went to the cabin of Madge Harker, the bootlegger, and bought rum and beer. He staggered home drunk and the kitchen resounded with his song:

Here's a cuckoo! There's a cuckoo!
Here's a cuckaroo!
Here's a cuckoo! There's a cuckoo!
There's a cuckaroo!

His cheeks the colour of pickled beets and his hair tumbling over his forehead, he sang and shouted in drunken ecstasy — and Mary and Kevin knew that he was mocking them. Mute and stiff with anger and frustration, they watched their dreams of foods and gifts and decorations gurgle into his mouth. And each time he drank, he laughed and peered at them with red, taunting eyes.

He was still singing when Kevin and Mary went to bed.

Oh, the Jones boys
They built a mill
On the top of a hill

And they worked all night
And they worked all day

But they couldn't make
That gah'damn saw mill pay

So the Jones boys
They built a still
On the top of the hill

And they worked one night
And they worked one day

And my Gawd didn't
That little still pay!

Kevin's eyes were wet as he wriggled down under the quilts on the cot in the living room. He shivered as the cold blankets covered his legs.

The grates of the stove were open and the reflected firelight cut a flickering, smokey-scarlet path to the kitchen door. He inhaled wood smoke and his mother's perfume.

Without knowing quite why, he giggled. His mother laid her palm on his forehead.

"What's wrong, Scampi? Are you feverish or something?"

He was giggling so hard he had difficulty in getting the words out. "Oh, I was jist thinkin' about how the things that are funny and the things that are sad are all mixed up together," he managed to blurt at last. "I mean, well, things happen — and you don't know whether tuh cry or tuh laugh."

And he giggled so loudly that he did not hear what his mother answered. He awoke without remembering how or when he had fallen asleep. It was night still, but he did not know if he had slept for hours or only for minutes.

From the open door of their bedroom came his parents' voices.

"Get away from me, Judd," Mary was saying. "For God's sake, get away from me!"

Judd's voice was as weird and chill as the wind that raked the window near Kevin's head.

"Git away from me, she says! Git away from me says the cheatin' little bitch! Eh! I'n jist hear her a-tellin' Ernie Masters tuh git away from her. A fat chance of her a-tellin' him that! No, what she'd be sayin' tuh him would be, Ernie darlin' would yuh please —" And here in a sniggering burlesque contralto, Judd inserted an obscenity.

"You'll wake Scampi, Judd. Please go and lie down, Judd. You're drunk and you'll wake Scampi."

Her words were half command, half supplication.

"You'll wake Scampi, Judd. Please go and lie down, Judd. You're drunk and you'll wake Scampi," he parroted. "Listen tuh the little bitch! Listen tuh her, will yuh! A helluva lot she cares about the boy — a helluva lot she cares about anythin'. Cheatin' little bitch! Dirty cheatin' little whore!"

Kevin strove to cover his ears, but his hands would not respond. *Oh, please God, make them stop and I'll never ask you for anything again. I promise I won't, God. Only make them stop, please.*

"And a lot you care! He's your son too! He's just as much yours as he is mine!"

The light streaming through the door staggered and weaved so that Kevin knew Judd held the lamp in an unsteady hand.

"Eh! I ain't so damn sure of that! I allus say that when yuh been cut by a crosscut saw it's damn hard tuh tell which tooth did the most damage!" Again he cackled in a hideous parody of laughter. "I got me a damn good idea that there brat's got a helluva sight more Masters blood in his veins than anythin' else. The snivellin' little bugger don't act much like no O'Brien!"

"Judd!"

Oh, please God, don't let him say anything more. Please, God. Please!

He heard the lamp being set on the floor or on a table.

"Mar."

Judd's voice was abashed, almost diffident.

"Go away! I hate you!"

Now Mary's voice was harsh and arrogant, Judd's plaintive and faltering.

"I guess mebbe I shouldn't oughta said that, Mar. I guess mebbe I didn't have no call tuh say that."

"Get out!"

"All right, Mar, I'll go back out tuh the kitchen and lay down and go tuh sleep. I won't drink anythin' more, Mar."

"I don't care what you do. Drink yourself to death if you want to. Go jump in the creek if you want to. *But get out and leave me alone!*"

"Look, Mar — in the mornin' I'll git me some more money and I'll see that you and Kev have the best Christmas yuh've ever had in yer life. I promise I will, Mar. There weren't no need of me gittin' drunk like I did. There weren't no need of it a-tall. I guess I'm gittin' tuh be jist nothin' but a drunkard. I don't know how yuh put up with me. But I'll go tuh the store in the mornin', Mar and I'll —"

"Just get out, Judd."

"Mar, I'll buy yuh a new dress. I'll git me some more money and in the mornin' I'll —"

"Just get out, Judd," she repeated wearily.

"All right, Mar." His voice was contrite, defeated.

A moment later, Judd lurched out of the bedroom, the lamp bobbing in his hands, and staggered into the kitchen.

In one part of Kevin's mind hate was an overturned lamp, spilling flaming kerosene. He did not fully understand Judd's accusation. But he had said that the blood of Ernie Masters flowed in his veins. This dark and inscrutable riddle frightened and shamed Kevin more than it would have done had its meaning been made stark and plain. He almost prayed that God would strike his father dead where he lay. Then he remembered how the man had begged and promised.

Never before had he heard his father so abase himself. To Kevin this was almost equivalent to a reversal in the laws of nature. It was like a total eclipse of the sun, like hailstones falling in May...

Twenty-Three

During the whole of the following day, neither of Kevin's parents spoke to the other. But Judd made much of Kevin. He called him "Kev," a name he used only when he was seeking to be expansive and friendly, and smiled almost shyly as he asked him little tentative, self-effacing questions about his reading and his schoolwork. This humility and strained heartiness embarrassed Kevin. Every day the gulf between him and his father widened, and Judd's attempts to bridge the gap were so pitiably inept that Kevin almost wept for him.

"Let's see now, Kev," Judd said, biting off a chew of tobacco, "I guess yer still makin' out good at school, eh?"

"Yessir, I guess so."

"What duh yuh like best — I mean which subjecks?"

"Hist'ry. I guess."

"Well, now. Well. I guess yuh've learnt about Wolfe and Montcalm and alla them there fellers, eh?"

Ever since Kevin's first year in school, his father — when he wanted to show that he shared his son's interests — had mentioned Wolfe and Montcalm. They were the only historical characters he remembered.

"Yeah," Kevin answered. "We learnt a little bit about them."

"I guess you'n remember where they fought that big battle, eh?"

"No, I guess not," Kevin lied. To repay his father for his friendliness he wished to give him this little honour.

Judd grunted with satisfaction. "Why, it were fought on the Plains a Abraham," he asserted. He smiled with the expression of one scholar conversing with another.

Kevin slapped his forehead. "Gosh, sure! I remember now!"

"Oh, the old feller still remembers a few things, Kev. I usta kinda like school. Graded ever' year I went."

He chewed tobacco, wiped his lips and blinked.

"Eddication's a mighty fine thing, Kev. Yuh can't git too much eddication, I allus say."

"I guess that's right." Each year it became harder for Kevin to call his father "daddy." But shyness and uncertainty kept him from changing the title. In recent months he had skirted the issue by calling him by name only when he had to.

In the afternoon, Judd announced that he had decided to sell the red cow. "The old bitch ain't worth a-nothin' anyways and I figger mebbe I'n talk old Biff Mason intuh takin' her off my hands. If I'n talk fast enough I might even get me a pretty fair price fer her." Rather sheepishly, he shuffled his feet and tugged at his cloth cap.

"Don't do nothin' foolish now," Grandmother O'Brien cautioned.

Judd's eyes widened comically. "Now, Ma, who said anythin' about doin' anythin' foolish?" He winked at Kevin, as though enlisting him as his co-conspirator.

The old woman shook her head vigorously and increased the speed of her rocker.

"Mark my words, son, yuh keep on a-drinkin' an' a-runnin' up store bills an' a-sellin' hens an' cows an' pretty soon yuh ain't even gonna have a shirt tuh put tuh yer back. Wilful waste means woeful want, son. We're poor folks — poor as dirt — an' we gotta remember it!"

"Now, Ma, yer livin' in the past. Times is changed."

"Some things ain't never gonna change, son. Yer poor — allus was an' allus will be. There ain't nothin's gonna change that. The Good Lord meant it tuh be. The Good Lord meant fer folks like us tuh take what's handed out tuh us an' be grateful fer it."

"This ain't got nothin' tuh do with what yer talkin' about, Ma. I'm jist gettin' rid of an old no-good cow. I been thinkin' a tradin' her off fer a long time now."

"There ain't no use in a-talkin' tuh yuh when yuh got yer mind set on a thing, son! I might jist as well save my breath tuh cool my porridge. Answer not a fool accordin' tuh his folly, the Good Book says. There ain't no earthly use in a-talkin' tuh yuh a-tall."

"Yuh wanta come with me, Kev?"

Kevin stared at his father in amazement. Normally, Judd would never have dreamed of issuing such an invitation.

"Huh? Gosh. Yes, I guess so. Sure," he stammered.

"Git on yer duds then, me laddie. Me and you is goin' cow tradin'."

Making a halter from a piece of clothes line, Judd led the red cow out of the barn and onto the road. There were only two colours in the world: the grey of the sky and the white of the snow.

"Break off a lilac switch, Kev, and switch her backside ever' time she gits balky."

Fetching a switch from the hedge, Kevin grinned; Judd slapped the cow's dropping ears lightly, almost affectionately. It was incredible that this same man had once seized a pitchfork and —

"Geddap up there, yuh old red fool!" Judd bellowed.

Judd leading the cow and Kevin trotting behind her with the switch, they went down the dry, white canal that was the road...

Biff Mason wore red garters on his sleeves and a pencil stub behind his ear. His lips were flaccid, perpetually moist, and his voice was a lugubrious singsong punctuated by whinnying laughter. Once, in the previous summer, Biff had caught Kevin pilfering peppermints and since then he had said often, in Kevin's hearing, that all of the mill hands' children were unblushing little thieves.

But, today, Biff ignored Kevin. While the men dickered in the yard, prodding and poking the cow, making her open her mouth and lift her feet so that they might examine her teeth and hooves, Kevin stood inside, imbibing the atmosphere of the store. The building was scarcely larger than the O'Briens' wood-shed and, like the woodshed, it was built of unbarked slabs and raw, unpainted boards. But the smells, sights, and textures were inexhaustibly intoxicating. Crates, cartons, and barrels stood on top of one another in grotesque, teetering towers. The smell was a compound of a thousand aromas, sweet and salty, vapid and pungent. There were the scents of kerosene, vinegar, molasses, ham, bologna, cheddar cheese, butter, clean new denim, tinfoil, chewing tobacco, and waxed wrapping paper. At this season, crates and shelves overflowed with oranges, grapes, nuts, and a dozen kinds of multi-coloured, fruit-scented candies. And, as always, there were big boxes full of gum rubbers, jeans, and black-and-red checked lumber jackets, and little boxes containing mechanical pencils, hairpins, playing cards, and pocket watches.

After thirty minutes of talk and gesturing, the men led the cow away, and Kevin, watching through a little clear space made by his breath in the opaque frost on the window, knew that the sale had been made.

A further ten minutes passed. Then Biff and Judd came back from the barn and entered the store. Kevin knew from the reek of his father's breath that he had drunk of the vanilla flavouring extract which Biff sold to the men as though it were liquor.

"This here young feller a yers is sproutin' up jist like a bad weed, ain't he, Juddie?" Biff whinnied.

"Yeah, I guess mebbe yer right, Biff," Judd said shortly, dismissing the subject. There were occasions, such as today, when Judd tried to be friendly with Kevin while the two of them were at home or alone together. But it was his unshakable conviction that small boys should be barred from the company of men. When they could not be excluded, Judd's etiquette demanded that they be ignored. Kevin had long ago been taught that the quickest and surest way to earn a strapping was to impinge on the conversations of men.

He sat on an orange crate, his mittened hands in his lap, as Judd and Biff transacted their business.

First, there was the question of a payment on the bill. Judd called credit buying "dealing on tick." Having been jobless for two months, he now owed Biff Mason $200 "on tick." A substantial part of the price of the cow was to be applied against this account.

"It ain't that I'm tryin' tuh dun yuh or anythin', Juddie — yuh know that, boy — but I gotta have cash tuh stay in business. Them there wholesalers wants their money ever' thirty days. Why, Juddie, iffin it hadda been anybody but you that owed me that there two hundred bucks, I'da cracked down on 'em long ago. But yer a friend a mine, Juddie, and I trust yuh. I'd say that behind yer back jist like I'd say it tuh yer face. Juddie O'Brien allus pays his bills, yessiree, Juddie O'Brien allus pays his bills!" Biff rubbed his hands together and licked his wet, flabby lips. Kevin squirmed with contempt for the storekeeper's slyness and greed. But Judd, warmed by the vanilla extract, seemed pleased.

"Yeah, Biff, I guess there ain't nobody in Lockhartville can say that Judd O'Brien don't allus pay his bills," he boasted.

"That's right, Juddie! That's right!" Biff neighed like a stallion. "And I'm the man tuh say it! Ever' man in Lockhartville will tell yuh that Biff Mason has allus said Juddie O'Brien is a man that pays his bills. I've allus said it, Juddie. Yessir. Yessir. Yessir..." Biff's voice trailed away as if he had exhausted this subject and could not think of anything more to say.

"Yeah, I've paid ever' cent I ever owed, Biff — ever' damn cent. I've paid ever' cent since I went tuh work — and that's twenty-six years ago."

"That's what I allus say, Juddie. That's what I allus say... Now, how much was yuh figgerin' tuh pay on this little bitty bill here, Juddie, eh, hay?"

For a few minutes they haggled. Bored and rather scornful, Kevin arose and went to the little glassed-in showcase near the door.

"Kevin!" his father said sharply.

"Huh?"

"Sit down over there! Don't yuh know no better'n tuh run all over the damn place when a man's tryin' tuh talk business?"

"Yessir."

Flushing, Kevin returned to the orange crate. He hated the little dark flicker of amusement in Biff's eyes.

But now Judd began selecting delicacies: round, smooth-skinned oranges; grapes that might have been picked from the trees pictured in the Bible; cashews, peanuts, butternuts, Brazil nuts; chocolate, coconut, caramel, butterscotch, and peppermint candy. Kevin's mouth watered as he watched Biff lay the little paper bags on the rough plank that served as a counter. And he noted that Judd prolonged the buying of these things, seemed to relish the privilege of smelling, touching, tasting, and ordering.

He bought a great red hunk of ham and a bag of sausages, and he bought pork and beefsteak. After hesitating for a long time, he bought canned clams and sour pickles and a bag of onions; these last items were the kind of food that Judd liked best: stout, vinegary, biting foods to be washed down with great draughts of black tea or buttermilk.

Then, stuttering and reddening like a young boy, he bought a frock for Mary. He did this hurriedly, staring around wildly as though afraid of being seen, barking a refusal when Biff invited him to feel the rich texture of the cloth. "It's all right! Put the goddamn thing in a bag or somethin'!" And as Biff wrapped the frock, Judd stared at it dubiously, as though it were a silly and useless thing.

Then: "Kevin, come here!"

"Yessir."

Judd pointed to a box. "Give him one a-them there goddamn watches," he ordered gruffly.

"Ah, yer makin' a good buy there, Juddie. Them there watches is worth three times what I'm askin' fer 'em! Why —"

"Jist give him one a the goddamn things!"

"Sure, Juddie, sure."

Biff extended the watch on an upturned palm. Kevin lifted it by its chain and held it gingerly.

"Seven dollar and fifty cents, Juddie, and worth thirty bucks iffin it's worth a cent," Biff Mason neighed.

To Kevin, seven dollars and fifty cents was a fortune. He felt that this gift was a rich and splendid thing.

"Gee, thanks, Daddy," he whispered.

"All right, put the goddamn thing in yer pocket and git over there outta the way and sit down!"

"Yessir," said Kevin, retreating hastily.

Back on the orange crate, he held the watch in front of his face, letting it dangle from its chain. He was rapt with admiration for its shining, silvery case and red-green-and-black face —

"Put that there damn thing in yer pocket, Kevin. I told yuh once."

"Yessir."

Judd blinked, straightened his cap and turned back to the corner. His voice had been harsh. But Kevin did not feel hurt. He understood.

Twenty-Four

Before leaving the store, Judd bought more vanilla extract. Seeking to conceal the transaction from Kevin, he signalled Biff with winks and little furtive movements of hand and head. But he was too clumsy to be cunning. In the field of guile and subterfuge, Judd was like a collie masquerading as a kitten.

The bottles hidden in the pockets of the denim smock he wore over his windbreaker, Judd loaded his arms with groceries. Kevin gathered up the remaining parcels. Their gum rubbers crunching the snow crust, they started up the road toward home.

As they reached the cabin of Madge Harker, Judd slowed his steps. "Seems like I'm fergittin' somethin', Kev," he drawled archly.

"Yeah?" Kevin's voice was dubious.

Judd stopped. "Eh! I remember now. I owe Madge Harker a few dollars. I guess mebbe I oughta stop in while I got the money on me." He glanced at Kevin as though appealing to his judgement in such matters. "It'll only take me a second or two," he added.

Kevin gazed at Madge's cabin: a squat, soot-coloured shack, half-hidden among tamaracks and willows. Smoke rose bleakly from the tilting stack.

"Can't I go with yuh? It's cold standin' out here."

"Eh? Why don't yuh walk on ahead? I'll catch up with yuh." Then Judd recalled his mood of friendliness and joviality. "Well, all right, then, come on!"

The path was so narrow that following it was like balancing on a fence rail. Twice, Kevin missed his footing and floundered in hip-deep snow. Laying his parcels aside, Judd lifted the leather latch: Lockhartville people did not knock on one another's doors.

The heat that struck Kevin's face smelled of coal oil, stale beer, and unwashed bedding. Madge Harker's cheeks were lacquered-red, as though from the cold. Her corpulent body was wrapped in a stained and rumpled housecoat. Exchanging greetings with Judd, she motioned him and Kevin to seats. Laying his packages at his feet, Kevin slumped down on the woodbox, by the bedroom door. Judd and Madge began the inevitable, ritualistic dialogue. Kevin fidgeted, sweltering in his wool breeches and mackinaw. He wondered how long it would take his father to tell Madge what she already knew: that he had come to buy liquor.

The cabin was heated by an old-fashioned stove, the legs of which bent like the knees of step dancers. The stove stood on a low platform made of slabs and covered with a sheet of wrinkled tin. Behind the platform lay an overturned carton and a pile of empty beer bottles. The cabin had not been finished: its posts and rafters were naked grey like those in a barn. From a spike in a beam opposite him hung a green-and-red windbreaker which he recognized as belonging to Madge's daughter, Nancy...

"Hello."

The whisper startled him more than a shout would have done. He turned in the direction of the voice. Nancy Harker grinned at him, her body, except for her head and shoulders, hidden in the blanket that served as a bedroom door.

He blinked and gaped. "Hello," he mumbled.

"Are you scared or somethin'?" she whispered.

He felt his ears reddening. "No, of course not. What is there tuh be scared of?"

"Nothin'. But you *look* scared. When I spoke to you, you turned as white as a sheet."

He scowled. "You shouldn't oughta sneak up on people that way."

"I didn't sneak up on you. I made myself invisible. I pressed a vein in my wrist and made myself invisible."

"I bet."

She laid her cheek against the blanket. "Why don't you ever talk to me at school?"

"Huh?"

"Why don't you ever talk to me at school?"

"I *do* talk tuh yuh. I've talked tuh yuh dozens a different times."

"Yes, but you don't *say* anythin'." She wrinkled her nose. "Did you know that my father was a merchant seaman?"

"Huh?"

"Why do you say 'huh' all the time?"

"Huh?"

"See! You said it again!"

He glared at her, feeling very hot and foolish.

"Yes, my father is a merchant seaman and he's sailed all over the world. He's in Haiti now. Do you know where Haiti is?"

"Yeah, I guess so."

"I should make you tell me, to see if you really know. But I won't. You see how nice I am? Did you know that in Haiti all the people are black and that they come out in the middle of the night and dance around fires and after a while the dead all get out of their graves and dance too. Did you know that?"

He decided that she was crazy. "No, I don't believe anythin' like that. It's only a story," he said, rather lamely.

"No. It's the truth." Again she laid her cheek against the blanket as though caressing it. "I'm a love-child, did you know that?"

"No. I didn't know."

He wondered who, or what, was a love-child. He supposed it must be a polite synonym for halfwit. Yet this Nancy Harker was reputed to be one of the smartest girls in school.

"Are you a love-child too? No, I guess you wouldn't be. Madge says I'm very lucky to be a love-child. She says most children are made outta hate — but me, I was made outta loads and loads and loads of love!"

He rather resented her assumption that she was a love-child, whatever that might be, while he was not.

"I was born in Halifax."

"Oh."

To Kevin, this was as though she had been born in Antioch or Jericho. Like her, he was whispering. Judd and Madge, ignoring them, continued their conversation at the other end of the room.

"It's a stupid place. I didn't like it much. I wish I'd been born in Haiti."

"I bet."

"I like you. I like you a lot. Did you know that?"

"Gosh, yer crazy —"

"I think maybe I'll fall in love with you. I'm thirteen. I guess that means I'm old enough to fall in love. Are you old enough to fall in love with me?"

His jaw dropped. His tongue writhed impotently in his mouth.

"Yes, I think I'll fall in love with you. You have the most

interestin' eyes of any boy in Lockhartville. I bet you see all sorts of things. I bet you can see in the dark like a cat." She grinned. "Did you ever see a vampire?"

He blanched as though she had discovered one of his shameful secrets. He thought of the dark fears that insinuated themselves into his mind on windy nights —

Her laugh was crystal. She bounced up and down, almost tearing the blanket from its rung. "Oh, yes! Yes! Yes! I should have fallen in love with you the minute I got in Lockhart-ville!"

"Yer crazy as a bed bug! Yer crazy as the birds! There ain't no use a-talkin' tuh nobody as crazy as you!"

She made a little pouting face. "Kevin!" Judd called sharply.

"Yessir?" He wanted to escape from Nancy Harker. No — he did not quite want to escape: he wanted to go off by himself and think.

Judd's lips were sly. "Why don't yuh and Nancy carry them parcels up tuh the house, eh? Me and Madge has got a little business tuh talk over here."

"I'n carry them. I don't need no help."

Madge chuckled and fingered her scarlet cheeks. "Well, then, you can just take Nancy along for company, Kevin."

"I don't need nobody tuh help me —"

"Hit the grit, young feller."

"Yessir."

He got to his feet, buttoned his mackinaw, picked up his groceries, and started for the door.

"Wait for me, Kevin! Wait till I get my coat."

Her laughter ringing like a bell, her empty sleeves flailing as she wriggled into her coat, Nancy ran after him —

Down the narrow path between the snowdrifts and under the willows and tamaracks, they walked in silence. When they came to the road, Nancy hopped, skipped, walked backwards, and leapt into the air. "Be careful, you'll spill alla that there stuff," he growled, thinking her very babyish and giddy.

"Your father is goin' to get drunk," she said mildly.

"Who says so?"

"Oh, of course he is. He sent us away because he wanted to stay alone with Madge and get drunk. All the mill men get drunk. Madge says it's the only time they're ever really alive."

"Humph!" He decided that he would not answer her again. He would stride in cold, aloof silence until they reached his home.

"Have you ever been drunk, Kevin?"

He tightened his lips to a bloodless line.

For a few yards, she skipped, the groceries swaying precariously in her arms. "Madge says I wake up drunk every mornin' a my life! She says that when you're as young as I am you're drunk all the time!"

They passed an open field: a sloping wasteland of snow. Sparrows flew up from almost beneath their feet. Their steps made the sound that horses made as they chomped their oats.

"What are you thinkin' about, Kevin?"

"Huh?"

"Don't keep sayin' that! I asked you what you were thinkin' about."

"Oh, nothin' I guess." Too late, he remembered his resolution to rebuke her with stony silence.

"When you look that way at school the boys say that you're stuck-up. They say you think you're too nice to talk to anybody."

His astonishment was thorough and genuine.

"They say that about *me*?"

"Sure, didn't you know? They say it about me sometimes too. But if you aren't thinkin' anythin', what are you feelin' then?"

"I ain't feelin' nothin' neither."

He wondered how the boys could possibly believe that he was stuck-up, that he did not wish to speak to them.

"Oh, yes! You must be feelin' somethin'. If you don't feel anythin' then you're dead. You aren't dead, are you, Kevin?"

"Don't talk so silly."

"That isn't silly. It's true. When you don't feel anythin' you're dead." She repeated the words with the air of one proclaiming a truth from Genesis.

"Well I guess I'm dead then," he snapped disgustedly.

"Then I guess you're just like the others. I guess you're just like Av Farmer and Riff Wingate and —"

No insult could have stung him more than this.

"No," he shouted, almost dropping his parcels. "I ain't like them a-tall!"

Her eyes glittered. "You're not? What makes you think you're not?"

"Because I'm not — that's why!"

He knew he sounded shrill and stupid.

"Oh yes you are! Oh yes you are! Oh yes you are too!"

Whooping, she danced around him like an Indian war party. He wished he dared drop his burden and slap her face.

"No, I'm not!"

"Tell me why you aren't, then!"

He was yellow with rage. The words burst out of him: "Because I'm gonna be a prophet, that's why!"

She stopped. "A prophet! You mean like the prophets in the Bible?"

Hot with embarrassment, he wished he could cut out his tongue. He had spilled his secret. Now she would tattle and everybody at school would jeer —

But he heard himself repeating it. "Yes, a prophet like Isaiah — and — and a king like David!"

"A king like David!"

Had he been able to murder her by will alone, she would have fallen dead in her tracks.

But she did not laugh. "No, I guess maybe you aren't like the others," she admitted slowly. "You do feel things. You're alive! Like me. But I don't guess I'm very crazy about prophets. Don't they just tear their hair and howl about sin? But a king...that's different. A king like David..."

They began walking again. "Did you ever think that maybe you aren't really Kevin O'Brien, that maybe you're somebody else who's just dreaming that he's Kevin O'Brien, and that maybe any minute you'll wake up and find out that everythin' that ever happened to you has been a dream?"

He gaped incredulously. "Yeah," he said. "Have *you* ever felt like that?"

"Oh, yes, yes, yes! And did you ever stop all of a sudden when you were doin' somethin' — oh, maybe somethin' like sharpenin' a pencil or pickin' a flower or tyin' your shoes — did you ever stop and think how funny it feels to be yourself and nobody else, how, how funny it feels just to be you and alive?"

"Yeah," he breathed. "Yeah, I've done that."

She pirouetted on the snow, her skirts billowing and rising. Her chant was almost a song. "You are different, Kevin O'Brien! You are! You are! You are!"

They were within sight of home now. He thought of what she had said about the dream, and about how it felt to be one's self and of how it felt to be alive. These thoughts were almost, but not quite, destroyed when one tried to put them into words. Trying to fit these thoughts into words was like trying to dip up the ocean in a basin. Yet if she had not spoken, he would never have guessed that —

"Tomorrow night after supper I'm goin' skatin' on the pond in the woods."

"Huh?"

"There you go again! You heard what I said. Tomorrow night I'm goin' skatin' on the pond in the woods."

"Oh." He wondered if she meant —

She laughed and bounded. "Oh, Kevin O'Brien, you're silly! Silly! Silly!"

He flushed. "But I like you anyway!" she crowed.

And he was startled by the realization that in talking with Nancy Harker he had quite forgotten the silvery new seven-dollar-and fifty-cent watch in his pocket.

Twenty-Five

Kevin did not go to the pond the following night, for by then he had convinced himself that Nancy had made a fool of him. Sick with dread, he thought of how it would be when school resumed a week after Christmas. Riff and Harold would meet him in the porch. Why if it ain't Key-von, the prophet a God! they would snigger. Come on in here and tell us what they been doin' in heaven lately, yuh prophet a God! He could almost see their wolfish, leering faces, almost hear their lewd, jeering laughter. And Nancy Harker would stand in the background, simpering. He wished he dared creep into her cabin at midnight and slay her; he wished he could drive a nail through her temple as Jael drove a nail through the temple of Sisera.

But the day before Christmas, Kevin and Mary waded through the snow of the heath to chop a fir tree. Mary wore a pair of Judd's overalls and one of his oldest lumber jackets. With the cuffs rolled into great bunches at her ankles and wrists, she looked like a little girl in a masquerade. They searched long and hard for a suitable tree and, wrestling it home, they tripped over buried windfalls, rolled in the snow, and pelted one another with snowballs until they were feverish and breathless. Kevin felt closer to her than he had felt in months. As they lurched through the snow, dragging the tree behind them like a log-boat, he almost forgot Ernie Masters and the jealousy and dark suspicion that preyed on his soul...

From one of the glacial, abandoned rooms upstairs, they bore dusty cartons containing the paper ropes and shreds of tinfoil and little glass balls that had decorated the O'Brien Christmas tree every year for as long as Kevin could remember. Mary washed the balls in warm water and baking soda and polished them with a clean flour bag. With Kevin handing them to her one by one, she stood on a chair and tied them to branches. Many of the balls were tied and untied a dozen times at as many different places on the tree.

"Oh, Scampi, I don't think it looks right!" Mary would wail.

And a solemn-faced Kevin would back to the other end of the living room and squint at the dangling bauble. "Mebbe not. Mebbe yuh better move it," he would announce at last.

And Mary would nod and purse her lips as she removed the trinket and attached it to a lower or a higher bough.

"How does it look there, Scamper?"

And once again he would back away and stare thoughtfully at the tree.

Judd growled that such folderol and fuss were damn foolishness. Confronted by the gee-gaws and tinsel of Christmas, he snorted like a man embarrassed by something infantile and sentimental. And he had no patience with ribbon and gay wrappings. When offering a gift it was his way to shrug and affect a look of boredom and distaste.

Kevin could not remember ever having believed in Santa Claus, although there had been a time, long ago, when he had pretended to believe because of his knowledge that the pretence would please his mother.

He never gave his father gifts. Judd said it was silly for a son to buy presents for his father from his father's own hard-earned money. But he had saved the nickels and dimes handed to him from time to time by his father, and at Biff Mason's store he had bought a bracelet costing almost a dollar for his mother.

On Christmas morning, she dug at her eyes and showered him with kisses. "Oh, thank you, sugar-baby!" she cried. Then she kissed the bracelet and slipped it on her wrist. She would never take it off, she said, she would wear it always, she would wear it even when she slept...

His father had already given him the watch. His mother's gift, wrapped in silverfoil and tied with golden ribbon, was a book, *The Star Rover* by Jack London.

"Do you like it, sweetikins?" she asked eagerly.

"Oh, Mummy! It's wonderful! I jist know by lookin' at it!"

And she glowed like a Christmas angel in the halo of his praise.

At noon, his body sprawled on the floor in front of the living room stove, his teeth burst grapes and his tongue tasted them — but his soul was in the world of a man named Ed Morrel, whose body writhed in a straitjacket in a clammy dungeon while his mind roved like one of the sword-swinging seraphim through the incandescent dust beyond the farthest stars.

And the O'Brien table was laden with food. Kevin masticated sweet, fat-rich pork and thick slices of spicy, smoke-fragrant ham. He cracked nuts with a claw hammer and gorged himself on their dry or oily meats. He laid-in candy until his teeth ached and devoured oranges until the acid of their juice stung his discoloured lips. All that remained of the money paid for the red cow, Judd had spent on rum and beer. Crosseyed and thick-tongued with drink, he made his Christmas dinner from cold canned clams, onion slices half-buried in salt, hunks of unbuttered bread, which he tore from the loaf with his fists, and blue-green sour pickles, all of which he washed down with rum from the bottle that stood open by his hand.

Grandmother O'Brien ate only bits of bread dipped in buttermilk. And throughout the meal, she rebuked Judd for his extravagance. "Mark my words, son, when yer poor yuh gotta plan ahead! If yuh don't watch yerself yer gonna eat and drink yerself right intuh the poor house! Yuh'll be huntin' up the poormaster a-fore spring — that's as sure as the skin on yer face!"

Mary and Kevin, their mouths full of food, scowled at the old woman. And to each of her admonitions, Judd gave the same reply: "Well Ma, I guess it's better tuh die a glutton than tuh starve tuh death."

In the afternoon, the clouds descended until it seemed they rested on the treetops, and the snow fell, soft and damp, spreading white cleanness over the world. Climbing the pole fence, Kevin tramped to the centre of the garden ground. Snowflakes disintegrating in his eyes, he saw the universe through a dancing kaleidoscope.

For an instant, as he stepped outdoors, he had smelled the snow, but its scent was so subtle that he could not retain it for longer than a second. Here, where the seasonal loam lay buried under two feet of snow — the soft, fresh snow lying on the brittle crust from earlier storms — he had to draw his breath almost to his stomach to catch a whiff of the suspended, secret aroma of the frozen soil.

There was an expectancy in the air, as there always was at the start of a snowstorm. He itched with excitement. His arms and legs tingled as though touched by electricity. He shaped a snowball in his hands, then rolled it on the ground, first kneeling, then creeping on all fours, then walking, then running. The snowball grew from a baseball to a squash, from a squash to a pumpkin, from a pumpkin to a nail keg, from a nail keg to a barrel. He decided that perhaps today he would make the biggest snowman since the beginning of the world.

Twenty-Six

As soon as he entered the school house, Kevin knew that Nancy Harker had not betrayed him. Riff tripped him, then asked what the hell was the matter with his feet, and Harold drew snickers from the boys lounging under the coat-hooks in the porch by wanting to know whether or not a new nipple for his nursing bottle had been among his Christmas gifts. But nothing was said about the secrets he had confided to Nancy.

He decided that he had been foolish to worry. What, after all, was there for her to tell? Thinking back, he told himself that he had not really disclosed any secrets. He had walked up the road with a giddy girl, and they had chattered nonsense. That was all.

Yet, as he took his seat and looked at her face, the small cheekbones, nose, and chin maturely finished and intact, devoid of even a suggestion of the fluidity normally seen in the features of children, he knew that she had somehow made him reveal himself. Meeting her bold, searching stare, he winced and turned quickly to his exercise books. He realized suddenly that what troubled him was not so much what he had told her as what she had known without having to be told. Even if he never spoke to her again, she would know every thought that rose in his mind, even those that came at night when he woke and took refuge in a softer and warmer darkness by hiding his face in the quilts.

And just as she knew without words, so he would know without words that she knew.

By some means she had made him naked and vulnerable. Because of this, he hated her. For he had been taught that all of the things that occupied his most intimate and fervent thoughts were cowardly and puerile nonsense, of which he ought to be ashamed.

But, beneath this hatred, like creek water under burning gasoline, there flowed a different and deeper emotion. His vocabulary held no word for this emotion. He suspected that no word in the language was big enough to contain it. It was one of those dark intimations that could only be hinted at in words so vague and inadequate as to be almost lies.

At recess, he sought to evade her. In the past, she had been only a misty fragment in the background: a head bending over a book, a swish of green-and-red-windbreaker cloth, a toss of ripe-wheat-coloured hair. Had anyone asked, he would have taken a closer look and said that this was Nancy Harker, just as in another case he might have answered that such and such a thing was a book, a table, or a chair. But, today, her wholeness confronted him everywhere...

At last, he came face to face with her in the path between the school house and the woodshed. In spite of himself, he met her eyes. Accusation and amusement mingled in iris and pupil.

"Why've you been tryin' to run away from me, Kevin O'Brien?" she demanded.

He fumbled for words; it was not his way to leap into communication like one diving into a pond. Like his father, like all the mill people, he preferred to wade slowly into the important matters, gauging the depth and testing the current.

"I ain't been tryin' tuh run away from yuh," he stammered untruthfully.

"Oh, yes, you have! All through recess you been sneakin' around like a mangy old dog with its tail between its legs!"

"I ain't been! I ain't been sneakin' around a-tall!"

"Yes, you have too! But it doesn't matter. I know why you've been runnin' away from me even if you won't tell me."

"Bet yuh don't!"

"Bet I do! Want me to tell you?"

He kicked spitefully at the blue-grey shingles of the woodshed.

"How duh yuh know I been sneakin' around unless yuh been taggin' after me?" he retorted. "Ain't nothin' I hate more'n anybody that keeps taggin' along when they ain't wanted."

She stuck out her tongue. He tore his eyes away from the disturbing little curve of her breasts.

"If you'll be good, I'll let you kiss me."

He gaped. "Who said I wanted tuh kiss yuh?" he said, humiliated by his shaking voice.

She laughed. "I don't have to have anybody tell me things. I just know. Listen, let's not fight anymore. Do you wanta come skatin' with me tonight?"

He kicked the heel of one boot with the toe of the other.

"I dunno," he muttered.

"You scared a the dark?"

"No!"

"You scared a me?"

"No!"

"Well, then, I'll see you after supper on the pond in the woods, okay?"

Shoulders slumping, he thrust his hands in his pockets.

"I guess so." He did not know whether he wanted to laugh or to snarl.

"Maybe I'll even let you kiss me!" she cried.

And, laughing, she skipped away.

For the seven hours that followed, Kevin writhed in the anguish of indecision. In one moment, he vowed that wild horses would not drag him to the pond. In the next, he sought to convince himself that even before receiving Nancy's invitation, he had planned to skate tonight. She did not own the pond, he told himself angrily. He had skated there long before her arrival in Lockhartville. If she happened to be there on a night that he chose to skate — well, then, she could stay at one end of the ice and he at the other! His mind swung back and forth like a pendulum.

At home, while his mother prepared supper, he determined to leave the decision to chance. Pulling two straws from the broom, he dropped them in his cap, held the cap above his head with one hand, and picked out a straw with the other. It was the shorter of the two. That meant he would stay home. Well, pulling straws was silliness, anyhow. Perhaps he should seek advice from his mother. No — she did not consult him before going to dances or prior to entertaining Ernie Masters in the living room! He would make up his own mind. Just let her try to tell him what he had to do!

"I guess the moon's gonna be bright tuhnight," he said. "I guess mebbe I'll go skatin' on the pond in the woods."

She did not look up from the stove. "Just remember to stay on the path, sweetikins, don't go off and get lost in the woods!"

So it was settled. He would go.

An hour later, he stood with Nancy Harker at the edge of the pond. Above the black and white firs and cedars, the moon seemed to float like a ghost ship across the murky ocean and through phosphorescent islands of cloud. Little glassy bell-flowers of ice tinkled on willows and alders. Skating out on the glittering ice was like running on the surface of the moon.

"I'll race you to the other end," she shouted.

And they were off. Lengthening his strokes, he felt the power of the moon ripple in his loins and belly. He had felt the pull of the moon before, but never so strongly. Everything was palpitant, lambent, changing, as in a dream. And the feeling it gave him was part joy, part pain: it reminded him of the times when his father, in drunken playfulness, had thrown him down and tickled him until he was almost delirious.

She could skate fastest. Already she was six or eight strokes ahead of him. Looking back over her shoulders, her hair flying like spun moonlight, she gave a little yelp of triumph and laughed. In the moonlight from the sky, and in the moonlight reflected from the ice, her face was wild and strange. A mad thought struck him: suppose she were a vampire? In the daytime, such a suggestion would have made him giggle. But tonight — tonight he could think whatever he wished without having to be ashamed. And with this realization came a surge of power and courage. Even the vast darkness around the pond held no terrors for him. For almost the first time in his life he was not afraid.

"Come on, you slowpoke Kevin O'Brien!"

If a pack of werewolves had come howling onto the ice, he would have run with a laugh to join them. This must be how God feels, he thought, and his throat opened in a little cry of wonder. God must live in a heaven of moonlight and ice. For, for a little while, he would be like God. And only a few hours ago he had been a frightened little boy!

Now he was gaining on her. He suspected that she had slowed deliberately so that he might catch her.

Strange! At all times he was called Kevin O'Brien, yet sometimes Kevin O'Brien was one person and sometimes another. There was Scampi and Kev and Namesake and young feller and Mister Big Breeches and laddie and Key-von — seven Kevin

O'Briens at least, and tonight, at this moment, he could look at all of them in wonder and pity!

Tiring, he slowed and looked up at the moon. He skated on the moon. Yet the moon still floated in the sky. In the worlds of Scampi, Kev, Namesake, young feller, Mister Big Breeches, laddie, and Key-von, this would have been impossible. In the world of this luminous, moonstruck Kevin O'Brien, nothing was impossible. In this world, the earth was liquid and the water was solid. Solid like the water that was ice. *And here, he was Kevin-David. King of Israel.*

Peter had walked on the water. Now he — Kevin-David — was running on the water! This was a miracle! Oh, he knew everything now. But most of what he knew could never be told, because there were no words; even in his own mind, he could not think of it in words: it had to be *felt.*

Nancy Harker turned and skated toward him.

"I decided you weren't ever goin' to catch up," she said.

She laughed, and the sound was that of the little bell-flowers of ice tinkling on the wind-shaken willows and alders.

"I'm a werewolf," he said. "Did yuh know that?"

"Oh, yes! Yes! Yes!"

"And I'm a prince and someday I'm gonna go into a country at the other end of the world and be king."

"Oh, I've known that ever since I first saw you!"

They laughed together, and — with scarcely any hesitation at all — Kevin O'Brien reached out and took her hand.

Twenty-Seven

Kevin awoke next morning with a jar of disappointment, like one shaken awake at the climax of an ecstatic and convincing dream. His first thought was that he was in love with Nancy Harker.

Dressing beside the kitchen stove, eating porridge with milk and molasses, and trudging up the white road to the school house, he thought of Nancy, and of love.

"Love" was a book word. No Lockhartville man ever spoke of love. Judd snorted whenever he heard the word mentioned. In Lockhartville there was only that other thing. Shuddering, Kevin remembered June Larlee on Kaye Dunbar's bunk and recalled certain dark passages in the Bible.

He and Nancy would never do an unclean thing. Their love would be as pure and golden as the love of the inhabitants of books. When he grew up, they would marry and — then he began to worry about whether or not he would get a chance to see her alone at recess.

But when their eyes met in class, he blushed and hid his face in a book, and at recess when they met in the schoolyard he shuffled his feet and fumbled with his mackinaw buttons and became so hot with embarrassment that he could only mutter a few choked monosyllables and lurch away. She looked after him with strange eyes, and a few minutes later, he saw her talking with Alton Stacey.

Alton leaned against the school house, hands thrust insolently into his pockets, a lazy grin on his choirboy's face. Nancy stood very close to him. Kevin hoped the school house would topple over and crush them both.

Then they both of them laughed and he reeled as though slapped. For he assumed immediately that they were ridiculing him. Nancy was a fool and a flirt and he hated her and wished that she were dead —

When she ran toward him, the last golden glimmer of last summer's suntan flashing on the bare skin between her wool stockings and the hem of her buoyant skirt, he felt a strange new stirring in his stomach, something that was part nausea, part hunger.

She halted, laughing, the little curve of her breasts rising and falling...

"Alton Stacey wants me to go skatin' with him," she said.

Kevin glared at her. "That ain't nothin' tuh me," he grunted.

"You mean you don't care if I go with him?"

"I don't give a hoot what yuh do." He strove to sound scornful but found, to his horror, that his voice quavered at the verge of tears.

"If I'da knowed you didn't care I wouldn'ta told him what I did."

"What?" he stuttered in incomprehension.

"I told him I couldn't go with him because I was your girl," she said.

And, her golden knees flickering, she whirled and skipped away.

In a few days, Kevin found the words jack-knifed into the walls of the woodshed and pencilled on the door of the privy. *Nancy is Kevin's Girl.* He pretended to be annoyed. But, in reality, the epithets pleased him and made him feel proud. He wanted to believe that Nancy was his girl, and the scrawled slogans assured him that she was.

But the walls bore other legends also. In the privy he saw his name linked with hers in words that he tried not to read and, having read, tried fruitlessly to erase from his mind . . .

On many nights and on every Saturday and Sunday in January, they went skating together. And he braved the derisive, envious laughter of Riff and Harold and the others by walking her home from school. He wished he could write her love letters like those he had seen in his mother's magazines. And he burned with self-hatred when he stood before her in red-faced and stammering incoherence.

"I had the most wonderful, wonderful dream last night," she told him one day.

"Gosh, what was it about?"

"Oh, I dreamt that a ship from Arabia sailed up the creek, from the sea, and that the Arabs broke into the school and took us all away to be slaves."

"Gee, that don't sound like a very good dream tuh me."

"Oh, but wait! It was, it was! Because the sheik had all of us girls stripped naked" — here her eyes frolicked and he blushed — "and he said I was the most beautiful of all his slave girls and he dressed me in beautiful, lovely, soft robes and golden bracelets and put a little golden crown on my head and made me his queen."

The dream disturbed him. It smacked of the darkness and uncleanness spoken of so often by his grandmother. It was indecent for a young girl to dream of being undressed by a man, still more indecent for her to speak of such a dream. And, besides, she was *his* girl. What right had she to dream of Arab sheiks?

"I don't think that was no kind of a dream a-tall," he growled.

"Oh, but listen! You was in the dream too. And the sheik made you the captain of his horsemen, and after we got to Arabia you rode into the palace and grabbed me and pulled me up on your horse and we rode away!"

"Well..." he said dubiously. That was better. Much better. Still, he wished that she had not dreamt of nakedness.

He was more shocked another time that she spoke of dreams. "Do you ever dream about girls, Kevin?" she asked him suddenly one afternoon as they sat at the edge of the skating pond.

"Huh? What duh yuh mean, duh I ever dream about girls?"

"Why are you blushin'?"

"I ain't blushin'."

"Oh, yes you are! And I know why!" she laughed and tossed her hair.

"You're bein' silly."

"No, you do dream about girls, don't you? About doin' things with girls?"

"What kinda things?"

"Oh, just — things."

"You ain't got no way a knowin' what I dream."

"Yes, I have: I'n see it in your eyes. I bet you dream about girls and when you wake up —"

"Come on!" he cried, springing to his feet, "I'll race you tuh the other end a the pond!"

She pouted. "It isn't any fun to race. I always get there first," she said.

"Oh, go tuh grass!"

She laughed, and his mind shrank in despair and dread.

Twenty-Eight

Kevin and Nancy sprawled on the floor in front of the stove. The wail of the wind was muffled by the snow that lay on the roof and against the walls of the Harker cabin. Never before had he been so intensely aware of her femininity. He was stirred even by the scents the heat stroked from her body. She wore maroon ski pants, and when he stared at the firm little mounds of her buttocks, the sensations in his chest and belly were so sharp and strange that he wondered if he were going insane. Then he decided that he was being tempted. Many of the mighty men of God had been tempted of the devil. What was it that Isaiah had said —

Nancy's voice was low, dreamlike.

"Do you ever feel as if there was somethin' inside you tryin' to get out?"

He stirred uneasily, thinking of the little, nervous, gnawing pains he felt sometimes in his loins and nipples. But these were things not to be spoken of: dark, shameful things of which one tried not to think.

"I guess so, mebbe," he answered aloud.

"That's how I feel all the time. I feel just like a butterfly startin' to flutter inside a cocoon. Up till now I've been a caterpillar but pretty soon I'm goin' to be a butterfly with beautiful shiny wings." She smiled and waved her arms as though she were already flying.

Then: "Why don't you ever kiss me, Kevin?"

He sat up, scowling. "Why duh yuh have tuh talk about kissin' all the time?"

"Other boys would like to kiss me. Alton Stacey — I bet he'd jump at the chance to kiss me."

"Go ahead and let him kiss you, then."

"Maybe I will."

"Go ahead — see if I care a hoot."

For a long moment there was silence except for the crackle of firewood and the muted wail of the wind.

"Kevin?"

"Yeah."

"Do you think it would be a sin to kiss me?"

"I ain't never thought nothin' about it," he lied.

She came so close that he edged away.

"Kiss me, Kevin."

"I don't want tuh." He hated the sound of his own voice, petulant and timorous.

"Don't you like me?"

"Gee whiz, sure I like yuh. But —"

"Kiss me, Kevin."

Before he could escape, she had cupped his face in her hands and kissed his lips.

"Oh, golly, yer silly," he muttered stupidly.

"Did you like that?"

"Don't ask so many stupid questions."

"Would you like to play a game with me?"

"Huh? What kinda game?"

But he was ready to play anything, so long as it had nothing to do with kissing.

"You'll be scared."

She gave him a sly little smile.

"No, I won't. I ain't scared a nothin'."

"All right. Put your hand there."

"Aw, this ain't no kinda game a-tall. This is jist some more a yer —"

"Put your hand there, I said."

He hesitated, blinking.

"Scaredy cat!"

"I ain't scared!"

"Put your hand there, then."

He obeyed. Her flesh was soft, warm, stirring.

"Do you like that?"

"I don't know." His lips were quivering.

She laughed. "Now, I put my hand there and — why are you blushin'? Are you scared?"

"No," the word was a croak.

"Now, this will be ever so much nicer —" Too astonished and frightened to resist, he let her put his hand between the buttons of her blouse.

"Madge calls them my little pears," Nancy laughed. "She says I'm a little ripe pear tree. Do you like that?"

He groaned.

"Oh, I bet your belly feels all funny and stirred up like creek water! That's even better than skatin', isn't it? Do you remember that first night we went skatin' and you said it was like runnin' across the moon? Well this is just as if you'd swallowed a little piece of the sun and it was shinin' all bright and warm inside you —"

"Don't," he whispered. She was unfastening buttons. "Don't do that!"

He wrenched her hands away.

"Kevin! You're hurtin' my wrists!"

"I better go home."

He would not have been more horrified and disgusted if her face had turned to a fleshless, grinning skull before his eyes. He thought of June Larlee and of Delilah and of Jezebel. He thought of how Eve had tempted Adam. In his mind there rose the figure of the serpent — a wriggling, hot, obscene thing...

Her blouse was half-open. He wanted to — No!

"What's wrong, Kevin?"

Her eyes were hurt, scornful.

"It's a sin!" he shouted.

"You liked it! You liked it!"

"No! That's a lie. I couldn't never like no sin. It's terrible wicked sin. People go tuh hell fer doin' things like that."

She drew her blouse together.

"Don't look at me that way, Kevin."

She sprang to her feet.

"Kevin, I wouldn'ta let any other boy in school touch me like that! I thought you wanted to, Kevin."

He pulled on his mackinaw. *And after they ate of the fruit of the tree of the knowledge of good and evil they knew that they were naked and they were ashamed...*

A moment ago she had been on the verge of tears, pleading with him. Now her voice rose in contempt and rage.

"You're just a baby! You don't know your — from a hole in the ground. I shouldn't never a had anythin' to do with you. I shoulda told Alton Stacey I'd be his girl — or Riff Wingate. You just wait until Monday, you'll see me with Riff and when you go by I won't even spit on you. You little —"

Blind with humiliation, he opened the door.

"Kevin! Don't be mad at me, Kevin! I won't really go with Riff. I promise, I won't. I —"

He lurched outside and stumbled along the narrow footpath to the road. The windblown pellets of frozen snow were like coarse salt hurled into his face.

Twenty-Nine

Judd had worked two weeks for a farmer, cutting and peeling pulpwood. But when he asked for his wages, the man told him impatiently that he could pay him nothing until spring. So Judd quit and went back to his futile wood chopping on the crown lands south of the creek. And, a few days after Kevin's twelfth birthday, Biff Mason informed Judd that he had reached the limit of his credit at the store. In relaying Biff's words to Mary, Judd howled with fury and muttered dark threats. Some morning, he predicted, Biff would wake up to find that his store had burned to the ground.

Martha urged him to seek help from the township overseer of the poor. The suggestion made Judd spring to his feet and shake his fists like a madman. "I'll fry in hell a-fore I'll ask for help from any man!" he roared. "We'll live on what we got or we'll starve tuh death. One thing's certain: Judd O'Brien ain't never gonna ask nobody fer nothin'!"

The pantry contained almost a barrel of flour and the cellar held a bin of half-frozen potatoes. So, three times each day, they ate butterless bread or biscuits and the wizened, green-tinged, bitter-tasting potatoes that were edible only when drowned in lard-and-flour gravy and drenched with salt. Judd affected to relish this fare. "Ain't nothin' puts meat on a man's bones like taters," he grunted as he dug his fork into the mud-coloured porridge before him. And every night he padded to the pantry in his socks and came back with a cold, dry biscuit which he covered with salt and washed down with water. As he ate, he smacked his lips and sucked his teeth like one enjoying a rich and hearty repast. Kevin was almost convinced that Judd ate such food through choice.

Mary refused to eat at the table. At mealtime she sat, chin in palm, in the chair by the window and stared at the naked lilac hedge and at the rose bushes, which the weight of the snow had borne to the ground. Two or three times a day, she stole into the pantry and nibbled a biscuit in secret. And, Kevin knew, her letters to her imaginary correspondents were filled with descriptions of banquets.

In mid-February, Judd sold the second cow to meet a payment on the house. Otherwise, he said, he and his family would be thrust out in the snow. As the cow was led out of the yard, Grandmother O'Brien stood at the window and watched, her brick clutched to her waist.

"It jist seems tuh me that God's put a curse on this here house!" she said. "It jist seems like God's tryin' tuh punish this here house fer some awful sin that's a-goin' on in it."

"Judd being out of work for three months has a helluva lot more to do with it than God has," Mary snapped. Kevin looked up in amazement: his mother almost never swore.

"Curse an' swear as much as yuh please, me girl. There ain't a sparrow falls without the Good Lord a-knowin' about it. And the Good Lord allus punishes sin. When a house is fulla sin, the Lord jist naturally reaches out His hand an' smites it —"

"Oh, what do you know about it! You aren't God!"

Grandmother O'Brien's voice was a whiplash of scorn, "No, I ain't God! I never said I was! But I know sin when I see it! I ain't blind, me girl — these old eyes is tired but they ain't blind. I know about the wicked, ugly, unclean sins a the flesh! I'n see 'em right under my nose! I know that God will punish an adult —"

"Shut up! You shut up your dirty old mouth! You foul old woman! Ever since I've been married, you've been sitting around here blatting about sin. To hell with you and your sin! I'm sick and tired of hearing about it."

Grandmother O'Brien turned to Kevin, who sat trembling in a chair by the table.

"Run out and help yer father, laddie."

Quivering with nausea, he got to his feet.

"Don't you tell him what to do! Don't you give my son orders!" Mary dug at her eyes, beginning to weep.

"Eh! An' a fine son he'll be with the likes a you fer a mother. Yes an' with the blood a God knows what a-burnin' in his veins. Conceived in sin! Conceived in godless, filthy lust! The fathers have eaten sour grapes and the children's teeth are set on edge! Oh, aye, a fine son he's like tuh be!"

"Shut up! Shut up before I kill you!"

"Is it a murderess yuh'd be, eh! Come ahead, me girl, I dare yuh. One more sin won't make no difference now. Yuh'll burn in hell! Yuh'll burn in hell with Jezebel and Delilah! Yuh hear me, girl! Yer gonna burn in hell!"

With a cry, Mary seized a stick of millwood from the box by the stove and advanced on the old woman. Martha made no move to raise her hands.

"Don't, Mummy!" Kevin screamed.

Babbling, his breath coming in great spasms, he ran to his mother and grasped her wrist.

"What the hell's goin' on in here?"

Judd stood in the doorway. The club fell from Mary's hand. Kevin clung to her, hiding his face. Martha swayed, then staggered to the rocker and sank down.

"Ma, what's wrong?" Judd bent over her. "Will somebody tell me what the hell's goin' on here?" He laid his palm on his mother's shoulder. "You all right, Ma?"

"Yes, son, I'n stand anythin' the Good Lord wants tuh hand out tuh me. Ain't no cross too heavy fer me tuh bear. Though he slay me yet shall I trust in him. Praise His name. Don't pay no mind tuh me, Juddie. It ain't yer old mother yuh got tuh worry about, boy."

Judd stared around wildly as though in search of a culprit. "Hey, you!" His big hands closed on Kevin's shoulders. "What are yuh! Nothin' but a little wizzenin' petticoat sucker? Eh? You hush that whinin' or I'll give yuh somethin' tuh whine about. Yuh hear me?"

Jerking him away from Mary, Judd shook him. Then — it was as though the wind lifted him and hurled him from a great precipice. Falling, whirling, twisting, he plunged into an eyeless and bottomless pit. Down...and down...and down...and down. From a ledge, hundreds of feet above him, came his mother's voice, growing fainter: "Scampi! Scampi! What's wrong?" His last conscious thought was that he was dying —

He regained consciousness in the living room. His mother knelt by his cot, holding cold cloths to his temples and chafing his wrists.

As he opened his eyes, she tried to smile.

"You fainted, Scampi. That's all. You just fainted," she said.

He tried to raise himself, tried to reach out to her, then fell back. He was like one come back from the borderlands of death.

"I'm going away from here, Scampi."

"Yeah."

Somehow he had known this for a long time.

"In a few weeks I'm going to live in town — in Larchmont. You'll have to stay here with your father for a while. But I'll come back for you. I promise I will, Scampi."

"Yeah." His voice was dubious. He did not have sufficient energy to pretend to believe.

"Oh, Scampi!"

Weeping, she lay her face on his chest. She shook his body with the convulsions of her sobbing.

He sought to lift his hand... sought to touch her... but he could not. And in this moment he knew as though God Himself had told him that never again would he be able to reach her.

Thirty

He walked in the windswept road and he did not know if he walked there in reality or in dream.

The world was too huge and strange. He could never hope to understand it. He wished he could crawl into the earth like a worm and hide there in the darkness where nothing could reach him. He wished he were a tree or a stone. He wished he were a single snowflake in one of the great drifts beside the road. He wished he were a fencepost, a blade of grass, a twig — anything that did not have to think and feel and struggle with the unanswerable questions with which God badgered human beings.

"I wish I'd never been born!" he cried. And he hated his parents for having brought him into this world. He could not put words to the thought, but it seemed he remembered a long-ago time in which he had lain in a dark, secret place where there were no terrifying questions to be faced, no agonizing choices — where there was only will-lessness and warmth and a great peace.

Thoughts whirled through his mind. His mother's hands soaping him before the kitchen fire. The ecstacy of surrender. He was no longer himself. He existed only as part of her body. Then the mill with its pulsating engine and shrieking saws. The oxen plodding forever before their log-boat. The old swaybacked nag floundering in deep sawdust.

There is a fountain filled with blood,
Drawn from Emmanuel's veins,
And sinners plunged beneath that flood
Lose all their guilty stains.

Blood ran from the nail-pierced hands of Jesus.

Blood dripped from the knife-tormented flesh of Hitler.

Blood from the throat of a deer. Blood from the pitchforked side of a cow. The blood of the orange-haired cat on the blade of a hatchet...

Oh, Daddy, don't kill me. Please don't kill me!

The clock-like gong of the strap. WHACK!

I love you, Daddy! I do love you. Please don't hurt me, Daddy!

Key-von O'Brien is a snotty-nosed little pimp.

Key-von O'Brien's mother still has tuh change his didies.

Key-von O'Brien's mother is the biggest old whore in Lockhart-ville.

Make 'im say it, Av! Make 'im say it, Av!

The skin torn from his palms, blood gushing from his nostrils and dribbling from his mouth.

Blood. Blood. Blood. Blood.

Have yuh had enough, Av? Have yuh had enough?

Well, if they ain't a-gonna fight, don't yuh think they oughta kiss and make up?

And as I passed by thee and saw thee polluted in thine own blood, I said unto thee that wast in thy blood, live: yes...

The nights of waiting for his mother. Counting the cars passing.

But what of the thing in the cellar that drinks so much blood?

A dead raccoon by the roadside. An empty rum bottle lying on a grave.

Wait! One more thing! They'll come for you! Some night when you're asleep in bed, they'll come for you, and they'll make you a living corpse like all the rest of us! They will! They'll come with knives and ropes and they'll drag you out of bed and they'll —

The gloss of darkness in Sarah Minard's parlour. Her fingers pinching his flesh. *You're a very pretty boy. Kevin. Do you know who I am? I am Death.*

Nancy Harker's hands on his body. *All the mill men get drunk. Madge says it's the only time they're alive.*

His mother's hands on his body. *Oh, Scampi, there isn't anything worse than being dead!*

Yes, laddie, when God was on earth, women like her was stoned tuh death!

Yuh'll burn in hell, me girl! Yuh'll burn in hell!

June Larlee's legs in red shorts. June Larlee naked on Kaye Dunbar's bunk.

June Larlee: *I guess yuh wouldn't have tuh look at him twice tuh know he wasn't a girl, would yuh, Mar?*

The pictures of nearly naked girls on the walls of Kaye's shack. Nancy Harker unbuttoning . . .

Cheatin' little bitch! Dirty cheatin' little whore! That snivellin' little bugger don't act much like no O'Brien!

Conceived in sin! Conceived in godless, filthy lust!

Put your hand there, Kevin. Put your hand there.

I'm a love-child, did you know that?

Put your hand there, Kevin.

Put your hand there.

Baby. Bay-bee. Sweet bay-bee. Sweet Scampi. Sweet Scampi bay-bee. Sweetest, sweetest, baby. Bay-beee . . . baybee . . . baybee . . .

Put your hand there.

I love you, Mummy.

Say it again.

I love you, Mummy.

— Again.

I love you, Mummy.

What are yuh, eh? Nothin' but a wizzenin' little petticoat sucker, eh?

Don't kill me, Daddy. Please don't kill me, Daddy.

Here's a cuckoo! There's a cuckoo!

There's a cuckaroo!

Here's a cuckoo! There's a cuckoo!

Here's a cuckaroo!

Saul has slain his thousands and Kevin-David his ten thousands.

Oh, please God.

Please.

Please, God.

Don't let Mummy leave me, God.

Don't let him say it again, God.

Don't make it so I have to fight him, God.

Make them stop, God.

I promise I won't ask you for anything else. I'll never ask you for anything again. Please God.

I'm gonna be a prophet a God.

Put your hand there.

Make me like David, O God. Like David and Isaiah and Jeremiah and Ezekiel and...like Jesus.

Do you ever dream about girls, Kevin? Do you ever dream about doin' things with girls?

Sugar-baby. Sweetikins. Scamper.

I'm going away, Scampi. You'll have to stay with your father for a little while, but I'll come back for you —

You should hear the music, Scampi! It makes you want to dance and dance and dance!

I am Kevin, the prophet of God.

I am Kevin, the prophet of God.

I am Kevin, the prophet of God.

Suddenly, Kevin knew what he had to do. The whirling galaxies of words and pictures that had been pouring through his mind vanished and were replaced by a great certainty and peace.

He knelt in the road, as he had done before, oblivious to the pellets that pelted his face.

"Oh God," he prayed. "Show me a sign! Open up the heavens, O God, and show me a sign! Show me that I'm one of Thy mighty ones, a king and a prophet, O God! Show me that I don't have to be afraid. Show me that I'll never have to be afraid again. Show me your face in the sky, O God!"

He had closed his eyes during this prayer. Now tremulous but smiling, he opend them, lifted his head slowly and looked up at the sky...

Afterword

This novel was sent to one publisher, rejected, and put in a drawer. It found its way to the public sometime after Alden Nowlan's death in 1983. It is a great novel — one written by a poet in his youth — and has a deep poetic sense. Poetry redeems its darker moments and enlivens its lighter. It is probably as good a first novel as most I've read, and better than most of the novels published anywhere the year it was rejected. So why was it rejected? And why didn't Nowlan, who fought whenever he had to, fight for it — and send it elsewhere? That is, did he believe the opinion of the editor who summarily dismissed it?

I doubt it. Nowlan knew more about literature than any editor did. He knew more about the novel, and that too is the secret. For this is a novel that stems from his youth, his growing up, his parents, and his village. It is a wonderful novel, filled with moments of unquestionable delight. Yet it also is a novel desperate with uncomfortable truths about his mother and father, his birth, and his solitude in the face of family and cultural violence. And I think this is why at least part of him might have been relieved by the rejection slip.

That long-ago rejection slip did Canadian literature and Alden Nowlan a great disservice, but no one in Toronto — or anywhere else — would know or care for almost thirty years. When I think of novels that have been dismissed in the century just past, I put this in the category of James Joyce's *Stephen Hero*, or Norman Maclean's *A River Runs Through It*, for the sheer blindness on which such decision making rests. In fact, I think *The Wanton Troopers* is a better novel then *Stephen Hero* — or what was managed to be saved of Joyce's manuscript — and, in many respects, as accomplished as *A River Runs Through It*.

The Wanton Troopers was rejected because of what it was — frightening and brave, at times utterly brave. It is the hopeful journey of a small, tremendously gifted boy born into a poverty-stricken Maritime family back in the 1940s. And that might have been too real for the editor who looked at it to contemplate. Of course, that tells us more about the incompetence of the editor at reading than Nowlan's ability to write. As Ralph Waldo Emerson said in *Success*, "'Tis the good reader that makes the good book . . . the profoundest thought or passion sleeps as in a mine, until it is discovered by an equal mind and heart." Far too many editors know nothing of great books — or at least how to read them. For this book, beyond everything else, has a deep, deep, enduring love for all things living, and a deep moral reverence for humanity no matter what. And nothing tells us this more than the poetry that crowns it. In this one way, then, *The Wanton Troopers* is a holy book.

If the book relied upon its poetry alone, then poetry alone would sanctify it. But its strength is greater than its poetry — for it is a book whose author understands humanity, character, and drama as well as most writers I have read. The human foible and false rebellion, the contrived bravery and final sadness of the father, Judd, make him as human as any of William Faulkner's men. The wondrous, self-interested delusion of Kevin's mother, Mary, gives her life the gift (yes gift) of tragedy. This is what the editor in some small office fifty years ago failed to see: the overflowing grace and human care of an artist determined to reveal at any cost those few elusive moments of tenderness among many terrifying hatreds — where Kevin is, like so many millions of solitary children, a scapegoat in a world he cannot control. No one was ever more careful to get it right, and to make it universal while doing so.

Nowlan was forever a major artist who needed to tell us not about his life so much as ours. And in the end, we celebrate this life he gives us as part of our own.

The Wanton Troopers recounts the 1940s Maritimes with a richness of expression rarely — if ever — found, and almost never surpassed. It is a book that exposes to forgive, forgives in order to celebrate — and in the end, begs us all to love.

David Adams Richards
Bartibog Bridge, Miramichi
July 2009

Reader's Guide

About the Author

In his preface to Gregory Cook's biography of Alden Nowlan, American poet Robert Bly praises Nowlan as "the greatest Canadian poet of the twentieth century."[1] Whether the adversity that Nowlan faced during his childhood (fictionalized here in *The Wanton Troopers*) nourished or impeded his literary development is a matter for debate, but the story of his life is indeed an inspiring one of triumph over difficult circumstances.

Nowlan was born during the Great Depression in January of 1933 in the village of Stanley, Nova Scotia. He was the first child of fourteen-year-old Grace Reese and Freeman Nowlan, a marginally employed mill hand who was twice her age. Nowlan's sister, Harriet, was born almost three years later, in November of 1935. Beset by poverty and Freeman's alcoholism, the couple struggled to feed and clothe themselves and their children.

As a work of fiction, *The Wanton Troopers* conflates, transforms, and omits material from Nowlan's life to create the world of Kevin O'Brien; still, the novel can be read autobiographically. Lockhartville and the shack in which the O'Brien family lives was, for Nowlan, actually two modest homes in the adjoining communities of Stanley and Mosherville. Each of these homes

---

[1] Robert Bly, "The Nourishing Voice of Alden Nowlan," preface to *One Heart, One Way: Alden Nowlan, A Writer's Life* by Gregory M. Cook (East Lawrencetown, NS: Pottersfield Press, 2003), 11.

lay under the powerful matriarchal rule of a grandmother: Grace's mother, Nora, and Freeman's mother, Emma, respectively. Both were strong, capable women who took care of Alden and Harriet when Grace went off to dances or Freeman went to work in the woods or disappeared on a drinking binge with his buddies.

Had their grandmothers lived, the children's lives might not have been so tragic. Of the two, Emma Nowlan most resembled Martha O'Brien of *The Wanton Troopers*. Although she was a pious, Bible-reading woman who eventually died of stomach cancer, Emma also earned notoriety as a village eccentric who amused children with her antics (which included impersonating a witch). She entertained adults with a talent for step-dancing — something the fictional Martha condemned. But it was Nora Reese who looked after the children the most up until the fall of 1939, when Alden started school.

By the time Nora died of Hodgkin's disease in the spring of 1940, Grace and Freeman's marriage had already broken up. Grace attempted to move the children in with her and her boyfriend but was blocked by Children's Aid, who assumed brief custody of Alden and Harriet until Freeman could move Emma into his house in Stanley. Once in the Stanley house, Emma took over as the children's principal caregiver. As her health deteriorated, she indulged young Alden by allowing him to stay home from school. He eventually quit after completing grade four.

By 1947, Grace's visits to Stanley-Mosherville had stopped, and Freeman's drinking had worsened. When Alden — by now housebound, depressed, and entirely devoted to reading books — fell ill, the Reese family forced Freeman to have Alden and Emma taken to the hospital in Windsor, Nova Scotia, where Emma died that summer. On the advice of doctors and with Freeman's consent, Alden was admitted to the Nova Scotia Hospital, a psychiatric institution in Dartmouth.

Although Nowlan could not resist using his experience at the Nova Scotia Hospital as sensationalist fodder for some of his later stories and poems, his treatment there — according to family accounts — was beneficial for the intelligent but socially awkward teen. When he was discharged early in 1948, Alden returned to Freeman's house to work with his father in the woods and at the mill. He also bought a typewriter with his meagre pay and began to write short stories, poems, and articles for the local newspaper. A reporter, recognizing the young man's talent, helped Nowlan make contact with a weekly newspaper, the *Observer*, in Hartland, New Brunswick. He was hired, and at the age of nineteen, he left Stanley for good.

During his Hartland years, from 1952 to 1963, Nowlan became known nationally as a poet and short fiction writer, producing five collections of poetry and earning praise from such figures as Irving Layton and Robert Weaver. On the day before he moved from Hartland to Saint John, New Brunswick, Nowlan married Claudine Orser Meehan, a divorcee with a nine-year-old son, Johnnie.

Nowlan's new experiences in a larger city working for the *Telegraph-Journal* and *Evening Times-Globe*, the joys of family life, and the tribulations of a near-fatal bout with thyroid cancer were the subjects of his breakthrough poetry collection in 1967, *Bread, Wine and Salt*. Canada's literary community rallied around the promising but stricken poet, securing him a Canada Council grant. In 1968, Nowlan was named writer in residence at the University of New Brunswick in Fredericton, and that allowed him to quit full-time newspaper work and devote his time to writing.

Despite living with cancer, Nowlan became the centre of Fredericton's cultural life, producing six more collections of poetry and two short fiction collections, completing the novel

Various Persons Named Kevin O'Brien, continuing his regular columns in newspapers and magazines, and even becoming a playwright with co-author Walter Learning. The university gave Nowlan a home at the edge of the campus, a location that reflected his role as a sometimes pugnacious and controversial mediator between artists, students, and professors.

Nowlan's prolific output was cut short on June 27, 1983, when he succumbed to respiratory failure. His legacy lives on in the many writers he influenced, in his posthumously published works (including *The Wanton Troopers*), and in his former residence on the UNB campus, which has been beautifully restored and renamed Alden Nowlan House in his honour.

Patrick Toner's interest in Alden Nowlan began in high school. He wrote his MA thesis at Carleton University on the religious and supernatural beliefs in Nowlan's poetry and, in 2000, a biography, *If I Could Turn and Meet Myself: The Life of Alden Nowlan*.

An Interview with Alden Nowlan

JON PEDERSEN

For three days in 1982, I interviewed Alden Nowlan for the National Film Board of Canada film production *Alden Nowlan: An Introduction*. The resulting half-hour film was completed in 1983, after Nowlan's death. The complete interview consists of approximately five hours of synchronized 16mm film shot by Kent Nason and full-track ¼" audiotape recorded by Art McKay, both of the National Film Board, Atlantic Region.

The following includes about half of the interview; a transcript of the complete interview is available from the Provincial Archives of New Brunswick or the Harriet Irving Library, University of New Brunswick.

Jon Pedersen
All writers complain of the constraints and difficulties under which they work. Is it a painful and difficult process for you?

Alden Nowlan
Well, writing with me is almost an inevitable process. I'm a writer almost in the same sense that I have grey eyes. I would write poems even if no one read them, but I wouldn't write stories or plays or newspaper columns if no one read them, obviously. But I would be writing poems even if nobody read them.

JP Is Fredericton a good environment for poets? Is poetry taken seriously?

AN I suspect it is, but it really wouldn't have made a great deal of difference to me where I was, as long as the place where I was wasn't actively uncomfortable, so long as I wasn't in a situation which was painful or humiliating. I mean, I'm not really an active enough participant in the community of Fredericton, in a sense, that it makes any great difference to me that I live here, you see. I mean, partly because of my background, I'm not the sort of writer who needs to be associated with other writers in order to be creative.

JP Could you elaborate on that?

AN Well, I grew up utterly alone in many ways. During my adolescence, I was so alone I might almost as well have been on a desert island. In fact I would have been happier on a desert island because then there would have been no one to torment me. And so I'm really a very self-sufficient person. I never mind, really, being alone.

JP Do you and your wife go out much?

AN I don't know, really, what's very much or what's little. It's all relative, isn't it?

JP What's the room like where you work?

AN A mess.

JP Do you have a window in it? Do you need absolute silence?

AN I read somewhere once that Alice Munro (whom I think is perhaps the best short story writer in the country) has said she couldn't write in a house in which there was another adult, and I'm very much like that. I couldn't really write anything, except for a newspaper column, when we have house guests or that sort of thing. Writing is a very private thing to me in the sense that if I were working on a poem and someone came into the room, I would automatically cover it with my hand, just as a reflex gesture.

JP And yet you can go on and publish that for the world to see?

AN Yes, but it's sort of like having a child in the womb and having it born. At one moment it's a very private part of the woman, in a sense, and then suddenly it has a life of its own.

JP When you first began to write things, why and to whom did you write them?

AN The very first things I wrote were attempts at Biblical revelations because I thought I was going to be a prophet. Then I started writing poems which I thought were enormously good. I mean, I thought I was intensely precocious, but looking back, the sort of things I wrote when I was eleven and twelve were the sort of things that anyone eleven or twelve could have written if they'd wanted to do it.

JP How successful are you at saying what you want?

AN Well, I agree with Paul Verlaine, who said that "no poem is ever finished. At best it's always abandoned." You never really say what you want to say.

JP Do you often feel frustration or disappointment?

AN Momentarily, but it's not prolonged because I think you have to make peace with your own limitations, actually.

JP How do you feel about criticism? Have you found professional criticism helpful or a hindrance?

AN The criticism in this country... First of all, I think the gift of being a genuinely fine critic is probably rarer than the gift of being a genuinely fine creative writer. But as it is, criticism can be done by anyone who wants to do it, and I think that the standards in this country have actually deteriorated since I've begun to write. When I started to publish things, my first little sixteen-page chapbook of poems, for instance, was reviewed by Northrop Frye, among other people. And now, you would be more apt to find a book by Northrop Frye being reviewed by some seventeen-year-old in the slow learners' class in Moose Jaw. That sort of thing has changed. Of course, many, if not most, of the book reviewers don't read the books anyway and generally just look at the jacket and flip it open and look at two or three pages. Also, in this country, where the reviewers and the poets and the fiction writers all tend to be the same people, obviously you get a lot of the business of "You scratch my back and I'll scratch yours," you know, and you even get people attacking your book because a friend of yours attacked a book of theirs, you see.

JP Have you ever been tempted to strike out at your critics?

AN I used to, but it's a loser's game. I probably would strike out at them if I could do it with the style of Irving Layton. I have one thought that has entered my mind, though, just recently. I've always felt that I could write a good horror novel, like Stephen King's. I had this wonderful fantasy recently of writing a horror novel which would become a bestseller and be made into a movie similar to *The Shining*, with Jack Nicholson, and make me an enormous amount of money. And I would buy a helicopter and I would fly from one end of Canada to the other, and I'd particularly stop for an afternoon in Toronto, and I would *piss* from my helicopter on every book reviewer in the country!

JP You told me last week you did something you've always wanted to do.

AN Last week I did a thing which I've been trying to will myself into doing for years. I received a fat envelope of clipping service reviews of my last book from Clarke Irwin, and I took out the reviews without reading any of them and threw them into a filing cabinet. Because the thing about it is, the good ones only make you feel good for about half an hour, whereas the bad ones, no matter how stupid they are, can make you feel bad all day. Because we're all so vulnerable that even if you know the person who wrote the review is, first of all, an idiot, and secondly, he didn't read the book at all, there's sort of a little voice inside you telling you you're probably as bad as he says you are. And even if you don't have that little voice, it's so frustrating because you can't retaliate. There's no way you can punch him in the mouth. There's no way you can answer him, really.

JP So being an artist — a poet — is really a very vulnerable place to sit.

AN It's often occurred to me how interesting it would be if people in other fields of endeavour were subjected to the same sort of public criticism that artists are. For instance, if you took a medical doctor and on Friday there was a review that said Dr. Smith's bedside manner leaves much to be desired and his knowledge of drugs is certainly not up to date, and as for his operating technique — it's a complete fiasco, and anybody who deals with him is in mortal danger of losing his life. Or if you reviewed the works of policemen, you know, and said, "In this investigation Sergeant Jones showed the utter incompetence to which his observers have now become accustomed." That is the sort of thing an actor or painter or writer — any sort of artist — has to cope with constantly. Politicians deal with all sorts of criticisms too, but the thing they do is not so private — it doesn't make them so vulnerable.

JP What sort of influence have you had on other writers?

AN That's a very difficult thing to assess. That would be something that's more for them to say than for me to say. I think one influence I could say that I've had is the influence of simply having been here. You see, when I started to write and publish things, there really was nobody else at all writing in New Brunswick and not many in other parts of the Maritimes, and so I think that I might conceivably have been an influence in that. You take a brilliant young New Brunswick-based novelist such as David Adams Richards, and I think there may well have been an influence on him, say, when he was in high school and starting to write, simply by seeing one of my books in the high school library and thinking, "Gosh, you *can* live in New Brunswick and you *can* write about New Brunswick," you know.

JP Do you keep a sort of abstract reader in mind when you write?

AN Yes, I suppose I do, because in a sense when I began to write poems, I was addressing them . . . Well, I did it partly for the same reason some other lonely children invent an imaginary playmate, and so I suppose in a way I address them all to some imaginary playmate — a kind of a sympathetic listener. And the best thing is when, through personal contacts — meetings with strangers or letters from people — I discover that someone has gotten the message. It's like putting a note in a bottle and throwing it into the ocean and it floats across and someone tells you they've received it.

JP So your poems, then — it's fair to say they always have a message or something specific you want to say?

AN Oh, I think so, yes. Otherwise, if it was completely abstract . . . if you had, for instance, an enormously precocious infant who, before it learned to speak, decided that the language, as it stands, is completely old hat and we no longer need messages and so on, well, that child, when it was hungry, instead of asking for food, might say, "Gobbledy gook." It probably wouldn't get anything to eat, you see.

JP Do you think people might sometimes think they understand your poems too quickly?

AN Oh, I think so. One of the wonderful lines from André Gide — which I would have published in the front of one of my books if Norman Mailer hadn't already done it — is "Do not understand me too quickly." I think that often happens, yes.

And another thing that happens with those few reviewers who actually read the books is that, because they see the surface simplicity, they first of all assume that that's all that's there and secondly assume that I just sat down and dashed the thing off. Whereas the fact is, in order to give the effect of immediacy and spontaneity, I may have written the thing as many as twenty-eight or thirty times.

JP So it's normal with you to write and rewrite?

AN Oh, yes.

JP Does the continual revising of your work sometimes work against you?

AN I suspect that it might but it's hard to tell. I find people who like earlier poems better than the later versions and that sort of thing.

JP Do you use any artificial helps — stimulants, drugs?

AN Well, I've... Some of my best ideas for poems have come to me when I was drinking. Of course I didn't set out to drink just so I could get the poems. It's also true, as Norman Mailer says, that most of his ideas come when he's too drunk to do anything about it. That has occasionally happened to me too.

JP Do you make a practice of trying to write when you're drinking?

AN No. There are a lot of drinking writers, of course. The late Hugh Garner said that he became a freelance writer because it was the job that interfered the least with his drinking. And there is an element of truth in that. If you have a nine-to-five job, you can't get drunk in the afternoon — you'll lose your job — but if you're a freelance writer, obviously you can. You just have to work a little harder the next day. Because you're in control of your own fate to a certain extent. And...what was I after saying?

JP Can you tell me — do you type or write? Do you have a word processor?

AN Well, I used to write everything by pencil, and I think in my experience most creative writers do write in longhand and then retype it, but now I do everything on the typewriter, which is great for me because I'm the sort of writer who — and I found out somewhere that Dylan Thomas did the same neurotic thing — that if I make a mistake and one line has to be rewritten, I start at the beginning and retype the whole thing. So I may have ten typewritten pages for one line. Also, if I'm writing prose, I sort of think on the typewriter. Flannery O'Connor, the great Southern writer, quoted, in comparison with herself, an old Southern woman whom she heard say, "I never know what I think until I've heard what I say." Well, I never know what I think, really, until I've seen what I've typed. So when I'm typing, if I've started a sentence in my mind and then abandoned it, I've already typed it, so there'll be a whole page with beginnings of sentences that trail off into nothing. I can't just sort of sit there as some people can and think a line out and then type it.

JP What are your work habits like? What sort of schedule do you keep?

AN Well, I work every day because I've found there's an immense amount of truth in what my friend the painter Bruno Bobak says. Bruno says a profound inspiration always comes to him when he's working. And I've found this too. I believe there is such a thing as inspiration for a painter or a writer, but invariably it comes, you know, when you're working.

JP So how much time each day would you spend working?

AN Oh, it varies an enormous amount. If I were working on a play, for instance, and we were getting close to the deadline, I might work twelve or fourteen hours a day. But in the normal run of things, I probably wouldn't work any more than four or five hours. Probably more often four than five.

JP Have friendships ever intruded on your work and given you cause for resentment?

AN No, no, I don't think so. Well, there have been times when the doorbell rang and I've said, "Damn!" but I'm always glad to see the person when I open the door.

JP Do you think that being a very practiced, very proficient writer sometimes blocks original thoughts?

AN I think there's probably a danger of it, yes. What I try to do with poems is, I try to write them as spontaneously as I would have done back when I started out as a poet, before I realized it was supposed to be hard work. Because when I started out as a poet, for instance, I would be covering meetings of the Hartland town council, and I would write sonnet after sonnet in my notebook, which pleased the members of the council enormously because they thought I was assiduously writing down what they said. I would write as many as four to six in an evening. Now, I try to write with that same spontaneity. And then I usually throw the poem in a drawer and leave it there — days, weeks, months, sometimes even years. And then periodically I go through all the things in this drawer and pick out something which appeals to me at that particular time and try to rework it, almost as though originally it had been done by someone else.

JP So when you publish a new book of poems, not all of them are recent poems.

AN Well, they're recent in the sense that the finished product is recent. But the first draft could have been done a year, two years …In fact, I think in the last book there's one that the first draft goes back twenty years.

JP How do you go about choosing the poems you'll submit for publication?

AN Well, to an extent, it's arbitrary, in that I simply choose those that I like best myself. But quite often in the interval since the last book, I'll have written quite a number of poems on a very similar theme that are essentially about the same aspect of life, and I'll have to pick out one of those which I think is most successful and include that in the manuscript and file the others.

JP In your childhood, what did the poet or writer represent to you?

AN I had an enormously romantic conception of writers. My great hero was John Keats, and if someone had told me when I was sixteen years old that I had consumption, I would have loved it. If I'd started spitting blood, I'd have felt just like Keats. I was eager to die in Rome at twenty-six. I'd have loved the idea when I was fifteen or sixteen.

JP Where did you go to get books when you were young?

AN In the neighbouring town of Windsor, there was a little public library run by a wonderful lady named Eleanor Geary, who allowed me to join even though I was outside the district and, if I kept the books overdue, didn't charge me any fines, God love her. And the marvellous thing about this library was that it was very small and old-fashioned and really hadn't been endowed with any money, so most of the books had been contributed. But since they'd been contributed thirty to forty years ago, the things that had been contributed were the complete sets of Dickens and Thackeray, and they had all the works of Charles Darwin. I'm probably the only living person in the entire world who's read the collected works of Charles Darwin. Whereas now they'd have ten copies of every current bestseller and none of those standard classics at all. I read Tolstoy and Dostoevsky there, and all that sort of thing.

JP Cocteau believed that sexuality is the basis of all friendship. What do you think?

AN I suppose it's probably true, if you use sexuality in the broadest sense.

JP Do you find that personally true?

AN Not consciously, no, but I don't deny that it might be true. It seems to me that is the sort of thing that would be unconscious anyway.

[interview section omitted]

JP You're a writer with a highly developed sense of professionalism. Do you think that is generally true of young writers today?

AN I don't think that enough young writers have a sense of professionalism. I think that a great many of them think that it is largely a matter of being inspired. Some of them, of course, have a highly developed sense of professionalism.

JP Where do you think your sense of professionalism comes from?

AN I think the young writers of today tend to have a greater sense of professionalism than the young writers back in the sixties, because in the sixties it was really fashionable to be a young poet. You had all sorts of young people with a certain amount of raw talent going around writing poems on the backs of envelopes and putting them in their pockets. But it isn't nearly so fashionable to be a young poet now. So I think that those who are young poets now are more serious to begin with, and inevitably that leads them to a more professional attitude.

JP Milton Acorn has said that there's no such thing as a young poet, that you have to have some years to be a poet. Would you agree?

AN I think it depends on your definition of a poet. Years and years ago, Irving Layton said to me that anyone could be a poet at eighteen, but in order to be a real poet, you had to be still writing poetry at forty-eight. And I now would agree with that, in the sense that during the years I've been around university campuses... in the early years around university campuses I would see some young person who had an enormous amount of basic talent and I would think to myself, "Well, if I'm remembered at all in the history of literature, it will probably be just as a footnote on page 180 of that person's biography." Well, a year after graduation that person could very well be selling insurance, and if he were reminded that he had written poetry when he was at university, he would probably laugh in embarrassment. Quite possibly, some other young person who didn't really show as much raw talent might have gone on to publish books and build up quite a body of work. I suppose it's the same as a musician or dancer or anything else. The people are divided into those that have a certain amount of raw talent that makes it comparatively easy for them to write poems or play a musical instrument, and there's the other group who are prepared to go through all the drudgery involved in improving themselves at doing that.

JP You told me a story once about a young poet from the university who came to visit you. Could you tell that?

AN Well, partly because of the various media, a lot of people — not just young people, but a lot of people in general — have very unrealistic ideas about the financial rewards involved in being a writer. And a number of years ago, a university student dropped in at my house to show me some of his poems, and I looked at them and said something about them. But several months later, I read poetry at the university where this young man was a student, and one of his teachers said to me that after young so-and-so visited your house he gave up writing altogether. I was almost devastated because I felt that I must have said something so unkind and so hurtful that perhaps I'd killed a future Yeats in the bud. I said something to this effect to the teacher, and he said, "Oh no, it's nothing like that at all. What happened was he came to me and said, 'Alden Nowlan has as much prestige as any poet in the country and he's living in a hovel in Fredericton. So if that's all there is in it, what is there in it for me?'" I think he expected me to have a butler.

JP What contact with other writers have you had throughout your development? [question not recorded]

AN One of the wonderful things about Canada, where the population is so small, is that the literary community is a large extended village, in a kind of way. Or, as Margaret Laurence calls it, "a tribe." The first time Margaret Laurence and I met, she kissed me and she said, "I always kiss members of my tribe." And some people have remarked that when you get a group of Canadian poets together, they never discuss poetry and certainly not literature. The first thing they do is gossip about all the other Canadian poets.

JP In your poetry and prose, Alden, how much importance does love hold?

AN Love plays an enormous part in all of my poetry and prose and, I think, in all good poetry and prose, because I think basically there are only two subjects anyone can write about, and one is love and the other one is death.

JP All writing is a form of comment on those two, you think?

AN I think so, yes.

JP Can you speak a bit about the importance of economy of words in poetry?

AN Economy of words is enormously important to me. It seems the natural way that I have of looking at things, perhaps because I'm the product of a culture which tends to use very economical speech. Just as Robert Frost was the product of a very similar culture, and he tended to use economical speech. I remember back in the early fifties when I developed an enormous admiration for the work of Dylan Thomas, whose work I still admire. But at that time, I admired it so much that I felt that this is the only way anybody could possibly write. And so for several months, I attempted to write Dylan Thomas poems. Of course, they were utter disasters because the ways in which Dylan Thomas and I tended to think and look at the world were entirely different. I think probably one of the most important things for a young poet is to find the people he can learn from. The ones whose work, whose characters, and whose outlook on the world is similar enough to his own that he'll be able to usefully learn from them.

JP Do you have any other advice for young writers and poets?

AN I think the most important advice of all to give any young poet or any young writer is to attempt to learn to distinguish the things that you really think and feel from the things you think that society expects you to think and feel. I've received poems from people in penitentiaries, and in the early days I always opened these with a feeling of excitement, thinking that here is going to be something that will give me an insight into the lives and attitudes of people whose lives and attitudes are very different from mine. But invariably I would find terribly senti-mental, sort of Edgar A. Guest type of poems. These people were in some place like Kingston Penitentiary and they were writing something like: "Oh, it's a glorious moon . . . shining in June," type of thing — "God bless the little daffodils that grow upon the greeny hills."

JP How do you choose the form of a poem?

AN I used to, when I began to write poems, use very metrical patterns. There was a time when every poem I wrote started out to be a sonnet. They didn't always end up sonnets because sometimes they turned into other things, but they always started out to be sonnets. And at one time, in the early days, I bought a book on English poetics, and I wrote one of everything in the entire book, you know, sestinas and ballade royales and all sorts of forms. But in more recent years, I've tried to let the poem choose its own form, and I've worked very, very hard on this, but sometimes the reviewers, being a careless lot, don't notice it at all and so decide that the thing is formless. While it sounds terribly naive, and I suppose was terribly naive, I think I learned a great deal in the process. Mind you, most of the poems were dreadful, but it was a learning experience.

JP What sorts of things trigger poems?

AN Well, with me, almost anything that happens to me can trigger a poem — conversations overheard in the doctor's waiting room, people I've glimpsed from the window of my car, things that I've seen on TV, things that I've read, pictures that I've seen — almost any part of the human experience. Mind you, they aren't all necessarily good poems, but almost any conceivable thing that would trigger a thought or trigger an emotion with me will trigger a poem.

JP Your poetry seems to appeal to a large audience. Why is that, do you think?

AN Well, I think my poetry potentially would appeal to a very large audience if so many people hadn't been put off poetry by poets who aren't really writing poems at all but are simply engaged in kind of incestuous word games. And the reason it does appeal is that it does express emotions and thoughts that we all share as human beings, that it basically speaks, I hope, about the human condition. That's the sort of response to my work that pleases me the most. It isn't praise, really, from a critic, although that's very pleasant. The response that pleases me the most is to encounter some person who has been moved in some way by something that I've written. I've been deeply touched, for instance, on the occasions when I've met some young person, a complete stranger to me, who has told me that, in the course of some relationship with a boy or a girl, one of my poems expressed what was felt at this particular time so well that he or she has sent the poem, you see, speaking for them. And in a lighter vein, I've had a woman come up to me after a poetry reading and say that she always quoted a certain poem of mine to her husband whenever he became too pompous. I've even had people tell me that they've framed certain poems of mine. That sort of human reaction is what's most important to me and, I think, what's most important, really, to any writer. Someone has said that the critics and the teachers are concerned with literature and that the writers are concerned with life.

JP What has your evolution been as a poet — in terms of form and theme?

AN I've moved from being a very traditional poet into much freer and looser forms. But I'm grateful that I did work in the traditional forms first, unlike a lot of young poets today, who start out trying to write free verse before they know what free verse is. They think all you have to do is simply blather away on the page. And from having written things like sonnets and villanelles I learned from very early on that you didn't blather away on the page.

JP Which of your poems do you feel closest to right now?

AN Invariably the poem I feel closest to is the last one I've written. Mind you, a few months or even a few days later, it may seem like a very inferior piece of work to me. But at that particular time, it's always the last one that I've done. I think the most devastating thing that can be said to any writer is for someone to come up to him and say, "I like the things you were doing five or ten or fifteen years ago much better than the things you're doing now." I think that's about the most devastating thing.

JP Does your poetry have a point of view or seek to answer a recurring question?

AN I think my poetry tries to answer questions, but not so much for other people as for me. It's sort of a process of organizing experience for me. Because all creation, I think, beginning with the creation of the world as described in Greek mythology or in the Bible, consists of taking chaos and giving it form. And I think that this follows through. That's what you do in a poem or a story. You take chaos and give it form.

JP It seems often that modern poetry sees man as a victim, as ordinary individuals pitted hopelessly against the world. How much do you assume that point of view?

AN Well, I suppose that, in the ultimate analysis, all of us are pitted hopelessly against the world in the sense that we all face an inevitable death, so that every life ends in defeat and all the stories have sad endings. But I don't think that's something we ought to be obsessed by. I mean, the mere fact that the journey ends in tragedy doesn't mean that we have to overlook or denigrate all the beautiful things we encounter on the way there.

JP Do you think that writers should confront society — the illusions and faiths of society?

AN Well, I think some writers should confront the illusions of society. It depends on the nature of the writer. There have been some very great iconoclastic writers, but it's an attitude that I don't think is central to me. It might be in certain societies. I don't know how I would feel if I were a writer in a country where writers are strictly curtailed by government agencies and that sort of thing. But in society as it exists now, I don't feel any great urge to attack it. I would have felt, I suppose, a much stronger urge when I was younger. And the reason I don't feel it strongly now, I think, isn't that I've changed so much as that the world has changed an enormous amount. There aren't nearly so many things to attack as there were in the fifties. I, at one point in the early fifties, was actually investigated by the Royal Canadian Mounted Police. During this whole McCarthy era, you know.

JP Could you tell me a bit more about that?

AN Well, it was funny in a way, because at the time I was actually investigated by the RCMP — I suppose the RCMP intelligence squad — it was just after I had left Nova Scotia and come to New Brunswick, so that I personally didn't encounter it at all. I simply heard about it from people like my father, the librarian, and the editor of the weekly newspaper, who had been questioned. And it was all because I'd written some letters to the editor of a newspaper which was then published in Cape Breton called the *Steelworker and the Miner*, which was a very left-wing newspaper — in fact, I think it was edited by a communist. And what strikes me as so funny in retrospect is all of this money and effort being spent to investigate the views of some poor little eighteen-year-old boy in a backwoods village in Nova Scotia… who couldn't have overthrown the government even if he had wanted to. And I think it's funny they could be that absurd and frightening that they could be that thorough.

JP How quickly do your attitudes and the way they reflect in your writing change?

AN I suspect that my attitudes tend to change slowly and almost imperceptibly, to me.

JP What writers have you learned the most from technically, and what sorts of things did you learn?

AN I think possibly the writer I learned the most from technically was William Carlos Williams. And I think this is true of a great many of my generation of Canadian poets and the generation of Canadian poets preceding mine. I think that many of the Canadian poets of the generation that's just a bit younger than I am — the sort of George Bowering-Lionel Kearns generation — learned a good deal of the things that they learned from American writers who had learned from William Carlos Williams.

JP Have you ever cribbed anything from other writers?

AN Oh, well. All writers, although not all of them would admit it, are shameless thieves. T.S. Eliot said that minor writers imitate, great writers steal.

JP D.H. Lawrence had a willingness to trust his instinct and follow it freely, so he said. And Forster, or Flannery O'Connor, as you mentioned, said, "How do I know what I think until I see what I say?" What do you think of this notion of an internal voice, a sort of primitive commentator inside you?

AN Oh, I think our ancestors, when they said that man was body and spirit and soul, were expressing a genuine truth. Obviously even Hugh Hefner would be prepared to admit that we are body, and I would take the soul to equal the conscious mind and the spirit to be an unconscious thing speaking inside us.

JP Does this "spirit" come into play when you write poetry?

AN Oh, I think so. And one of the fascinating things about writing poetry is the inspiration often comes when you're trying to do the most disciplined form. I think that I've come up with some of my best individual lines when I was working with strict metrical forms. When I simply started out, for instance, simply knowing that the line had to be iambic pentameter — five distinct beats — I would work and work simply to get a line that made sense and had five distinct beats. But in the end, suddenly, a line sort of leaped through that was perfect from my point of view but which wouldn't have come at all had I not had to go through all that straining.

JP Robert Bly says that you are psychically brave because you skate out along "the edges of fear" in your poetry. What do you have to say about that?

AN Well, I think we come back there to the business of the importance of being able to distinguish what you really think and feel from what you think that society around you expects you to think and feel. In other words, to admit to yourself what it is — the way that you react to things. And I think it's not only important in poetry and in fiction but it can be enormously important to a journalist. Simply to admit that he finds something boring or tedious or the emperor wears no clothes, you know.

JP In the poem "There is a horrible wing to the hotel" what are you really talking about?

AN Well, there are various types of ideal poems, but one of them would be a poem which expressed something as a poem which you couldn't express in any other way. And I think in "There is a horrible wing to the hotel" and in many of my darker poems — because I sort of have daytime poems and nighttime poems — I'm striving to express something in the poem which really couldn't be expressed outside of the poem. So, therefore, to attempt to explain it would be to destroy it.

JP What value is there in the exploration of such strange and far-out ideas?

AN I don't really think that any ideas are strange and far-out. Possibly because so much of life has seemed strange to me, I'm prepared to accept as quite normal almost any degree of strangeness. I have certain moments in which I'm quite prepared to believe in vampires and werewolves. If it's a really good horror movie on TV, I don't like to watch it when I'm alone in the house.

There's a definite association, I think, in our society between alienation and the artist, but I don't think that that needs to be at all. And I think that the historical period during which there has been that feeling of almost the necessity of the artist being alienated from society is comparatively brief. You know, through the eighteenth century, writers didn't feel at all alienated from society. And then, of course, during the Romantic period of Keats, Byron, and Shelley, they did. But then again, during the Victorian age, they didn't. And I don't think it is essential to be alienated from the society around you in order to be a great writer because obviously Shakespeare was very much a part of the society around him. He wasn't alienated at all. And he's still generally conceded to be the greatest writer in English.

JP They say that as a writer you must be super observant of your environment. Can you comment about that?

AN I don't think that it's necessary for a writer to be super observant. I think that it's probably very necessary that he compensate for his areas in which his observation is weak by exercising the areas in which his observation is strong. In my own case, I am very weak visually — in the sense that I tend not to notice what people are wearing, you know. I've known people for months and didn't notice that they had some physical deformity until some friend pointed it out to me. But I'm very aware of the things that people say and the nuances of their voices and the idiomatic expressions they use and how the words they use don't always have their dictionary meaning. So that in the audio section I'm very strong.

JP Do you write poetry every day?

AN You really can't write poetry on a nine-to-five basis as you can write prose. On the other hand, you do work at it every day in the same sense that people who are clergymen point out, rightly, that they are really working on their sermons every day because they are observing things from life and listening to people, which will eventually become material for a sermon.

JP So you write poetry, then, at certain times of the week or month, or is it every couple of months you would begin to write poetry?

AN It varies. Usually, if I'm involved in some lengthy prose project such as working on a play, I try, for instance, to have it so that if I work for three weeks on the play, I work a week on nothing but the verse.

JP Just one week concentrated.

AN Yes.

JP When you switch from journalism or prose to poetry, do you make special preparations to prepare the ground?

AN Well, the hardest part of all of being a writer who writes in a great many genres as I do — plays, journalism, short stories, and poetry — is the switching from one to the other, because it's not something that you can do very quickly. If I've been working for a week on poetry and then try to write a newspaper column, the problem I have is that I work too hard at it. I'm too meticulous, you see. Because often a newspaper column is much better if it's dashed off than if it's written carefully. If you write it carefully, being conscious of the subtleties of the language and the nuances of the words, the reader will probably miss the point entirely. Because, obviously, the reader is going to be dashing through that and he smells the toast burning and he tosses it to one side, whereas people will perhaps read a poem over and over. And yes, it's very often very difficult to switch from one to the other, very frustrating.

JP Alden, can you tell me a bit about the way you find words that juxtapose in a poem to create a sort of haiku feeling — a sort of unexpected feeling?

AN Well, it's mostly a process of trial and error, actually. And often it seems almost purely accidental, although I suppose there's something that's simmering in the subconscious.

JP Do you ever find these sorts of juxtapositions almost independent of a poem and sort of catalogue them in a book or something?

AN Oh, yes, I make all sorts of notes of, sometimes, just meta-phors and of odd terms and that sort of thing. I used to make lists of rich, mouth-filling words, but I tend to use a much simpler vocabulary now. In fact, I found, three or four years ago when I was preparing a collection of selected poems, that in some of my earlier poems, there was a word or two that I'd now forgotten what it meant, and I had to look it up in the dictionary.

JP Do you keep a journal, a diary of sorts?

AN I have at various times. I used to start a diary every January first and some of them would go as far as January seventh. I think the longest any of them lasted was probably the first of February.

JP You told me that you sometimes have to set yourself a deadline to finish a poem. Can you tell me again about that?

AN Possibly because I'm an old newspaper man, I'm very dependent upon deadlines. And so, at various times, I have created completely imaginary deadlines for poems — telling myself that I had to have a poem done by Saturday. There was a period when I forced myself to write a poem a day. And when I was doing it — in the sense of saying that I had to have it done by Saturday — often it was very imperfect, but at least it was finished. And I had something to work on later. Whereas if I hadn't set the deadline, I probably would have abandoned it halfway through.

JP You sometimes paint pictures — watercolours. Could you talk about that?

AN Well, I don't paint much anymore. I used to paint a little — sort of in keeping with Gilbert Keith Chesterton's wonderful observation that anything that's worth doing at all is worth doing badly. And I think that's very true in the sense that, while I was always a very bad painter, I think that I learned to be much more observant of good paintings as a result of doing bad ones than I would have been if I hadn't done any at all.

JP The little watercolour that you have hanging in your living room, could you describe it and tell me what it's about?

AN The watercolour that I have framed in my living room is basically there because I decided that it was the weak best of a very bad lot. And I felt so good about it that I framed it.

JP And what does is show?

AN Oh... basically, a woman sleeping.

JP Does it have any particular meaning for you?

AN Well, one night during the period when I was doing watercolours... I suppose, actually, I should give some very philosophical explanation of how and why I did it. But, in fact, one night, during the time when I was doing watercolours, I was sitting in the living room of our house and my wife was asleep on the chesterfield, and I was sitting there getting increasingly sloshed, and I simply did watercolour after watercolour and that was the best of the lot. I was the sort of painter who always did it better when he was half sloshed. Which means I was pretty amateurish.

JP Would you care to say anything about what you're writing now?

AN The last project that I finished was in collaboration with Walter Learning — a radio adaptation of George du Maurier's novel *Trilby*. The radio play is called *La Svengali*. It looks into the whole business — well, of course, in *La Svengali* or *Trilby*, a hypnotist — a mesmerist as they called them in the nineteenth century — takes a little girl who's tone-deaf and turns her into a great operatic singer. But in the play, we try to carry it a bit beyond that and, by implication, go into the whole business of how someone creates someone else or uses them as an instrument. You know, like Colonel Tom Parker with Elvis Presley or Brian Epstein with the Beatles. To a degree, you have created them or you could certainly imagine that you had. But I could visualize Tom Parker standing in the wings, accepting all that adulation as being for him.

JP You've always written plays in collaboration with Walter Learning. Do you think you'll ever write one by yourself, and if you do, what sort of subjects would you choose?

AN I don't know if I'll ever write a play on my own or not because I think of it so much in terms of it being something that I do with Walter. If you collaborate with someone — particularly if you collaborate as much as Walter and I have done, because we've finished three stage plays and started half a dozen others and done quite a number of TV plays and radio plays — in a sense, there exists an entity which contains part of Walter Learning and part of Alden Nowlan and is independent of us both. At one point we thought (I think perhaps we were right) that we ought to use a pseudonym to represent this character

— this author who was really neither of us but kind of a combination of the two. It's sort of as if we'd had a child together and he were the mother and I were the father.

JP The character of the creature in your play *Frankenstein* — once you said that character was one of the most autobiographical things you've ever written. Could you explain that?

AN Often people have taken it for granted that Kevin O'Brien in my novel *Various Persons Named Kevin O'Brien* is a straight autobiographical figure, and I've told many of those people (only half jokingly) that the creature in our stage adaptation of *Frankenstein* is much more autobiographical than Kevin O'Brien is.

JP In what way?

AN All of us are alienated to certain degrees at certain times, but the creature is utterly alienated. And he, as he appears in the play, I think, personifies exactly the way I felt when I was fifteen and sixteen years old. I, in effect, was the creature. During that period, I never strangled anyone (as the creature does), but I can tell you that I often was tempted to do so and sometimes wish that I had.

JP Could you talk a bit more about your alienation as an adolescent?

AN The worst forms of alienation are . . . the worst results are not that other people think that you're inferior. The horrible thing is when *you* begin to think that you're inferior. I think this is true of minority groups. For a long time, I think, this was true of many Blacks or many of our native people. They'd been told for so long that they were inferior that they'd come to believe they *were* inferior. And in the individual case, it's not so bad really to be unloved as it is to convince yourself that you are utterly and permanently *unlovable*. And that's what the creature feels, and that's what I felt during my adolescent years.

JP Could you be even more specific about the factors in your adolescence that contributed to this feeling of alienation?

AN Well, I've written somewhere that the worst sort of indignity is loneliness without privacy — loneliness in a crowd. It isn't so bad to be alone (or I shouldn't imagine it to be) if you were a hermit or a monk or if you were marooned somewhere. But it's desperately hard to be utterly alone in a situation where you also have to deal with encounters with other people. And that's the sort of situation that I was in, really. In retrospect, I think that it probably was good for me because I've found that there's an enormous amount of truth in what Nietzsche said. Nietzsche said that "what does not kill me, strengthens me." And I've found that to be very, very true.

JP What's the sensation a writer has when he hears his own words from the mouth of somebody else — a really good actor?

AN At least in my case, when I hear my words from the mouth of a really good actor, I always develop an enormous affection for that actor. And if he or she does an appalling job of delivering my lines, I (perhaps irrationally and unfairly) develop an intense dislike for that person. I can't help but emotionally take it very personally, even though I know that's not very rational. But a person could be an excellent individual and still do a very bad job of delivering my lines. I believe that rationally, but I feel in my heart that anyone who can't deliver my lines well is a black-hearted villain and ought to be driven out of the theatre.

JP You asked me earlier on not to interview your family — your aunts and uncles back home and even your wife. Could you talk a bit about that? Why would you feel reluctant?

AN Well, I think it's because it's essentially irrelevant to my role as an artist. I think it's probably much more noticeable in politics than it is in the arts and probably much more noticeable in the U.S. than it is in Canada, but we get this whole business that when Jimmy Carter was president, his brother Billy became a celebrity, which was really unfair, you know, in many ways to brother Billy, who would have been very happy running a little service station down in Plains, Georgia. If it were not for the pure accident that his brother became president of the U.S., he would never have become a celebrity. And my point is that it was pure accident and it's utterly irrelevant. Many of the people who know me and are related to me either by blood or by marriage are only vaguely aware that I write at all. And certainly they have no conception of what being a writer is.

I could probably give a better . . . a fairly good example of this business of being unaware of what somebody does. There's a wonderful story that Walter Learning told me. During the second production of *Frankenstein*, Walter played one of the minor comic relief characters — a character who did a bit of slapstick humour to give the audience a chance to laugh so they wouldn't laugh at the serious parts. Well, the play went to Newfoundland, and Walter's dear old grandmother came to one production. After the production, she came to him and, in tones of great relief, said, "Now at last, boy, I know what you does for a living." Obviously, from her point of view, she thought he spent all his life playing slapstick parts on the stage. But at least that gave her something to hold onto.

It's very hard for people who are illiterate or semi-illiterate to form any conception of what it is that a writer does. You see, they would have less conception of what I did than I would have of what an astronaut did. So it would be just as relevant to interview me about the NASA project as it would be to interview some of my cousins about my writing.

JP Your only novel, *Various Persons Named Kevin O'Brien*, dealt with your childhood in a sort of fictional way. Were you satisfied with that approach, or do you think you'll go at it again in some other form?

AN Well, I suppose, actually, like all writers, or like most writers, all that I ever write about is what it's like to be me. I don't really think of *Kevin O'Brien* so much as being autobiographical, or semi-autobiographical, as I think of it in terms of it's being a study of personality and a time. And of how, as time passes, we constantly are developing into different people, almost like a caterpillar developing into a butterfly, except that the butterfly then perhaps changes into a bird and the bird changes into something else. But at the same time, all those previous selves are inside us, you see. And inside each of us, somewhere, there's a five-year-old who's apt to get out at any moment and throw a tantrum...I've thought at various times, in fact, of doing a play in which all of the characters were various past selves of the central character, and they were encountering and interacting with one another on the stage in the same way they really do encounter and interact with one another inside us.

JP Did you write *Kevin O'Brien* with ease or . . . ?

AN It was very difficult for me to write *Kevin O'Brien*, just as it's very difficult for me to write a play, even in collaboration. Because I think that all writers are divided into marathon runners and sprinters, and I, essentially, am a sprinter. And to be a good novelist, you have to be a marathon runner, and so *Kevin O'Brien* as a novel is written in a very episodic style. Some reviewers said that it was a book of short stories masquerading as a novel. That doesn't worry me, really, because I don't care how it's defined as long as it works. But it was, yes, very difficult for me.

JP Did you work on it each day or in really concentrated periods?

AN I worked on it mostly in periods of intense concentration in which I would do one section of it, and then there might be an interval during which I did other things, and then I would go back to it and work on it again for a week or two weeks, very hard.

JP When you were writing *Kevin O'Brien*, how many words roughly would you expect to write in a day?

AN With me, it's almost impossible to measure how many words I write a day because I rewrite so extensively. And I might very well, say, write two thousand words on Monday and throw fifteen hundred of them away on Tuesday. So it would be difficult to say whether on Monday I'd written two thousand words or only five hundred.

JP Do you think in ideas? Or do you think in words, pictures, or what?

AN I'm...not sure, really, how anyone thinks. I tend to think that we probably all are essentially like primitive man, and we really exist on a purely emotional level, in that we feel things in our guts. The only difference being that as civilized men we feel we must give some plausible verbal formulation to this feeling, so we invent words and make it into a plausible theory, but it really originated in what we felt here [he indicates his gut].

JP Do you take your dreams seriously? Do they affect your work?

AN It's funny about dreams. One of the most frustrating things about dreams that I've found as a writer is that on several occasions I've had a dream which, while I was dreaming and during the first few seconds after I woke up, seemed to me to be the nucleus of an absolutely great poem. And sometimes I've even scribbled it down in the night, and almost invariably the next day, it turned out to be absolute gibberish. So while I think that dreams may have meaning, it's probably just a meaning that applies in the dream. I have very interesting dreams. I think I have a far more interesting life when I'm asleep, in some ways, than I do when I'm awake.

JP You were telling me this morning about a poem that actually did work out that came from a dream.

AN Yes, I have one poem which actually came straight from a dream. Well, in fact, it was a nightmare. And I had the nightmare and woke up and wrote it down and didn't change a word of it. And not only was it...not only did I use it in a book, but it's probably been reprinted more often than any other of my poems. It's called "The Execution."

JP You came very close to death. How did that affect your work and your life in general?

AN Well, the effects of coming close to death weren't nearly as radical as you might expect, simply because we're mercifully able to put death out of our minds so easily. I probably find it harder than most people, and I think it's probably a very healthy thing to think about death. I think that far from it being a morbid thing, if I were one of these people like a maharishi, instead of suggesting that people sit down and meditate, I would suggest that they sit down each day and think about their own death for five, ten, or fifteen minutes. And I think they would be much happier during the rest of the day and probably much kinder to the people around them.

JP And that's the effect it had on you, basically?

AN I think so, yes.

JP What do you think happens to you after you die?

AN I'm not sure. I would be inclined to think that the same thing happens to us after we die as happens to a rose or a bird or any other thing that's alive. The only kind of afterlife which I find emotionally plausible is the kind of afterlife which the ancient Greeks believed in, in which the dead exist in a kind of shadow land in which they're perhaps not completely aware that they are dead. You know, I find the traditional kind of Christian eschatology completely implausible.

JP No pearly gates for you?

AN I'm afraid not, though it's been a wonderfully useful imagery and great things have been said about it. Chesterton, a man whom I admire enormously and, of course, a man who was a Catholic, said a marvellous thing once. He said that there is a hell, but God never sends anyone there.